THE
APOCALYPSE
CLUB

A NOVEL

THE
APOCALYPSE
CLUB

A NOVEL

BRIAN KOSCIENSKI & CHRIS PISANO

tpg

Treehouse Publishing | St. Louis, MO

tpg

Treehouse Publishing | Saint Louis, MO 63116
Copyright © 2019 Brian Koscienski & Chris Pisano
All rights reserved.

For information, contact:
Treehouse Publishing
An imprint of Amphorae Publishing Group
a woman- and veteran-owned business
4168 Hartford Street, Saint Louis, MO 63116

Manufactured in the United States of America
Set in and Adobe Caslon Pro
Interior designed by Kristina Blank Makansi
Cover designed by Kristina Blank Makansi
Jacket Images: Shutterstock

Library of Congress Control Number: 2019902875
ISBN: 9781732139152

For everyone
who believes in the magic of the world,
feels the magic in themselves,
and wants to learn more
about the magic in others

A FEW MONTHS AGO

LILA HAD BEEN MISSING for three months, and Strongbow had searched everywhere, using every tracking spell he could learn. Nothing. His little sister had disappeared like smoke on a summer breeze. Until two days ago, that is. Now he and four of his classmates were on an unnamed mound of jungle, rocks, and sand off the coast of Brazil.

"We shouldn't be here," Cassidy whispered, huddled behind the largest of the boulders that lined the beach.

Tierney squeezed her hand, Cassidy's lithe fingers barely half the width of his. The light of the full moon emphasized how pale her porcelain hand was against his stark ebony skin. "We're here for Strongbow," he whispered back. "He would do the same for any of us."

"One thing he's not doing is flapping his jaw," Willem hissed, English accent thick. His normally fiery red hair now muted by the moonlight to the faintest hint of orange while every freckle along his cheeks and arms stood out against his blanched skin. "You've been yippin' like a purse dog ever since we got on this bloody island."

"Since we don't have a plan and none of us are telepathic," Nicholas whispered, "we need to communicate somehow."

Tendrils of his long, ink-black hair floated on the breeze and his dark eyes looked ethereal against his wide cheekbones and square chin.

Strongbow didn't listen to the bickering. He couldn't. All he could hear was the pounding of his heart. From behind the boulder, he peered out to assess the situation. Two rows of six-foot tall torches flickered with amber flames, tipped with curls of black smoke, and led to clearing with a waist-high stone altar on which his sister lay. It was less than fifty feet away. And Lila wasn't moving. Worse yet, three Mesos danced around the altar, their tanned skin aglow in the torchlight. They wore headdresses that looked like a nest of snakes had taken up residence atop their hair while dull white serpent bones and colorful feathers dangled from ties around their necks, arms, and thighs.

From his vantage point, Strongbow could see images of snakes painted so they were twined around their arms and legs and in striking positions on their backs. *This looks like something out of a bad movie*, he thought as he watched the boys dance around the altar, each holding a spear and singing in a Mesoamerican language probably not spoken for centuries. Then the dancing stopped. The exuberant singing softened to a melodic chant. Two Mesos stood next to the altar, one on either side, swaying while waving their spears in the air. The third stood at the head of the altar and produced a knife with a rippled blade. Using both hands, he raised it above his head, blade down. Moonlight glinted off the polished steel.

"No!" Strongbow screamed. Sand sprayed from his heels as he leapt from behind the rocks and sprinted across the beach.

Surprised, the other four chased after him. Willem yelled, "This? This is the plan? Great! So excited to be a part of it!"

"Shut up," Nicholas barked. "Do something with their fire!"

"Still too far away, genius! And where are your creepy-crawlies?"

Strongbow waved his arms and mumbled a few words in his people's native language. Too worried to concentrate, the gale force wind he tried to conjure was nothing more than a strong gust. It was enough to get the Mesos' attention and interrupt the ritual, but the trio swiftly moved in front of the altar to protect their sacrificial offering. Spears up and ready, one of the Mesos whisked his hand through the air and snapped his arm forward as if throwing a ball. In an instant, a raging inferno shot forward from the torches creating a wall of fire speeding toward the five interlopers.

But just as quickly, the wall of fire split in half, clearing a path for Strongbow and his friends. Willem's work.

Panting, the five youths skidded to a halt and stood before the three Mesos. Strongbow stepped forward and growled, "Release my sister!"

The Meso in the center stepped forward, his face partially hidden by a serpent mask. In perfect English, he said, "I believe tradition dictates you finish your sentence with 'or else'."

"Your overconfidence will be your demise, Meso."

"Our overconfidence? *You* are mere students attacking an unknown enemy in an unfamiliar environment."

Strongbow couldn't agree more about the environment. This was not his home, his lands. He was uncomfortable here, but he could still work his magics. He was more worried about Cassidy since her magic was so closely tied to home. The nearby jungle provided plenty of foliage, but it was so foreign she was probably struggling to use her abilities. If he were more tactful, more of an expert in strategy, he would drag out the conversation as long as possible to give Cassidy more time to find something familiar, a tree, a plant, a vine. But he was too close to his sister to think that clearly. Instead, veins bulging under the skin of his neck, Strongbow ground his teeth, then bellowed, "I said release my sister!"

The Meso leader removed his headdress and calmly said, "No."

Strongbow's eyes widened, but Cassidy's sharp gasp rose up in the air. "Talo? But … but … How?"

The young man, straight black hair slicked back with ceremonial oils, regarded the blonde girl. His lips twisted, stopping between a smirk and a sneer. "How? Yes, I have another three years until my ascension and you have another three years to train before we face each other in battle. I know full well that is the reason you were chosen. Students my age. My *peers*, right? It's because of me that—"

Talo paused, distracted by vines creeping from the jungle and slowly wrapping around his ankles. Cassidy had found something familiar to control, but it wasn't enough. With little effort, Talo kicked the vines away. Bloodlust in his eyes, he hissed at Cassidy, "Stupid girl! I may not be ready to accept the gifts from my gods, but that doesn't mean I'm powerless!"

As fast as the wind, Talo threw his spear. As soon as he released it, the other two Mesos each waved their hands at it. Halfway to Cassidy, the spear split into two, then four. Willem reached out with his hand and yelled, "Stop!" Two of the projectiles dropped two the ground, but the number of spears in flight doubled again. Two missed, but the other two hit their target.

Trembling, Cassidy looked down and reached for the spears—one through her waist, the other sunk deep into her thigh—but pulled her hands back as if touching them would worsen the situation. Her legs buckled. She dropped to her knees and reached out for Tierney. A cough of blood painted her chin.

Tierney rushed to her, dropping to his knees as well and catching her as she fell back. She tried for one last, "I love you," but could only croak a frothing gurgle. Her lashes fluttered as her eyes lolled back. Tierney closed her eyes for her.

Strongbow knew this mission was dangerous, knew the institute was training its students to defend against the Mesos and stop their mad plans to bring back their ancient gods of blood sacrifice and destruction. But knowing about danger and diving into it were two different ideas. Fiction versus fact. A scary story versus reality. Thinking about faceless monsters versus watching a friend die because of them.

The pain of loss twisted through his insides just at the same anguish contorted Tierney's face. Mouth open, but no noise came out as tears traced the lines of his silent scream. Then he retaliated.

Still on his knees, he whispered words that could only be found in the darkest jungles of Jamaica. Strongbow was unfamiliar with the spell, but knew that these words should never be uttered. Tierney's eyes swirled into a milky white as he communed with spirits all too willing to listen to the pleas of mortals. The sand around one of the Mesos puffed into the air, swirling and spinning about him. In one instant the cloud of sand became so thick, he was lost from sight, the next instant the sand dissipated, floating away harmlessly on a gossamer breeze. There was no trace of the Meso. Dead. Gone as if he had never existed.

Nicholas attacked as well, using the shadows of the nearby jungle to summon forth spiders. Inch wide patches of blackness sprouted eight legs and scuttled from the foliage. Wave after wave, thousands of spiders descended upon the second Meso. He wriggled and screamed, trying to swat them away or stomp them beneath his feet. Dozens of spiders burst into flame and ash from a minor spell he cast, but he quickly lost concentration as they scurried about his eyes and ears, crawling into his mouth. Black webbing oozed about his body until he fell to the ground, mummified.

Strongbow centered his anger. His sister had been kidnapped. Cassidy had just been killed. He called upon his own spirits to listen to his prayers. And they did. Pulling his arms tight against his body and touching his ankles together, he fell to the sand and writhed. Squirming, his body stretched and twisted, scales replacing skin, teeth turning to fangs, as he transformed. Within seconds, Strongbow morphed into a ten-foot long rattlesnake, as thick as a thigh. Coiling and ready to strike, he hissed as the noise of his rattle filled the night air.

"Oh my. A scary snake," Talo said, sarcasm dripping from his words. "Look what I can do."

Talo ran toward his attackers, and within three steps, dove at them. As quick as a whip snap, he was a twenty-foot anaconda with black scales that shimmered green in the torchlight. Feathers from his discarded headdress floated serenely to the ground. Strongbow in snake form dodged the attack. Voice distorted, he yelled, "Willem! Get Lila!"

Willem acted immediately. He skittered around the Meso mummified in black webbing, keeping as far away as possible. With no one to guard the altar, he ran to it uncontested. However, Strongbow's heart broke from the next set of words from Willem's mouth.

"Lila's not on the altar! There's nothing on the altar!" Willem screamed, running toward his friends. "She was never here! It was a set up! We were set up!"

By the time Willem was close enough to help fight Talo, it was too late. The monstrous anaconda feigned a lunge toward Strongbow. Still in a coil, the rattlesnake sprung to avoid the perceived attack. As soon as Strongbow shot the opposite direction, Talo lunged at Nicholas. Within the blink of an eye, Talo's jaws clamped onto Nicholas. Strongbow knew that he would be forever haunted by the look on Nicholas' face, frozen with the terrifying knowledge of what was coming next. The crunch of snapping bones stole his chance to scream.

Willem stopped between Tierney and Strongbow and whispered, "Bloody hell." From the torches, he conjured fireballs, but they simply burst into puffs of smoke against Talo's scales. "We gotta get outta here!"

Not letting go of Cassidy, Tierney constructed the framework of the portal. Rolling black smoke bubbled from the sand like oil. The smoke folded in on itself, doubling in height every second until it reached six feet. Willem then turned his attention to the smoke, wriggling his fingers and spouting an incantation. A burst of white light flickered in the center of the roiling smoke, bright and stark against the blackness. The light expanded, forming a portrait framed by billowing darkness. As if opening a door, the light gave way to expose a room with a couch and chairs.

Viciously shaking his head, Talo tossed Nicholas's dead body like a broken toy. With a spitting hiss, he turned his attention to the trio of survivors. Willem screamed, "He's going to attack! Strongbow! Turn into a bear! Turn into a bear!"

"Go!" Tierney yelled at Strongbow.

Strongbow transformed again, this time into a large eagle. He took flight, talons out.

Talo attacked, striking just as fast as before.

Strongbow as an eagle grabbed Willem by the shoulders all the while Willem screamed, "No! Talo! Attack Talo!"

A flurry of scales blurred across the beach, spraying geysers of sand.

Even though Strongbow couldn't completely lift Willem, he had enough strength and momentum to get both of them through the portal, safely into the room. Willem screamed his protests as Strongbow turned back from eagle to human, powerless to do anything more than watch as the portal closed. The last image of the beach he saw was the black serpent wrapping itself around Tierney, smiling as it constricted.

CHAPTER 1

BREE MOORE HAD HOPED for more out of her sophomore year of high school. Summer vacation was less than three months away, and she felt like she had accomplished nothing she'd had set out to do from her freshman year, other than "not be a freshman." She found a sense of pride in her high GPA, but that had been a constant for her throughout her school career. During the summer between freshman and sophomore year, her freckles faded, her braces came off, she had laser eye surgery to liberate herself from glasses, and fate had bequeathed to her one full cup size. She even made an effort with styling her hair. It was still long and the color of light caramel, but now it flowed and shimmered in the light rather than resembling strands of rotting hay.

These changes were supposed to help her through high school, and she'd had hoped to relish them with her closest friends, Chelsea and Amanda. Instead, they'd been drifting further from her all year. Did they feel abandoned by her? Chelsea still had a mouth full of metal, both she and Amanda still needed glasses, and they each still had middle school hairstyles. They'd always teased her about being a bit odd, but recently, they'd accused Bree of trying to be *popular*.

But Bree didn't seek out popularity. She didn't even understand the power dynamics required for it. Now and then, she would daydream about turning every head in the room when she entered, but that desire never grew beyond a vague whimsy. What she really wanted was to be normal, or at the very least, to be invisible from overly critical eyes, namely Brittany and the other cheerleaders. No such luck. Especially today.

Bree stood at the front of the room while her science teacher, Miss Harkins, held up two flourishing plants. The forest green and bright emerald explosion of stalks and leaves were so profuse they hid the pots they were in. For five weeks, each student had watered two pots of newly sprouted plants, one with water and the other with some form of clear soda. Every experiment garnered the same results— the plants given water grew to heights from six to eight inches and sprouted a couple dozen leaves while the plants given the soda were nothing more than withered parodies of their counterparts. Except for Bree's. Both of her plants looked like handheld jungles.

Most of her classmates stared at her with appalled confusion. Some glared with jealousy, while the remaining few could care less. None were happy for Bree, except for Miss Harkins. "Bree, these are amazing! I … I don't know what to say. I think botany may be in your future."

"Or gardening," Brittany blurted. "My parents just lost their hedge man. Want to take over?"

Half of the class laughed, and a rush of unwanted warmth flowed to Bree's cheeks.

"Now, class, settle down," Miss Harkins said. If it were any other teacher publicly sticking up for her, Bree would have been even more embarrassed, but she had always had a bit of bond with Miss Harkins. Her youngest teacher by far, Miss Harkins had sparkling eyes and long brown hair, which, even though unstyled, was beautiful. Bree guessed she was in her mid-thirties and hoped she'd look just as good when she was that age.

Residual chuckles danced about the room while Miss Harkins continued, "I think these are lovely. What's your secret? What did you do?"

Fighting the sudden dryness in her mouth, Bree knew a simple answer would be best. "Nothing special."

"Just like you," Brittany interjected again, this time to a chorus of laughter. Even though Miss Harkins called her out on the comment, Brittany's self-satisfied smirk haunted Bree for the rest of the day.

When the last bell rang, and the weekend officially begin, Bree was still thinking about the cuttingly casual tone in Brittany's voice. As she opened her locker, she heard a familiar laugh, one she'd grown up with but had heard less and less of over the past few months. Turning, she smiled, but Chelsea and Amanda walked by as if she didn't exist.

"Hey," Bree said, hoping her tone wasn't too desperate.

The two girls stopped and glanced at her, both offering an expressionless, "Hey."

Bree hadn't talked to them for over a week, not because she hadn't wanted to, but because she'd felt unwelcome the last time they'd hung out. Maybe she was reading too much into it. Maybe she was just self-conscious. Maybe they were still her best friends and she was being too hard on them. Too hard on herself. Whatever … right now they were her only hope for the human interaction—for the *friendship*—

she needed. She wanted things to be like they'd always been before. She wanted to spend the weekend laughing and joking and gossiping and watching movies and talking about books and boys and forgetting about snide comments and derisive laughter. "So ... what are you guys doing tonight?"

Chelsea answered, "Probably something you'd consider boring."

"I never think you—"

"Yeah," Amanda cut her off. "We don't want to hinder your quest to be popular."

"I don't want—" Bree started.

"Besides, I'm sure you're probably too busy washing your hair and plucking your eyebrows or something," Chelsca chimed in.

"Stop!" Bree squeaked. Her plea louder than expected, she looked around furtively to see if anyone was else was close enough to hear. "Please," she whispered as she felt her nose prickle and a tear slip down her cheek. "I just ... I just miss you guys. This year was supposed to be the best year yet for us and now it's almost over and all I wanted was to fly under the radar so Brittany wouldn't make fun of me but somehow I've lost my best friends because I think you think I abandoned you or something but I didn't and I'm not trying to be popular and I'm all alone even though I'm standing right here." She punctuated her statement with a sad laugh that came out more like a choked sob.

Chelsea looked to Amanda, then back to Bree. "So ... you still want to hang out with us?"

"Yes. Of course," Bree said, putting her whole body behind her reply. She wiped the tear away and sniffled.

"And you're not trying to ditch us for Brittany and her evil friends?" Amanda asked.

Bree went rigid. "Oh, God, no!"

"Then why have you been ignoring us?"

"I haven't been! Or at least I didn't mean to. It seemed like you guys were mad at me and didn't want me around anymore, so I … I don't know. I guess I pulled back because I didn't want to hear you say you didn't want to be friends with me anymore."

"We aren't mad at you. Well, we were because we thought you were avoiding us. But now I guess all we are is confused."

"I'm sorry. I didn't mean to confuse you. I guess I got confused, too."

"Okay," Chelsea said, hugging Bree. "I'm sorry I haven't been the nicest to you."

"Me too," Amanda said, taking her turn to hug Bree. "We're gonna watch vampire movies at my place. I've already got the snacks. Be there in an hour?"

"Yeah," Bree said, her bottom lip quivering as she smiled and wiped her eyes with the back of her hand. "I'd like that. I'll be there."

"Okay. Good. We gotta go catch our bus, but we'll see you soon! Maybe you can let us in on your secret and tell us how you get your hair so shiny all the sudden," Chelsea said as she and Amanda made their way out the exit.

"Okay," Bree whispered as she waved, and then used her sleeve to wipe away the remaining tears.

Bree started her walk home, a short five blocks away. Clutching three books against her chest, she followed the sidewalk, admiring the beautiful early Spring weather and reveling in the fact that her best friends were still her best friends and that maybe the year would turn out better than she feared. Maybe she and Chelsea and Amanda could fall back into their old routines. Maybe it was a chance for them all to blossom anew, like the world around them? She drew in a long breath. Flowers were blooming and everything smelled good and the sky was blue and the sun was warm and she was happy.

The trees lining the suburban streets weren't too tall, their leaves beginning to fill in with fresh new green. Planned out, each tree had a match directly across the street, each pair inviting, like the arms of an old friend waiting for an embrace. Every house was a moderate two story, square edges with little creativity in design, but every neighbor had different landscaping. The ruby reds of the Mullers' azaleas popped in comparison to the sprinkle of white pansies around them. Tulips of every color surrounded the Gundersons' house like a rainbow palisade and were often the topic of conversation during many a neighborhood cookout. Vines ensconced the latticework and gazebo of the Thorpes' yard, transforming it into a grapeless vineyard. As Bree passed Mrs. Erskine's house, she once again admired her landscaping choices—roses mixed with blueberry bushes.

That combination created a unique bouquet; it was the aroma of her childhood. It was a longstanding ritual for neighborhood kids to dare each other to pilfer blueberries from Mrs. Erskine's yard. When she was seven, Tommy Smith dared Bree to grab a handful. She'd done it, but after getting a dozen plump berries with ease, she went for the unlucky thirteenth and a thorn sliced the base of her thumb. In a low ominous whisper, Tommy had told her that Old Widow Erskine was going to use Bree's blood as a means to ensnare her soul. Bree had believed him and for weeks suffered through nightmares in which Mrs. Erskine was a witch who kept children's souls in glass jars in her basement. When she finally realized it just couldn't be true, she stopped talking to Tommy Smith and had avoided him ever since. Poor Mrs. Erskine. The mean stories about her had been circulating through the neighborhood as long as Bree could remember.

After the blueberry incident, Bree had thought of Mrs. Erskine as a terrifying witch, but after she grew out of that phase, she viewed her as the crazy cat lady, more suited for the company of the unknown number of felines that inhabited the house with her. More recently, Bree's view had shifted again, realizing that Mrs. Erskine was simply a lonely old widow. A chill ran down Bree's spine as a terrible thought infiltrated her mind—was it was her destiny to become a sad old woman like Mrs. Erskine?

Maybe when the old woman was in high school, the popular clique had ostracized and ridiculed her as she tried to reinvent herself and she had inadvertently pushed her best friends away? What was happening to Bree now *couldn't* have that profound an effect on her so many decades from now, could it? No! That couldn't happen. Bree wouldn't let it. Besides, things were looking up, her friends finally giving her another chance, inviting her back into their friendship. Things were going to get better!

And then she collided with Brittany.

The impact was so hard that both girls stumbled backward, Bree's books falling from her grasp.

"Bitch! Walk much?" Brittany said. Her books had fallen to the ground as well, but she still had a firm grasp on her cellphone.

Bree froze. Half of her wanted to collect her books, now mingling on the sidewalk with Brittany's, and then run. The other half just wanted to run.

"Well, look who it is. My new gardener," Brittany said, her glossy lips twisting into a wicked smile. "Where are you going in such a hurry? A gardening emergency?"

Bree said nothing. She knew no matter how she answered, Brittany would continue to attack. Unable to find the courage necessary to take three steps and grab her books, Bree was at least able to find her voice. "Home. Just going home."

Still keeping her prey frozen with a predatory glare, Brittany bent and picked up one of Bree's books. "Home? To cheat? Like you did with your science project?"

Swallowing hard, Bree could only muster a dry whisper. "I don't cheat."

"No? So, you just work really hard to break the curve like a good little ass kisser?" Venom dripping from her caustic words, Brittany carried the book over to a nearby tree. "Because you have no life, you make the rest of us people suffer. You'd rather go home and bury your nose in this book than go to a party."

Bree had no response until she noticed a big pile of dog poop at the base of the tree. She started forward and reached out for her book. "No!"

"Stay!" Brittany yelled, pointing at Bree.

Bree stopped and gulped, dropping her arms to her sides.

"Good bitch." Smiling from ear to ear, Brittany purred

and waggled the book over the dog feces. "I wonder what would happen if you couldn't bury your nose in this book? I think, for the greater good of our fellow students, I need to do something to stop you from ruining the curve in all our classes. Who knows, maybe someday you'll thank me for saving you from yourself."

Tears welled up for the second time in one day as Bree tried to think of something to say. Her throat tightened as images of arriving in class holding an armload of feces-covered books flipped through her head like a slideshow. Her mind reeled, scraping to grasp any form of logic she could use to convince Brittany to stop this cruelty. And then Brittany screeched, flinging Bree's book into the air and across the yard.

Bree ran to grab her book, which had landed in a forsythia bush, and then turned to see Brittany flapping her arms like a crazy person. *What in the world?* Hurrying back toward the sidewalk to pick up the rest of her books, Bree stopped when she finally saw what was freaking Brittany out—a blacksnake was curling around one of Brittany's outstretched arms. Bree knew blacksnakes were harmless but seeing one showed up out of nowhere made her nerves squirm. And then she stopped in her tracks and nearly dropped her book. There was a dozen or more snakes slithering down the tree trunk, forked tongues flicking toward Brittany like they couldn't wait to taste her.

Shrieking so loud her voice cracked, Brittany stood rooted to the spot, eyes wide, arms flailing.

"Brittany! They're blacksnakes. They're not poisonous," Bree heard herself yelling over the sound of her heart thudding in her ears. *Where had all these snakes come from?*

But Brittany only screamed louder. She grabbed the snake on her arm and flung it away and then took off running, leaving her books scattered on the sidewalk.

Fear constricted Bree's lungs as she stared at the writhing serpents on the tree. They seemed to have multiplied! Breathless, unsure what to do, and terrified that the snakes would soon be slithering toward her, she stared down at the ground and backed away toward the sidewalk. When her feet hit the sidewalk, she bent to gather her books, absently picking up Brittany's as well. And when she stood, she cast a fearful glance toward the tree.

Nothing.

Not a single snake.

Then she heard voices behind her. Bree whipped around to see Miss Harkins standing next to two kids about Bree's age—a boy with flame-red hair and clusters of freckles on his nose and cheeks and an Asian girl with sleek, black hair flowing over her shoulders. The boy held out his hand to Bree, but she didn't take it. He glanced at Miss Harkins and the girl and then looked back at Bree. Hand still extended, he took a step forward.

"Come with me if you want to live."

CHAPTER 2

THE RED-HEADED BOY dropped the beaker, and the plastic container bounced on the floor, banged against one of the metal chair legs, and slowly rocked back and forth to an eventual stop.

"You suck," the girl said, sticking one hand out palm up, the other planted on her hip.

"Wait! Give me a minute. I can do this!" The more agitated the boy got, the thicker his British accent became.

"No, you can't. Thus, this is you losing the bet."

"Just give me another try and—"

"No, no, no. No best of three. No best of five, or eleven, or a hundred and one. Pay up."

"But—"

"But nothing. You said you could juggle three beakers. I knew you would suck, so I made the wager. Sure enough, you do indeed suck at juggling three beakers. Now pay up."

Bree stared as the short, redheaded freckled boy slapped a one-dollar bill into the waiting hand of the foot-tapping Japanese girl.

"Stop it, you two," Miss Harkins said.

The girl pocketed the money and turned to look at Bree. Her shimmering black hair went past her shoulders and flowed like a curtain of finely spun silk with even the slightest move of her head. Eyebrows perpetually furrowed over her dark almond shaped eyes and her tiny lips always pursed, she held a constant expression of restrained anger.

Feeling lost in a torrential sea of insanity and looking for any form of life raft, Bree turned to Miss Harkins. Her biology teacher leaned against her desk at the front of the classroom and shook her head while pinching the bridge of her nose. She gave the sigh of disgust only an experienced teacher could muster and said, "You know, you two were supposed to be mentors for Bree. Instead, you scare her half to death with ridiculous dramatics and nonstop arguing!"

The girl crossed her arms and turned her back to the boy. "It was the ginger genius who scared her, not me."

"Oh, come on!" the boy argued as he fought not to smirk. "That was funny! She thought it was funny. Right, Bree?"

Bree did not think his joke was funny. Terrifying. Confusing. *Maybe* exhilarating. But not funny. Well, in retrospect, Brittany screaming her head off and running away was funny. The snakes appearing and disappearing, though? Unnerving. Then after all of that excitement, turning around to see Miss Harkins standing right behind her with two strangers? Disorienting. Top off the experience with the boy reaching out to her with a menacing quote from the *Terminator* movies? Frightening. After that, Bree just wanted to run and scream as well, until Miss Harkins stepped forward and explained that the snakes weren't real and her life wasn't in danger.

Ignoring the two teenagers with her, Miss Harkins had put an arm around Bree's shoulders and said, "Bree, I can explain everything. In fact, there is quite a bit that we need to talk about. Do you mind coming back to the school with us?"

Stunned into a zombie trance, Bree had followed her teacher and the two other teenagers, back to school, down the hall, and into her science classroom. Miss Harkins had shut the door and motioned for Bree to sit, but before she could explain anything, the boy had grabbed three plastic beakers and bragged about his juggling skills. Now that he'd lost his bet with the girl, Bree looked up at Miss Harkins, hoping she could offer an explanation before Bree collapsed to the floor in a screaming fit. "What? Is? Happening?"

Miss Harkins nodded toward the other two teenagers. "Bree, please meet Ryoku and Willem, two students of mine I hoped would help me explain what's going on."

"Students of yours?" Bree had never seen the two teenagers before in her life. They didn't go to this school, she was sure of that.

The expression on Miss Harkins' face softened as she regarded Bree. "Ryoku and Willem go to a different school. One at which I teach other subjects. Let me ask you something, Bree. Do you believe in magic?"

Bree's eyes widened. "What? Magic? What does that have to do with …?"

Miss Harkins drew in a long breath and gave Bree a sympathetic smile. "It has everything to do with what just happened with Brittany, and I suspect, with what happened with your science project."

Bree frowned and shook her head, completely bewildered. "I don't understand."

"Bree, I know this is hard to believe, but magic is real." Miss Harkins' voice was soft and soothing.

"What do you mean real? As in Harry Potter real? As in *real* real?"

"Yes. That's exactly what I mean."

"Of course, Harry Potter was fiction," Willem said. "We're not."

Bree ran her fingers through her hair and rubbed her temples. Her head hurt, right behind her eyes every time she blinked. "That's impossible."

With an audible sigh, Ryoku walked to a sink embedded in a lab table and turned on the water. As the thin stream flowed from the faucet, she moved her hands and wiggled her fingers. Her movements possessed a tense gracefulness, as if she participated in a beautiful and angry dance with the world around her. Then the water flowed into the air.

A small column of water floated, rippling as if in an unsteady tube. It split into two columns, each twirling around the other, a dancing double-helix. Ryoku's arms and hands and fingers moved as fluidly as the water she commanded, now transforming the liquid into an undulating sphere small enough to fit in the palm of her hand. With one final snap of her arms, the ball of water flew across the room, splashing Willem in the face.

"Bullocks!" Willem yelled. He showed that the fire of his temper matched the color of his hair as he performed a conjuring of his own. Foot long geysers of flame erupted from each of the dozen Bunsen burners in the room.

"Enough!" Miss Harkins snapped, slapping her desk for effect.

The flames disappeared. Mumbling to himself, Willem walked to the nearest roll of paper towels to dry off. Without a word, Ryoku turned off the faucet.

Bree's heart thudded and she struggled to breathe. What she just witnessed defied any sense of logic, unraveled any bonds of science and reality that she knew to be true. Maybe the stress of the day was too much and caused her to have vivid hallucinations? Perhaps this girl, Ryoku, merely threw a handful of water at Willem, but Bree's overtaxed mind saw it flow through the air first. Maybe Brittany punched Bree? Or pushed Bree to the ground and she hit her head against the sidewalk? This was all an illusion; an illusion in response to brain damage. It had to be. Right?

"Bree? Bree, look at me," Miss Harkins said. "Take deep breaths. In through the nose, out through the mouth. That will help with the shaking."

Not even aware that she was shaking, Bree did as instructed. A deep breath. Another. Her breathing sounded loud to her, against the pulsing heartbeat in her ears. Another breath. Bree felt better, less panicked. But still very confused.

"Better?" Miss Harkins said, encouraging and calming.

Bree gave a few jerky nods, still breathing deeply.

"Good. I know this is a lot to process. I thought bringing these two bundles of fun would help you digest the information and get you comfortable with the idea. Silly me. I won't make that mistake again." Miss Harkins glared at Willem and Ryoku. Willem glowered and turned away while Ryoku examined her nails.

Finally calm enough to find her voice, Bree said, "I ... I don't understand what this all means or what it has to do with me."

Miss Harkins left her desk and joined Bree, sitting at a neighboring student's desk. She placed a hand on Bree's shoulder. "Bree, you have the gift."

"Gift? What gift?"

"We certainly have a quick one here," Ryoku snorted.

"You can really be a jerk sometimes," Willem mumbled.

Ignoring the quibble, Miss Harkins went on. "Magic. The gift of magic. The gift to manipulate the environment around you in wonderful ways. The gift that very few have."

"Magic? Me? What are you talking about?"

"Yes, you, Bree. Think about our most recent science experiment with the plants. You saw how everyone else's turned out. Yours flourished, even the one that was supposed to be half dead. I'd be willing to wager that has happened to you all your life."

Bree frowned, her gaze shifting away as she thought about all the plants in her house and the yard. Always busy with her career, Bree's mother neglected them, going weeks without even watering them. Bree had stepped in to take care of them, but she never did more than give them water and a bit of plant food now and again. They'd always flourish after Bree intervened. To no one in particular, Bree whispered, "Mom says I have a green thumb."

"Injuries, too?" Miss Harkins asked, still smiling, her hand comforting on Bree's shoulder.

"Yeah," Bree said, the word falling from her mouth as she remembered Bun-Bun. Five years ago, a young rabbit hopped to Bree as she played in the backyard. Seeing that its back leg was injured, she took it in to the house and immediately set up an ersatz emergency room using a cardboard box and a bath towel. It took three days before her mom noticed and demanded that it be released back into its natural habitat, but by then Bun-Bun's leg was perfectly healed. Bree had been too young to realize that speed of the healing process was unnatural.

"That's because of your magic," Miss Harkins said.

Bree looked at her hands as if for the first time, new tools with no instructions. Even though she doubted the words, she said them anyway, "I have magic in me?"

Both Willem and Ryoku extended their arms and offered the quick, soft applause reserved for golf courses.

"By George, I think she's got it," Willem said, thickening his accent on purpose.

"Indubitably," Ryoku said. "A dollar says she cries now."

"Naah. That's a sucker's bet."

Bree offered a quick sneer to the two jibing her and then turned her attention back to Miss Harkins. "So, who are they? And who are you?"

"I'm your teacher," Miss Harkins gestured to the classroom in which they sat, "and I'm a teacher at another school. Ryoku and Willem are students from the other school."

"Like Hogwarts?"

"Yes, but this school is real, and I think you—"

"And you want me to be a student at your magic school?"

"Hey, she's getting faster and faster," Willem said.

"Oh, she certainly is," Ryoku added.

"Almost as fast as Cassidy."

Ryoku's expression changed and her head snapped around toward Willem. He recoiled from the slap of her glare as she mouthed the words, "Stop being stupid."

Quickly speaking before Bree could ask about Cassidy, Miss Harkins said, "For you, it would be more of an 'after school,' program. You would still attend school here and live with your mother. But after school, you would come to our institute and explore your gifts, your skill sets."

"Skill sets?"

"Not all magic is the same. Different regions, different cultures, different backgrounds breed different magic."

"So, my ... magic ... is different than Ryoku's or Willem's?"

"Certain aspects, yes, but there is some overlap as well. Think of it like trees. No pine trees grow along the equator and no palm trees grow in the tundra. But both are trees. The same goes for the magic energies of the world. Different areas have access to different energies with lots of overlapping. Since there are many different cultures that have evolved over the millennia, there are many different interpretations of those energies."

"So, since I was born in North America, I ... what ... am in tune with plants and healing? Like some kind of hippie Wiccan with herbs and crystals or something?"

Miss Harkins chuckled. "We call it New American magic. Willem is from England, so he has access to Western European magic, something akin to what Merlin popularized. Ryoku's parents came from Japan, the magical energies of her native country are strong within her."

"There are things they can do that I can't?"

"There are things that come easier for you than others and vice versa."

"It's like slam dunking a basketball," Ryoku said. "It's easier for a person who is seven feet tall than someone who is six feet tall. The person who is six feet tall can do it, but it takes a lot of work, time, practice, effort, and energy."

"Unless you're like me and you can sink three-pointers all day long," Willem chimed in. To show off, a basketball suddenly appeared in his hands. His tongue poked out from his mouth in concentration as he arced the ball through the air toward a hoop that popped into being on the other side of the room. As the ball swished through the net, both the ball and the net exploded into confetti while the sound of a cheering crowd filled the air.

"What the hell is wrong with you?" Ryoku snapped.

The confetti disappeared and the crowd noise ceased. Willem shrugged his shoulders. "What?"

"What you just said makes no sense! It didn't fit into my analogy! A three-pointer is not the same as a slam dunk. And basketball in England? Really."

"It made sense! You like to dunk and I like three pointers!"

"My analogy had nothing to do with 'liking' something and everything to do with the work involved in compensating for ability. You just performed an illusion. That magic comes naturally for you, like the seven-foot tall person in my example. Illusion does not come naturally to Bree and her New American magic energies. Like the six-foot person in my analogy, if she wanted to learn how to harness illusion, she'd have to work very, very hard at it."

"Yeah, but my illusion makes your analogy better."

"No! No, it doesn't! Your analogy making skills are as terrible as your beaker juggling skills!"

"I'm sorry, Willem," Bree said with a slight smirk. "Ryoku is right."

"Bullocks!" Willem crossed his arms over his chest and pouted.

BRIAN KOSCIENSKI & CHRIS PISANO

Still not sure what to make of the information given to her, Bree looked back to Miss Harkins and asked, "So, where is this … institute … located?"

"It's tucked away in the Massachusetts countryside."

Bree was surprised at the sudden feeling of disappointment. "But we're in Pennsylvania. My mother would never let me go. You said I would still go to school here, like usual."

"Oh, Bree," Miss Harkins said with a smile, "did you forget we're talking about magic?"

Standing, Miss Harkins waved her hand through the air. A small patch of air rippled, like a pebble disturbing a pond. Within seconds, a hole the size of a door appeared in the middle of the science classroom, opening to a room furnished with antique furniture. Bree couldn't breathe, doubting her eyes, her vison, her sanity. Her science teacher opened a hole in the air just by waving her hand!

As if walking through a regular doorway, both Ryoku and Willem entered the furnished room. Miss Harkins followed and once through, she gestured to Bree. "Would you like a tour?"

A scratchy static filled Bree's ears, a white noise warning that a nervous breakdown was imminent. All her life she'd felt lost. She always wanted an opportunity to find herself, wanted to be normal, wanted to understand where she fit in with everyone else. Even her best friends thought she was odd. Now her favorite teacher said she was one of the most extraordinary people .on the planet. She would never fit in now? As fear and anxiety started to throttle her, she realized that fitting in might not have been her ultimate goal. What she really wanted was not to be lonely. And now, as she peered through a magic portal, she saw three people who were odd just like her. With a big gulp, she stepped through the door.

CHAPTER 3

BREE TURNED THE PAGE. The color of the paper was eggshell and she treated it as such, using just the tips of her fingers. The book was far from brittle, but she decided to err on the side of caution, reverent of the history laid out before her. Her fingers slid over the page while her eyes scanned the content. She loved the texture of the paper, the faint roughness of the uneven divots and the dark ink of the handwritten font. The book was over five-hundred years old, and even though it was written in English, she stumbled over the odd spellings, the proliferation of "e"s at the end of so many words and using a stylized "f" where she knew an "s" should be. The illustrations captivated her the most. Hundreds of plants and beautiful flowers—she marveled at the detail given to every picture, each one precisely annotated. She turned the page.

"I told you this would be her favorite room," Ryoku said, leaning against the doorway between the hallway and the small library.

"Bullocks," Willem mumbled, slapping a crumpled one-dollar bill in Ryoku's extended hand. "Seriously, who at our age enjoys a library over a game room?"

"Ummm, people who can read."

"I can read! I read all the time!"

"Oh, I'm sure. All those quote-unquote articles in those magazines you have hidden in your—"

His cheeks reddened to match the color of his hair as Willem waved his hands as if they could erase Ryoku's words. "Whoa! My preferred reading material doesn't need to be a topic of discussion!"

Ryoku stiffened. "Ew! I was joking! I didn't think you actually had any ... you know."

Willem turned and made a hasty retreat into the hallway. Aiming for the kitchen, he said, "Hey, I'm thirsty! You thirsty, Bree? Of course, you are. I'll go get us some drinks. Be right back!"

"Get back here, you pig! How could you perpetrate the degradation of women? Just another example of how misogynists think women should be nothing more than two dimensional playthings for men's libidos!"

Bree chuckled at the fading sounds of Ryoku tearing into Willem as she chased him down the hallway. Ryoku was right, though; this was so far Bree's favorite room. With her tour guides abandoning her, she decided to stay where she was.

Walking through the doorway opened by magic (a door-port, as they called it) from her science classroom into the lounge of the institute had been a bit disorienting. Bree suffered no dire effects except for the difficulty of wrapping her mind around the fact that she traveled hundreds of miles with one footstep. After stepping through and finding herself in an exquisite sitting-room, she immediately felt woozy. Dizziness spun within her head while nausea poked at her belly. "Whoa."

"Here. Over here," Miss Harkins said as she took Bree by the arm and escorted her to a nearby canapé sofa, upholstered in supple crimson leather, and had deep scrolls carved into the rich mahogany wood trim. Other equally opulent couches and ottomans were placed around the large room, carpeted with a filigree pattern of scarlet and gold. "We've all felt the same way the first time we door-ported. Willem? Could you get a glass of water for Bree?"

Willem did as he was asked, but before he gave the water to Bree, he seized the opportunity to be contentious, and said, "The first time Ryoku did it, she threw up."

"Liar!" Emphasizing her lack of appreciation for the joke, Ryoku commanded the water to leap from the glass and splash Willem's face. By the time Willem returned from the kitchen with a towel and a dry face, Bree felt better.

Despite the overwhelming evidence that shenanigans might ensue, Miss Harkins asked Willem and Ryoku to show Bree a few of the institute's thirty rooms. Willem insisted on the game room first. Bree certainly enjoyed it—a pool table in the center flanked by a foosball table and air hockey table, pinball machines and large screen televisions plugged into the most current video game systems lined two of the walls, dart boards hung from the third wall, and the fourth wall had a fully stocked soft-drink and juice bar while tables were interspersed throughout. But she could tell that the institute held so much more.

Ryoku took over tour duty and showed Bree some of the classrooms as well as several different libraries, varying from rooms with rows of towering shelves to small, cozy reading rooms that invited a visitor to settle in with one of the hundreds of intriguing books tucked here and there. Which was exactly what Bree did.

Bree turned the next page. She shook her head in awe when she saw there was a whole section on how to use poison ivy in potions, complete with benefits and encumbrances. As she turned to the next page, a slight chill passed through the air. Hugging herself, she looked up to see a girl sitting in one of the other chairs.

With a jolt, Bree said, "Oh! You startled me. I didn't see you come in."

"No, you did not," the girl replied.

Bree inhaled so quickly her chest hurt when she realized why she didn't notice the girl enter. Skin the color of toffee, the girl wore a hooded cloak, thin and silken, emerald green with golden swirls along the edges. Long black hair flowed from under the hood, well past her shoulders. Her eyes were dark brown with flecks of bright green. Offering a subtle smile across her full lips, her face possessed an inviting warmth, yet a quiet confidence that bordered on aloofness. However, what unnerved Bree was the fact that she could see through the girl sitting in front of her. "Are you ... a ghost?"

The girl's chuckle made Bree feel dimwitted. An exotic accent adding mystery to her melodic voice, the girl replied, "No. I am very much alive and in good health. This is my astral projection, a visual manifestation of my spirit."

Bree continued to stare. Questions bounced around in her head, but she felt stupid for not knowing the answers. The girl remained silent and simply gazed back, clearly not giving up any information unless asked. Well past the awkward stage of silence, Bree suppressed the desire to fidget, afraid of making the situation worse. "So ... my name is Bree, and I'm new here."

"I know," the girl said. "My name is Siza."

"You said that this is your ... spirit? Where's your body?"

Siza's smile changed, but it made Bree feel like she asked an acceptable question. "I am in my bedroom."

"Where is that?"

The smile shifted and Bree felt stupid for asking that question. "Here. At the institute."

"You live here?"

"Yes. There are many rooms. Do you not believe they could spare a few for bedrooms?"

Bree slouched back in her chair. "Sorry. I just thought everyone ... what'd Willem call it? ... door-ported?"

Siza tilted her head and Bree felt like a clumsy kindergartener. "As you learn about magic, you will come to find that it takes energy, concentration, and skill to door-port. Coming from my home in Egypt to the institute each day would take a considerable amount of all three traits, making it impractical to do on a consistent basis. Secondly—"

Sitting up, Bree blurted, "Egypt is in a different time zone, so meeting here after school would be impractical as well." She smiled, excited that she made that deduction. Until Siza's smile shifted ever so slightly, as if exhibiting a courteous disappointment.

"Yes. You are correct." With no previous experience in conversing with astral spirits, Bree remained unsure of what to do next. So, she tried another question, hoping she wouldn't come off sounding stupid. "I take it other students live here, too?"

An inviting smile. *Good question!* Bree thought.

"Yes," Siza replied. "Willem lives at the institute as does Strongbow. I believe there will be more students starting on Monday."

"Everyone's parents are okay with this?"

Siza's expression soften to that of pity. *Dumb question!*

"Of course. Most of the students who participate in magic come from families steeped in the tradition. Both of my parents practice the arts and are contributors to this institute. However, like you, Ryoku's family is unaware that she spends much of her free time here. Willem does not talk about his family much, but Strongbow's entire family is involved in the arts."

"Strongbow. I haven't met him yet."

Siza's expression remained unchanged. "He is back home with his tribe in New Mexico at the moment. He is still grieving from his last encounter with the Mesos."

"Mesos?"

Even though Siza was largely transparent, her whole demeanor shifted, and her body tensed. *Bad topic! Really bad topic!*

"'Mesos," Siza said, "is a colloquialism we use to refer to a cult of magic users who worship the ancient pantheon of mad Mesoamerican deities. Their beliefs are misguided at best and their practices are abhorrent … including human scarifies. Strongbow believes they are involved in his sister's disappearance."

"He and a few other students decided to attack them," Miss Harkins interrupted, leaning against the doorway with her arms crossed. Bree jumped, surprised that she didn't hear her arrive, and blushed as if she got caught spreading gossip. Even Siza looked startled by Miss Harkins' arrival. With the earnest tone of a teacher, Miss Harkins continued, "It went horribly wrong and we … lost … a few students. Which is why we have rules."

Siza bowed her head enough for the hood to hide her eyes. Even Bree felt guilty, until Miss Harkins entered the small room and continued with a milder tone, "But that is the whole purpose of this institute. To allow young people to learn about their abilities responsibly in a safe environment as well as to meet and learn from students from different cultures."

One word caught Bree's attention, flitting around her mind like a hummingbird. Nervously, she asked, "What do you mean … lost?"

Miss Harkins turned to the astral projection of Siza and said, "Thank you for talking to Bree, Siza, but I think I need to talk to her alone."

Siza pulled back her hood to expose her face. Her bright eyes regarded Miss Harkins with respect as she said, "Yes, Miss Harkins. I understand."

Siza stood and gave a slight bow, then faded away leaving behind a handful of raining sparkles that quickly dissipated. Unblinking, Bree whispered to herself, "So coooooooool."

Miss Harkins sat in the now vacant chair and turned to Bree.

"You said 'lost,'" Bree whispered.

Heaving a weighted sigh, Miss Harkins reached out and put her hand on Bree's. "Yes. Yes, I did. Unfortunately, I mean that in the gravest of ways. But the students we lost took it upon themselves to break the rules and willingly participated in dangerous activities. What they did was no different than drinking and driving. It's okay to be here, Bree. As long as you follow the rules, you'll be perfectly safe here."

Bree assumed that magic could be dangerous, but to hear that students—people her age—lost their lives from carelessness sent a shiver down her spine. If they came from families who used magic and ended up dead, what chance did Bree have of surviving? Then there were the Mesos....

"So ... there are evil magic users?"

"Magic use is just like any other profession or religion. There are those who use their skills for selfishness and greed while others only use their abilities for the betterment of their community."

"But these Mesos ...?"

"Are nothing for you to worry about. There is a lot more to magic use than this institution. However, this institution will be a very good starting point for you, Bree. This is a place where I believe you will excel. Don't forget, I see you every day at school. I know your potential, and I would love to help you reach it."

Familiar warmth tingled in Bree's cheeks as she blushed. "You think I'd be good at this?"

"Absolutely. The purpose of this institute is more than just learning about magic and how to use it. It's a place to connect with others like yourself, to make friends, to—"

As if her chair became electrified, Bree jumped up and yelled, "Oh my God! Amanda and Chelsea!" Her skin paled to the color of milk as she looked at her cell phone. "I'm late! I'm sorry Miss Harkins, but I have to go now!"

Eyebrows knitting with concern, Miss Harkins stood as well and said, "Bree? Is everything okay?"

"I … I … yeah. I'm supposed to hang out with Amanda and Chelsea, and I just need to get home."

"Okay. Think of your bedroom in your house." Grasping Bree's hand and uttering some well-spoken words, Miss Harkins created another mystical door-port, this one right to Bree's bedroom. Wringing her hands together, Bree started for the door-port, but stopped to look back at Miss Harkins for permission. Her teacher handed her a business card and said, "Please think about taking advantage of what we have to offer. This is a great opportunity to learn about yourself and how you fit in the world around you. Here is my number. Just text me anytime you want to come back and I will open a door-port right to you."

"Thank you." Hand shaking, Bree took the card and then stepped into her bedroom. The magic portal closed behind her. Fear and questions about the institute and the Mesos were squashed by the fear of losing her newly re-found best friends.

CHAPTER 4

THE ALARM WENT OFF and Bree hit the snooze button within half a buzz. Already awake, she stared at the glowing red numbers and assumed her tear-burned eyes were just as red and glowing. Mary Fuffle was tucked under her arm and she gave the stuffed bunny an extra squeeze, cuddling it closer to her face, the dirty yellow fur scratchy, yet somehow still comforting.

She'd been given the stuffed animal before she was two, so she had no memory of receiving it, but she had many, many memories of having it. The off-white belly had once been snow white and the bright yellow fur had long since faded to a dull canary, the floppy footed and lop-eared stuffed animal had been her best friend. They shared many good times and many tears.

Her mother told her that its original name from the manufacturer was "Mister Snuggle", but Bree could only muster "Mary Fuffle" and the name stuck. Bree yearned for the days of making choices and changes with little to no consequences. Not that she remembered too many of those days either, she just knew that there was a time when she could change the name of her best friend and everyone thought it was adorable. Now, she made one honest mistake and her best friends hated her.

The alarm sounded again, and again she slapped the snooze bar. Monday morning announced itself and showed no sign of allowing her to wallow in her own pity, so she decided to get out of bed and start her day.

All through her morning routine, the memories of the weekend haunted her, restless spirits of recently dead relationships. As soon as she'd returned from the institute, she'd called Chelsea. There was no answer, so she called Amanda. No answer. Then Chelsea again. Then Amanda again. She texted and emailed and reached out to them through every social media network she belonged to. Nothing.

Using her entire Saturday, she repeated the process to no avail. By Saturday evening, both Chelsea and Amanda shunned her electronically, reversing friendship statuses on every mutually traveled website. Virtually, she was alone.

Sunday morning, she went to Amanda's house, knowing Chelsea would be there. Bree tried to explain, saying she was looking into an after-school program that gave her an opportunity to experience different cultures from around the world, and then apologized with every fiber of her being. Since Amanda's parents weren't home, no courtesies were extended and no filters were observed. Chelsea asked questions like, "Why didn't you call to let us know you couldn't make it? At least a text or something?" but Amanda answered before Bree could with responses like, "Because she no longer views us as important enough to waste her time!"

It wasn't true, but no matter how many times Bree apologized or different ways she explained her actions, Amanda became more and more agitated. Yelling and swearing, Amanda kicked Bree out of her house, banning her for life.

Now it was Monday and Bree trudged down the stairs and into the kitchen to make a bowl of cereal. The room was bright, mostly windows and skylights, transforming the space into a pseudo-solarium. A chic black and white pattern of tiles raced along all of the countertops while the gray and white faux marble flooring worked smartly with the cupboards and the chrome high-end, name brand appliances. As she so often did, Bree ignored the kitchen table as well as the table in the dining room. Instead, she opted to sit on a stool at the butcher's block counter in the center of the kitchen. She took long maudlin scoops from the bowl to her mouth as she stared absently at the cuts and gouges in the counter's thick wooden top. So apathetic, even her mother's morning tirade about a client didn't bother her.

"He said he doesn't like what?" Bree's mother, Allyson Moore, yelled. Wearing an earpiece, she looked as if she were irritated with the chicken Caesar salad she was making herself for lunch. "He's an idiot! You're with him at the property, right? Well, you keep him there, I'll be right over."

Obviously frustrated, she ran her hand through her short hair, clipped close at the base of her neck and getting longer the farther up her head it went, leading to thick cinnamon colored locks strategically styled to look happenstance. She removed her earpiece and placed it into the pocket of her suit jacket, the same shade of black as the skirt that stopped a few inches above her knees. Her lips shifted from a blood-red scowl to a warm crimson smile as she turned to greet her daughter. "Good morning, Bree."

"'Morning, Mom" Bree pouted into her cereal bowl.

"Oh my. That salutation is far from warm and inviting," Allyson said as she slid her plastic salad container into her designer lunch bag. "Is it about a boy?"

A slight smirk tugged at the corner of Bree's mouth as she thought about how ridiculous it was that her mother always missed the target by asking if a boy was the cause of any problem in her life. Bree could be carrying a severed head and her mom would undoubtedly ask, "Is it about a boy?" Why would it be about a boy? Bree's last date had been a "friend-date" with Sci-Fi Sam at the end of last school year. He went away for the summer and when he came back, Bree had changed—"blossomed" according to her mother—and Sci-Fi Sam hadn't hung out with her since, hadn't even tried to talk to her. Rumor had it that she became too attractive and that made him uncomfortable. Yet, the "normal" boys still viewed her as the awkward girl from her freshman year. So, her mother would always, always, always be wrong when she asked, "Is it about a boy?"

Keeping her thoughts about her mother's off base question to herself, Bree mumbled, "No. Amanda and Chelsea. I don't think they're my friends anymore."

"Oh. Them." Bree could tell that her mother tried to hide her feelings about them. She failed, though, the tone of her voice revealing that she didn't hold either of them in high regard. "If they don't appreciate you, then the answer is obvious. Just make new friends."

With that, Allyson kissed her daughter on the forehead and left for work.

Bree felt numb. Her mother's words held little meaning since they trivialized her emotions and offered a solution that bordered on the impossible, like suggesting that a trip to the moon was no more difficult than a trip to the mall. She finished her breakfast and went to school.

Everyone stared, all day. Bree knew that half of the student body didn't know she existed, but she felt as if all eyes trained on her. Any time she passed close to any of the cheerleaders or athletes, they stopped and watched her walk by. Undoubtedly, Brittany told everyone in her cliques about the weirdness of the snakes Friday after school, probably even embellishing the tale more with every telling. Then there were the students that she sometimes associated with. They stared as well, hearing how poorly she treated her lifelong friends and how pathetic she had become by begging their forgiveness. Even Miss Harkins seemed to stare at her in science class.

Bree returned home to an empty house and a voicemail from her mother stating she wouldn't be home until after 8:00. A text followed to make sure she got the voicemail. As she ate her insipid microwaved lasagna, she replayed the day's events and concluded that her life had less flavor than her dinner. Could she go through another day like that? Tomorrow? Just existing, ambling from class to class like a hallway zombie? At least zombies had a hunger for brains as motivation. What did she have? What did she live for? Her mother's approval? Her mother, the "man-hating, hear her roar, pulled-herself-up-by-her-bootstraps-after-her-husband-left-her and became a real estate attorney" woman? It didn't seem likely to Bree that she would ever grow into a woman her mother would respect. However, her mom's parting words this morning did stick in her head.

Bree reached into her pocket and pulled out the business card from Miss Harkins. "Make new friends," her mom had said. Shrugging her shoulders, Bree mumbled, "What the hell," and sent a text to the number on the card.

Before she had a chance to formulate a plan, even before she had a chance to feel anxious about her decision, a door-port opened in her kitchen. Shocked, she jumped back as Miss Harkins walked through. "Oh, I'm sorry, Bree. I didn't mean to startle you."

"That's okay," Bree whispered, forcing a smile.

Miss Harkins returned the smile and placed her hand on Bree's shoulder. "I am very happy that you contacted me. I was a little worried about you in school today. You seemed so withdrawn."

"I'm okay," Bree lied. "I was just thinking about the institute all weekend."

"Am I to assume you'd like to see what we have to offer?"

Bree's fake smile became real. Someone wanted her. "Yes. I think I would like that."

"Wonderful! It's a very exciting day, too. We are getting more students today. Are you ready?"

Biting her bottom lip, Bree nodded. New students! Possibly like her, taking a new step into a new world, trying to find answers to questions she couldn't even articulate. She took a step and followed Miss Harkins through the door-port.

They walked into the lounge, just like the last time she visited. However, there were seven adults sitting around, talking. Plates of hors d'oeuvres adorned the tables. Bree tried to appear as if she had done this a hundred times before, but she was pretty confident that she had a wide-eyed, deer-frozen-in-the-headlights gaze. So concerned about trying not to look like the neophyte she was, she paid no heed to conversations, or that any of them stopped when she arrived.

"Bree, these are some of the other instructors as well as the parents of our newest student who will be staying with us."

Blushing, Bree offered a weak smile and a quick wave. "Hi."

The adults all returned warm smiles and various greetings. Some nodded, some waved, depending on their cultural preference. Wishing that they wore silly "Hi, my name is…," name tags, Bree wondered how to differentiate between parent and instructor. Miss Harkins placed her hand on Bree's back and guided her out of the room. "I'm sure you didn't contact me to chat with adults all night, so how about we get you to the other students? They're in the game room. Do you remember how to get there?"

"Yes," Bree said. As Miss Harkins headed back to the lounge, inevitable anxieties crept into Bree's mind as she walked down the hallway. What if the others didn't like her? Siza and Willem had been friendly, but what if it was all an act? Ryoku had a certain level of abrasiveness, but Bree saw some commonality with her—both had to sneak away from home to spend time at the institute—but what if Ryoku didn't see that? Were there cliques here like in her high school? Butterflies flitted about her stomach as she entered the game room.

Ryoku sat on one of the stools at the juice bar playing a game on her phone. Close to her were Willem and another girl, tall with hair so black that tints of blue shimmered under the right light and eyes the crystal blue of newly formed ice. A tall, broad shouldered Native American boy with anger perpetually etched into his face threw darts, sinking them deep into the cork dartboard. Bree assumed that he was Strongbow.

As Bree started to walk toward Ryoku, Siza appeared in front of her. "Hello."

Trying not to appear taken aback, Bree said, "Oh, hi. Siza, right? I didn't see you come in. Nice to finally meet you."

Other than being opaque, Siza looked exactly the same way she had as an apparition—smooth, dark complexion, ethereal hazel eyes, and a green silk cloak with gold designs along the edges. She still displayed a smile that conveyed more than her words. Right now, it told Bree that she'd said something stupid. "We have already met."

"I know. It's just nice to meet you in person."

Siza's smile made Bree feel as if she were five. "It hardly matters if you converse with my corporeal form or my astral spirit, I am still the same being."

Exasperated from being on the losing end of a war of wits and not wanting to lose a friend before she'd even made one, Bree tried to change the topic. "I see. So, I'm assuming the guy trying to throw the darts through the wall is Strongbow? I haven't met him yet, in either corporeal form or astral spirit."

A slight head tilt accompanied Siza's smile and showed that she appreciated Bree's little joke. "You are correct. However, I would counsel against trying to do so now."

"I gathered that. Still no luck finding his sister?"

"Luck can be altered. But neither luck nor hard work have brought him any closer to his goal."

Strongbow threw three darts, one at a time, and grouped them close together. As soon as the third dart left his fingers, he strode to the dartboard and removed all three with one angry yank. Returning to his original spot, he repeated the process, his brow furrowing and jaw jutting the entire time. Bree felt bad for him, but didn't know what to say, so she looked over to Willem and the new girl, who stood a good four inches taller than he did. Bree couldn't help but giggle to herself as she heard the frustration grow in his voice as he said, "Okay, spell your name again?"

With a thick Irish brogue, she replied tersely, "S-I-O-B-H-A-N."

"That spells See-O-Ban!"

"It's pronounced Shi-vawn."

"Chiffon?"

"Siobhan."

"Sea Bond?"

"Siobhan."

"Chevron?"

"What is so hard for that toffee nugget bouncing around in the English head of yours to grasp?"

"Well, with a temper like that, I think I'll call you She-Bear!"

"Of course. You're English and think you have a God-given entitlement to everything you lay your eyes upon!"

"Why don't you have red hair?"

Ryoku looked up from her phone and twisted her face, sneering in confusion. Even Strongbow stopped throwing darts to look over at the argument. Siobhan squeezed her eyes closed and shook her head. "What?"

"Seriously, what kind of Irish girl doesn't have red hair?"

"The kind that actually lives in Ireland."

"I have red hair. An English boy has red hair and an Irish girl doesn't. Seems a bit wonky to me."

"There are plenty of Irish girls with black hair."

"You should dye it to show that you're Irish. If you don't want red, then go with blonde. Blondes have more fun, you know."

"Gingers have no souls, you know." With that, she spun on her heel and walked away from him, not seeing Ryoku kick him in the back of the knee, buckling his leg, as she said, "Idiot. No wonder you don't have a girlfriend."

Strongbow smirked and went back to throwing darts as Siobhan crossed the room to introduce herself to Bree. "Hi. If you didn't catch my name, it's Siobhan. I don't blame you if you abandoned that muddled conversation at any point."

Bree chuckled. "No, I definitely caught your name. I'm Bree. I think your name is beautiful, Siobhan."

Siobhan shot a glare to Willem, now rubbing the back of his knee. "Hear that, ginger? Not only can she say it, she likes it."

Willem opened his mouth, but Ryoku cut him off, "Think about what you say before you say it, genius. Words have consequences, and with you, the consequences are usually negative."

He crossed his arms over his chest and pouted, until he glanced to the entrance of the game room. His eyes widened, and his jaw fell slack.

Wondering what could possibly leave the gregarious Willem speechless, Bree turned to the doorway. There stood a boy with short black hair and coffee colored skin, similar to Strongbow's. His brown eyes held anxiety and he smiled meekly. Confused, Bree was unsure why Willem reacted the way he did to such a timid looking boy. Then he articulated it. "Meso!"

CHAPTER 5

A BEAR. Bree blinked, and sure enough there was an eight-foot grizzly with a thick coat of brown fur and two-inch claws standing on its hind legs where Strongbow had been throwing darts. Raising its front paws over its head, it roared, lips curling back to expose glistening teeth as streams of saliva sprayed from its muzzle.

Terror squeezed her chest as Bree tried to back away only to trip on a chair leg and fall, landing hard on her posterior. Hands and feet worked as she crab-walked across the floor toward the door. Fear-injected adrenaline blocked the pain in her backside, but she knew she'd have a bruise later.

What was going on? Seconds ago, a Hispanic boy walked into the room and then Strongbow disappeared and a grizzly appeared in his place. Now, out of the corner of her eye, she saw Willem lift a lighter, spark it to produce a tiny flame, and then whoosh it somehow until it billowed and shot forward toward the new boy as if propelled from a flamethrower. The thrumming heartbeat in her ears muffled the shouting from everyone else in the room.

"No!" Miss Harkins shouted over the commotion, jumping in front of the cowering boy. Whisking her left hand through the air, the flames swirled and dissipated into nothingness even as she wiggled the fingers of her right hand toward the bear. The air warped and wavered and then, writhing, the bear gave one last roar, and then shrunk in size, its fur retreating into its skin, claws returned to fingers and toes while the elongated face of the enraged bear surrendered to the equally enraged face of Strongbow.

Panting and patting at his clothes as if to make sure they were still there, Strongbow wobbled and struggled to stay on his feet. "Miss Harkins!"

"Strongbow, listen," Miss Harkins said, still holding her hands out, shielding herself and the new boy. "He is one of the new students."

Strongbow's face contorted as if he was trying to not cry. "But he's a Meso!"

"He is a teenage boy with the ability to tap into the magic of his culture, just like you. He …."

"Whatever," Strongbow growled, turning his back to Miss Harkins. With an angry wave of his hand, he opened a door-port to his bedroom. Before anyone could say anything, he stepped through and disappeared.

With no smile, Siza asked, "Shall I send my astral spirit to him?"

Miss Harkins lowered her arms and relaxed her whole body. "Thank you, Siza, but no. It's best we just let him cool down a bit."

"Well, I for one agree with him," Willem said, his accent thick with anger. "Or did we all of a sudden forget who murdered Nicholas, Cassidy, and Tierney?"

"Willem, none of us forgot about them, but this boy was *not* there. He and his family are *not* a part of that cult."

"He's. A. Meso." Willem growled.

"That's it," Miss Harkins said, slipping into the teacher mode that Bree had seen when students in her biology class became too rambunctious. "Everyone into the lounge. Siza, please ask Strongbow to join us."

"Hell of a first day, huh?" Siobhan mumbled to Bree as they filed from the game room to the lounge.

"Yeah," was all Bree could muster. Her heartbeat still throbbed in her ears, muffling the sounds around her as tunnel vision squeezed her sight like a clenching fist. Trying to be subtle, she took deep breaths in through her nose followed by a slow exhale past her lips.

Once in the lounge, Siobhan sat on one of the ornate couches with plush cushions. Bree was quick to sit next to her, briefly wondering if the perceived strength she admired in the Irish girl was real, or a misconception due to her height and stern features. She recalled how the girl refused to back down from Willem, and Bree decided Siobhan was indeed a strong person. *Maybe I can gain strength from simply being near her*, Bree thought.

The adults in the room blurred together. Feeling like a boat on choppy water, she anchored herself to Miss Harkins, standing in the center of the room next to two boys. The one boy was the "Meso" who caused the uproar simply by appearing in the room. The other, dressed in a black T-shirt and black pants, was tall and thin with a slim nose and dull brown eyes. Thick dark hair hung over his ears and temples and was cut so it rested like a shaggy mane over the top of his collar. His hands were stuck deep in his front pockets, which emphasized his slouch, and his shoulders rolled forward slightly, as he slowly shifted his weight from leg to leg as if swaying in a gentle breeze. The frown on his face made him look like he had been sent to the principal's office for shooting spitballs or something. The young Meso didn't look any happier.

Even though the boy in the limelight was short, he was still taller than Willem and a bit stockier. He, too, wore a black T-shirt advertising a rock band Bree had never heard of, jeans, and snakeskin boots. Miss Harkins put her arm around his shoulders and said, "This is Javier. He's from Mexico and like many of you, he'll be living at the institute."

"Why is he here?" Willem asked. Refusing to sit, he stood near the far wall with his arms crossed. Ryoku stood next to him. Even though she hadn't verbalized her opinion, her crossed arms, cocked hip, and scowl let everyone know what she thought.

Keeping her voice even, Miss Harkins explained, "Lately, you have been using the word 'Meso' in a derogatory fashion, branding all Mesoamerican magics as evil because of what one cult is doing. That's like saying all terrorists come from one country. We all have '-isms' associated with each of us. Our religion. Our skin color. Our nationalities. Let's not forget, each of our magics ties *all of that* together. Our magics are who we are."

"How do we know he's not a spy?" Willem asked.

One of the other teachers started to step forward, but Miss Harkins waved him off, answering the question herself, "Because his parents are both on the council, just like Siza's."

The anger in Willem's face dissolved as he accepted Miss Harkins's answer. He kept his arms crossed as he turned to Siobhan and said, "Well, I don't trust her either."

Siobhan conveyed all she needed to with a snarl, her cold blue eyes glaring.

Too focused on Javier, Bree missed Willem sticking his tongue out. She appreciated the new boy's situation. He was alone. Different. An outsider. People who should be supporting him accused him of something he didn't do and made assumptions about him even though he did nothing to warrant them. He was clearly nervous, and Bree figured he just wanted to be accepted by people like Willem and Strongbow. But instead of seeing the institute as a bridge between cultures, he'd arrived to find a wall.

Maybe she still had adrenaline coursing through her. Maybe Javier's plight spoke to her even more deeply than she suspected. Maybe she just felt like it was the right thing to do. Whatever the reason, Bree stood and walked up to Javier. She stuck out her hand and said, "Hi. I'm Bree. I'm new here, too."

Brown eyes glinting, he smiled, teeth bright white. In an unsure voice he replied, "I'm Javier."

Ryoku held out her hand to Willem. "Pay up. I told you she'd be the first one of us to befriend him."

"Bullocks, Bree!" Willem whined as he slapped another crumpled one-dollar bill into Ryoku's hand. "Betting on you is gonna cost me a bloody fortune!"

Bree smiled, encouraged that Ryoku used the word "us." She had wondered where she fit into the puzzle, but Ryoku's subtle hint helped—she was a part of "us." Her smile grew as Siobhan stood, stuck her tongue out to Willem, and introduced herself to Javier. Siza greetedhim as well, but Ryoku and Willem stayed where they were. So did Strongbow.

As silent as a shadow, Strongbow had appeared at the threshold between the lounge and the hallway. He leaned against the doorway with his arms crossed. The gaze from his dark brown eyes bored through Bree, stripping away layer after layer of the persona she displayed and the person she thought she was until there was nothing left but her soul, so deep that even she didn't know what he saw. The muscles at the back of his jaw flexed, adding extra angles to his already chiseled face. After what seemed like eons of judging her, Strongbow gave a slow and deliberate nod. Bree blinked, and he was gone. Her heart slammed around inside her rib cage, as if it had been chained during this strange communion with Strongbow and leapt about like it was excited to be free. What did he find when he peered into her? What did the nod mean? Did he respect her for doing what she thought was right or was it a dismissive nod? Or was he signaling somehow that Javier was *her* responsibility now?

Miss Harkins cleared her throat, garnering the students' attention, still standing next to the other new boy in black. "As you can see, Javier is not our only new student today. This is Rumiel. He's from Transylvania."

The room fell silent; the only sound Bree heard was her own heartbeat. She had completely forgotten about Rumiel's arrival, and after she put so much effort into breaking out of her own shell to give even a modicum of comfort to Javier, she doubted she had anything left for Rumiel. She hoped one of her peers would step forward to introduce themselves so all she had to do was smile again and repeat her name. Unfortunately, Willem was the first to speak.

"Transylvania? Are. You. *Kidding*. Me? We have a vampire now?"

Rumiel winced. His accent wasn't thick, but it was detectable. "Transylvania is now a small region in Romania. Lots of forests. No vampires."

As if he didn't hear a single word, Willem turned to Ryoku and said, "We've got bloody vampires in our school now."

"Willem! That is absolutely not—" Miss Harkins began to scold but was cut short by the appearance of black mist forming in the middle of the room.

Bree's heart skipped, but noticed that no one else moved, or even looked surprised. She wondered how much more weirdness she could take, but then came to an epiphany—she still felt more comfortable here than at high school.

Like smoky vines sprouting from a lone seed, wispy tendrils unfurled from the floor and rose upward. The tips curled and unfurled, dark fingers grasping for the unknown. Once they reached the height of a person, they interlocked and flowed outward, creating the wavy frame of a doorport. Through the mist walked two large black men.

While one was older, they had similar facial features, close enough that Bree correctly assumed them to be father and son. The stern face of the older man scowled so hard that he seemed to be wearing a mask. His head was clean shaven and shone in the lounge lights. His ink black eyes, high cheek bones, and a tapered chin gave him a stern, aristocratic look. His son looked just as stern, minus the timeworn lines and crevices around the older man's mouth and eyes. Finger-thick dreadlocks flowed evenly past the young man's shoulders, a black mane on a hungry lion.

Handsome, regal even, he was the most beautiful man Bree had ever seen.

Father and son both wore leather vests and pants, but neither one had on a shirt. The older man wore tan with primitive style snakes of red, yellow, and green embroidered along the sides of his pants and front of his vest while the son wore black snakeskin, scales glinting in the light. They were both broad shouldered and well-muscled, and Bree couldn't help but notice the younger man's taught rounded muscles and smooth, glimmering skin.

Willem and Ryoku both went slack jaw when they saw the young man. Finally finding her voice, Ryoku asked in a whisper, "Tierney?"

"No," the older man said in a voice deep and rumbling. "This is Tierney's twin, Lucien. I trust this institute will do a better job of keeping him safe than they did with his brother. I, for one, will certainly be keeping a more watchful eye."

"Yes, Mr. St. Martin," Miss Harkins said, offering a smile along with a slight bow. Deftly, Miss Harkins escorted him toward the other adults congregating at the one end of the room as she continued, "We appreciate you offering your services to the council and becoming an instructor here. Your extensive knowledge of voodoo will benefit the students."

Rigid posture adding to his air of haughty disposition, Mr. St. Martin growled out a response. "I'm here to be close to my son, to keep him *safe*. I would prefer he stay at his home institute, but he insisted on coming here."

"We believe that he can learn a lot from being exposed to the magics from different cultures," Miss Harkins said, extending her hand like a game show model to the other instructors in the room.

"That is what you told me I brought Tierney here. And now—"

"And now *you* are here as an instructor, to teach other young men and women about your culture's magics. So, let's leave the students to get to know each other while we adults come to some agreements and work out a plan for the rest of this semester."

No sooner did Miss Harkins turn her back and escort Mr. St. Martin out of the room with the other instructors, Willem and Ryoku, along with other students lining couches and sitting on chair arms, turned to focus on Lucien.

"So you're Tierney's twin," Willem said.

"That I am," Lucien replied. "And you are Willem."

Willem straightened up and smiled. "Yeah. I'm assuming Tierney told you all about my smooth nature and sharp wit?"

Lucien looked Willem up and down. "Tierney told me that your brash words, erratic behavior, and quick temper mask feelings of inadequacy, limited intelligence, and even more limited height. I believe he referred to you as Ryoku's yippy purse dog."

Ryoku threw back her head and laughed as Willem turned beet red. Everyone else stared in stunned silence. Finding his deep voice hypnotic, Bree wanted Lucien to talk again. Laced with a Creole accent, his words held a level of authority and confidence she found simultaneously comforting and exciting. Lucien continued, "My brother also told me about Ryoku, Siza, and Strongbow. Although, I do not see Strongbow?"

"He's in his room," Ryoku said. "Did Tierney tell you that he's moody?"

"He described Strongbow as one who acted upon his emotions and, even though they flowed like a twisting river, they were often justified. He described *you* as moody. More intelligent than you let on, but not quite as clever as you think, quick to choose sarcasm over wit."

The smile jumped from Ryoku's face to Willem's.

Lucien turned to Siza. His eyes held neither anger nor malice, but a level of seriousness that Bree had never seen in person her age; an adult in a teenager's body. Siza smiled and nodded slightly, the hood of her cloak exposing only the lower half of her face. "I believe I would prefer to remain ignorant about your brother's thoughts of me."

"Tierney told me that you talk less than the others, but say far more. He held you in high regard." He punctuated his statement with a warm smile as Siza blushed. Bree melted. She couldn't pry her stare away from this new student.

Lucien addressed Rumiel and Javier. "As the newest additions to this institute, I am sure we will get to know each other well. I hope we can learn much from each other—and that our interests and goals align."

"Siobhan and I are new, too!" Bree heard her voice cut through the air. Lucien and the other students turned toward her just as she felt her face heat up in what she knew was an obvious blush. But no one had time to respond or laugh as Miss Harkins poked her head back through the door.

"Our meeting will likely go on for a while, and it's getting late. Ryoku and Bree need to return to their homes while all the other new students who are staying here need some time to settle in. There'll be plenty of time to introduce yourselves to your new classmates tomorrow."

Siobhan stood and held a hand out to pull Bree to her feet. Leaning in, she whispered, "Down, girl. Or you'll drool on yourself."

Bree blushed even more and looked away from Lucien. She whispered back, "I don't know what you're even talking about."

Siobhan gave a knowing smirk and nudged Bree with her elbow. "Oh, please. I'm surprised you haven't escorted him to his room yet."

Siza approached Bree with a similar smirk on her face. "You are not the only one to find Lucien alluring. Nor are you the only one being less than subtle." With that, Siza offered a quick glance to Ryoku.

Bree almost giggled when she saw how Ryoku looked at Lucien, the forlorn longing of a puppy waiting for a tasty treat, until she realized that she probably looked just as ridiculous mere seconds ago. Ryoku stared with a sweet smile and a sparkle in her eyes, as if remembering a favorite dream, until she noticed that Bree was watching her. Mood soured, Ryoku's face twisted to a scowl, harsh enough to make Bree suddenly happy to be leaving soon.

CHAPTER 6

"YIKES," BREE WHISPERED as she pulled on her workout pants. It had been a while since she'd worked out and back then they hadn't been quite so tight. She slipped her matching shirt—black with pink stripes down the sides—over her head and realized it, too, was more formfitting than she remembered. For a while, she'd worn this same outfit, or one like it, to spin classes, kick boxing, yoga, Pilates, and Zumba, and she'd jogged in them, but with everything going on in her life combined with the lethargy accompanying the recent winter months, she hadn't worked out lately.

Self-conscious, she wondered what the other students would think. Miss Harkins had told her that they were going to start some exercises today, so Bree figured the other students would be wearing similar gym attire.

Turning sideways, she regarded herself in the mirror, seeing the similarities she shared with her mother. She'd perused magazine articles about how girls could use their best "attributes" to attract boys, but she'd been so skinny for so long that she never thought she'd have any attributes at all. Now, her old workout outfit revealed curves that seemed to have appeared overnight.

Even though she knew that her mother wouldn't be home for another four hours and that her bedroom door was closed, Bree peeked over her shoulder to confirm her privacy. She turned back to the mirror and struck a magazine-cover pose.

Hand behind her head, she puckered her lips and arched her back. Giggling, she imagined Chelsea and Amanda laughing with her, striking ever more ridiculous poses. Then she stopped and dropped her hands to her sides. Chelsea and Amanda. What were they doing now? She frowned at her reflection. Her former best friends probably wouldn't laugh at all, but instead say she was trying too hard to be beautiful and popular. Sighing, she reached for her cell phone and sent a text to Ryoku.

Until she could make one herself, Miss Harkins instructed Bree to contact Ryoku for a door-port. Lacking both the strength and skill necessary to do it herself, Ryoku would use it as a training assignment and would rely on one of the more advanced students for help. Bree assumed it would be Willem. Even though neither Ryoku nor Willem had been to Bree's house, they at least had been to the area, familiarity aiding in the ability to door-port. Within a minute, one appeared.

Now acclimated to this mode of transportation, Bree stepped through without taking notice to what was on the other side. She assumed she would walk into the game room with all of the other students there. She assumed correctly. However, she also thought that everyone else would be wearing workout clothes. She was wrong.

At first, she noticed that everyone was wearing street

clothes like jeans, T-shirts, and skirts and boots. Then she noticed the stares, a form of bewilderment etched on every face. Playing cards at a small table, Javier and Rumiel both went wide-eyed and looked away. Javier blushed while Rumiel stole brief glimpses. Strongbow smirked, then went back to tossing darts in silence. Lucien looked her up and down, but then he turned away as well. Willem leered, a slick smile slithering across his face. As usual, he was the first one to speak.

"Why, 'ello poppet."

A smack to the back of his head from Ryoku followed. "Eww! Pig!"

Still smiling, still leering, Willem continued, "Seriously? Look at her! I mean, she's ... she's ..."

"Don't say it!" Ryoku scolded.

"But wow! I mean ... wow!"

Blushing, Bree crossed her arms over her chest. Embarrassment mixed with anger. She had hoped to find a new start at the institute, be someone new with these people. Instead, she felt stupid and clumsy, just as she did in high school, and Willem's immaturity only made it worse.

"I think she looks nice," Rumiel said, unsteady voice barely above a whisper. Moving as one, all eyes shifted to him. His cheeks pinked, and he hunched forward, turning his attention back to the card game.

Ryoku turned to Bree, her lips twitching in an obvious attempt at stifling a laugh. "But seriously. Other than to show off, why are you dressed like that?"

Forcing herself not to panic or cry or run and hide, Bree focused on keeping her voice steady and even. "Miss

Harkins said that we were going to start exercises today."

Ryoku's eyebrows rounded to frame the pity withing her eyes. The sincerity of that look, though, Bree could not deduce. "Oh, Bree. She meant *mental* exercises. We're going to be meditating today."

"If you really want to work out, I'd be more than happy to be your partner," Willem said, waggling his eyebrows.

"Down, you English dog," Siobhan said as she put her hand on Bree's back to guide her out of the room. "Bad dog. Bad!"

"Bite me, Sea-Bear," he replied.

As Bree left the game room with Siobhan, she heard Ryoku say to Willem, "You are such a pig!"

"Ignore him," Siobhan said as they ascended the curved staircase to the second floor. "He's English. Manifest Destiny hasn't been bred out of his blood yet. Although, England does have a good music scene, and some fun night clubs."

"Night clubs?" Bree asked, skin tingling from uttering the words.

"Yeah. Lot of fun. I think one of the first things I'm going to do when I learn how to door-port is head over and hit the clubs. Only problem is it takes a long time to build up the strength to door-port that far. Though, everyone says if we work together, we can door-port farther than if we tried it by ourselves. We should go some time."

"We?" Adrenaline rushed through Bree's veins. It was energizing to think that she befriended someone her own age who had been to clubs before. Now her new friend wanted to take her to a club! "Really?"

Siobhan chuckled at Bree's reaction as they entered

her room. Even though it was as small as a dormitory, she kept it clean and organized. Posters of female bands as well as Celtic crosses and knots adorned the walls. Her desk contained pencils and pens neatly in a mug with Irish swirls on it in one corner and an autographed photograph of Lucy Lawless as Xena in a frame on the other corner while her laptop was centered on the desktop. Even her bed was made. Opening her closet, Siobhan said, "Of course 'we.' It'll be fun. Ryoku seems like she would be into the idea as well. Maybe make it a girls' night?"

"Umm …." Bree mumbled, not knowing how to reply.

Siobhan grabbed a large black tee shirt. "Do you think Siza would be interested?"

"Umm …." Bree replied again, trying to wrap her head around the conversation.

As if cued, the astral projection of Siza suddenly appeared in the middle of the room and asked, "Interested in what?"

Bree brought her hands to her mouth to stifle a squeak as she jumped backward and Siobhan threw the shirt in her hands at the translucent image of Siza. The shirt passed right through Siza and flopped onto the bed. Siobhan placed her hand to her chest and yelled, "Good God, girl! You scared me!"

"Me, too," Bree said.

Siza lowered her head, clearly ashamed of her actions. "I offer my humblest apologies. I meant neither disrespect nor harm. I merely wished to convey that our meditation exercises will begin shortly in the yoga room. It's at the end of the game room hallway."

Siobhan looked to Bree, both girls still wide-eyed from

being startled. As they calmed themselves, they smiled. Then chuckled. Then laughed. Wiping a tear from her eye, Siobhan said, "You need to give some kind of astral warning before you appear out of nowhere. Like, astral knock or something!"

Siza offered an apologetic smile. "I will do my best to provide some form of advance warning in the future."

"Good. We need some boundaries, girl."

"So," Siza started, curious, "May I ask what you were talking about before I arrived? You had mentioned my name, after all."

Siobhan peeked out her open door to make sure they were alone. She grabbed another tee shirt from her closet and handed it to Bree. With a wink, she said, "Bree and I were wondering, after she and I learn how to door-port that is, if you would be willing to help us make one to London some time to go clubbing."

Siza's eyes widened, expressing surprise to be included in the planning stages of such a covert operation. "That sounds rather duplicitous, but I believe the resulting camaraderie might be worth it."

"Good! Bree and I can't wait to learn how to door-port. Anyway, let everyone know we'll be down in a minute."

Still maintaining her mischievous smile, Siza offered a slight bow and then disappeared.

Thoughts swirling, Bree put on the tee shirt, large and loose, stopping mid-thigh, and followed Siobhan to the yoga room. Bree had admired Siobhan when she first met her, but she never imagined that in a matter of days they would end up co-conspirators. Excitement and fear tumbled through her chest. Other than breaking curfew a few times with Amanda and Chelsea, Bree had never broken the rules. Now she was thinking about going to another *country* to go clubbing! A chill flowed down her spine as she wondered if she truly had the wherewithal to do that. The small notion of not knowing the door-port spell, or *any* spell for that matter, comforted her.

By the time they reached the yoga room, Bree had wrangled some of the butterflies in her stomach. The room was open and airy with evenly spaced columns and skylights through which rays of sunshine flowed in to brighten the room. The hardwood floor was streaked with thin beige and brown planks and potted philodendrons rested on pedestals next to each pillar.

Everyone else was already there, all sitting on mats. Siza sat in front next to Miss Harkins and they faced everyone else. Javier and Rumiel sat next to each other in the front row while Strongbow and Ryoku sat behind them. Willem sat behind Ryoku with an empty mat next to him. Behind Willem was Lucien with an empty mat to his left. All the students still wore what they were wearing when Bree first door ported into the game room, except for Lucien. He had changed into different clothes, now wearing a plain black workout shirt, his muscles stretching the flexible material to its limit, and loose black nylon shorts.

Siobhan glanced at Lucien, then to Bree and winked. She sat on the open mat next to Willem and scowled at him. Confused as to why Siobhan would willingly sit next to Willem, Bree sat on the last empty mat, the one next to Lucien. She tried to pay attention to Miss Harkins and Siza as they spoke, but she couldn't stop herself from stealing glances of Lucien. Why did he change? She was certain he was mocking her, teasing her for her misunderstanding.

Even though she didn't like that he was making fun of her, she was grateful that he was more subtle than Willem's lasciviousness. She then noticed that everyone else closed their eyes and shifted to a kneeling position, tucking their feet under their backsides.

Following along, Bree closed her eyes and tried to replicate the same pose, starting with her right ankle over her left. Uncomfortable, so she switched to left over right. Not enjoyable, but not painful. Having missed the instructions or secrets on how to do this properly, she cursed herself for not paying attention. She placed her hands on her thighs. Palms down didn't seem right. Palms up made her feel as if she was trying to get a suntan. Palms down. She then slid her hands to her knees, but that seemed too far, so she drew them back to where they fell naturally, but then she felt lazy. Then her right foot felt numb, so she tried to lean to the left to untuck ....

She felt a warm, strong hand grip her forearm. Jerking as her eyes snapped open, she saw Lucien leaning over toward her. Even though he whispered just loud enough for only her to hear, his accent thickened his words. "You seem to be having a difficult time understanding the simplicity of closing your eyes and relaxing."

Bree looked into his eyes, so brown they seemed black and endless. Having never seen eyes so dark, she was surprised at how warm and welcoming they were. Embarrassment bloomed within her chest. She was unsure if it originated from not being able to do such a simple task or the fact that it took her so long to answer. "I can't sit like everyone else."

His full lips spread into a warm smile, exposing his perfect teeth. "Then simply sit in a way that makes you feel comfortable."

"Okay. But what ... what do I think about?"

His grip tightened ever so slightly and her whole arm tingled. "You don't. That is the whole purpose of meditating."

"I can't not think. My mind is racing nonstop with all of this. This is so new to me."

"Your magic is nature based, right? Maybe you can find solace in that. Start there and let your mind drift." Lucien released her arm, returned to his modified kneeling position, and closed his eyes.

Bree sighed and tried again, this time sitting cross-legged, her hands simply resting on her lap. Listening to Siza's and Miss Harkins' soothing voices, she thought of the forest near her neighborhood. She loved playing in it when she was young, and she still loved visiting it. Now that spring had arrived, the flowers in the adjacent field would begin to bloom. She smiled, feeling the softness of the grass between her toes, the tenderness of the flower petals against her fingertips. The smell of wildflowers filled her heart and mind. Lost in those sensations, nothing else mattered. Until she once again felt a strong, warm hand on her forearm, and she opened her eyes.

Lucien was leaning toward her, but this time, there were nine other pairs of eyes staring at her as well with just as many mouths agape. Starting to ask, "What ...?" she looked down and saw why she was the center of attention.

As if in an embrace, she was wrapped loosely from head to toe by leafy philodendron vines.

CHAPTER 7

"I'M FINE. I SWEAR," Bree said.

"How could you be fine?" Willem asked, making sure to stay at least one person removed from Bree. "The plants came alive and attacked you!"

Miss Harkins plucked a stray leaf from Bree's shoulder and said, "Now, Willem. They did no such thing."

Bree felt a bit claustrophobic from all the bodies standing so close to her, their hands unwinding remaining leaves and stalks from her body. The minor calamity even started to play tricks on her mind. Lucien pulled a leaf from her hair, taking a few strands with it, but as he wiggled his fingers to dislodge the leaf, she swore that he kept her hair. Raising her hands in front of her, Bree backed away from everyone. "Guys. Please. A little space."

As sheepish as usual, Rumiel dropped his eyes and backed away. "Sorry. It was just really cool what you did. I'd love to be that good with my talisman."

Confused, Bree looked to Miss Harkins and asked, "Talisman?"

Miss Harkins, voice as soothing as ever, said, "Each form of magic has a talisman, a totem, so to speak, that the practitioners of that magic easily control or commune with. For example, yours is flora. Plants and flowers."

"I thought my magic is nature based?"

"It is. That is what we call the core of your magic. Many magics overlap in different ways. Siobhan's, Ryoku's, and Strongbow's are nature based as well like yours, whereas you and Siza belong to magics that both have strong healing spells. But your talisman is unique to your magic, a part of you."

Bree turned to Rumiel and asked, "So ... what is your talisman?"

Obviously trying to keep his voice from cracking, he replied, "Insects. I can, or will, learn to control insects. Insects and spiders."

Without realizing, Bree twitched her upper lip into a slight sneer. "Oh. So, what is everyone else's talisman?"

Miss Harkins answered for everybody. "Well, Siza is spirit, Siobhan is earth, Strongbow is air, Javier is reptiles, Lucien is darkness. As I'm sure you could guess, Willem is fire and Ryoku is water."

"I can control flowers too," Ryoku hissed. Arms crossed over her chest, she leaned against one of the pillars and scowled. "Cherry blossoms."

"True," Miss Harkins said, still talking to Bree. "Since cherry blossoms are such a deep rooted aspect of her culture, her land, her history, they are part of her core magic."

"Reptiles can be found in both jungles and deserts, much like my culture," Javier chimed in.

"Really?" Willem asked, sarcasm dripping as thick as his accent. "I thought reptiles were your power animal because all you Mesos are lizards and snakes."

"Willem!" Miss Harkins snapped.

Frowning, Willem said, "Sorry, Javier."

Even though Strongbow sat on one of the window sills away from the group, a smile slid across his face upon hearing Willem's words.

Bree wanted to interact with Strongbow more and took this opportunity to take a few steps closer to him and ask, "So, what about what you did the other day? Turning into a bear?"

He continued to look out the window without acknowledging Bree or her question. Miss Harkins answered instead, "That's polymorphing. It's a part of his core magic. His magics are tied so directly to the spirits of the land and nature that he can change into many of the indigenous animals of North America."

"Before you ask, I know what's bouncing around in that frisky little mind of yours," Willem said, "his clothes become part of his fur or scales or feathers. That's why he's still in them when he shifts back."

Bree scowled at Willem and lied, "I wasn't thinking that."

"Anyway," Miss Harkins continued, "Other magics contain the ability to poloymorph as part of their core magic."

"Like mine," Javier jumped in again. "But I don't know how to do that yet."

Willem said, "I'm sure you'll learn your core magic soon enough to turn into a snake. Or a lizard. Or a snake. Just sayin'."

Knowing very little about the reasons behind the perceived notion that Mesoamerican magic was evil, Bree couldn't help but feel sorry for Javier. Even if the magic was evil, which she highly doubted, she knew that this awkward boy certainly was not. She also knew all too well what it was like to be on the receiving end of such hateful words, especially since Willem's previous apology possessed the warmth of a dead fish. "Well, Willem, following your logic that means since illusion is a part of your core magic, you're trying to hide something. A … shortcoming, maybe?"

Miss Harkins brought her hand to her mouth to hide her grin. Most of the other students laughed. Lucien smiled. Even Strongbow turned his head to flash a smile in Bree's direction. Willem's eyebrows knitted as he tried to think of an appropriate comeback. They drew together even tighter when Ryoku held out her hand and said, "Give me a dollar."

"What? Why? We didn't have a bet on this!"

"No, but she owned you so good I feel it should cost you."

"*What?*"

"Seriously. Give me a dollar."

Rolling his eyes, Willem mumbled, "Bullocks to this." He reached into his pants and handed another crumbled up bill to Ryoku.

"Nice one," Rumiel said to Bree, offering a shy smile.

"Thanks."

"Way to stick it to the British dog," Siobhan said.

"Now, Siobhan," Miss Harkins said. "That's just as bad as what he said."

"Sorry, Miss Harkins," Siobhan said, as Willem stuck his tongue out at her.

Bree turned back to Miss Harkins. "So, how did it happen? I get that plants are my talisman, but I didn't tell them to do that."

"Well, what were you thinking about while meditating?"

"There's some woods by my house that I like to go to. I was thinking about that."

"How did that make you feel?"

Bree looked away and thought about the joy that the memories brought her. . Unconsciously, she wrapped her arms around herself, a solo hug. "Warm. Comfortable. Happy."

"That certainly explains why all of the flora in the room was embracing you, don't you think?"

Still confused, Bree asked, "But how did I do that? It wasn't a conscious effort."

"Magic comes from emotion," Lucien said. "Because emotion itself is magic."

Lost in his dark eyes, Bree felt like she was trying to run with no traction. Hearing his words dried her mouth out and sent flutters straight to her heart. She begged herself not to say something stupid in return, but every response that she mentally conjured she deemed unworthy. Not wanting to create an awkward silence, she just blurted an overly girly, "Really?"

"Our bodies are made of water and proteins and calcium and sugars. We are all nothing more than elaborate chemistry experiments. Yet we feel. Our emotions are moved by perfect sunsets and we find wonder in the stars on a clear night. We find joy in the laughter of children and hold hope that we ourselves can find such exuberance again. We tingle over the notions of romance and yearn for the soft touch of love's fingers. What we are capable of feeling is infinite, yet we are such incredibly finite beings. *That* is magic."

The world rippled around Lucien, nothing else existed beyond the tunnel vision of Bree's distorted peripheral. After a dry swallow, she whispered, "I totally agree."

"Whoa," Javier whispered to Rumiel. "That's really cool."

Rumiel clenched his jaw and grimaced, lowering his gaze to his feet.

"Yeah," Willem laughed, "And we feel stupid when we find ourselves caught in the rain with no bumbershoot and anger when a car drives by to splash us with a mud puddle and satisfaction when we flip it off."

Upset that Willem so rudely interrupted her moment with Lucien, Bree began to work on her look of derision, until she noticed one being shot at her. From Ryoku. Again. However, now that the spell Lucien cast with his beautiful words had been broken, Bree turned back to Miss Harkins and said, "Okay. Emotion drives magic. Got it. But judging from everyone's reactions, what I did was … unusual?"

"Definitely impressive for someone who has never used magic before, that is for sure," Miss Harkins answered. A sense of pride bloomed within Bree..

"Then how was I able to do that?"

"That just means you're a natural, or you came from a family very strong in magic."

Bree chuckled atMiss Harkins' last comment. She imagined her mom and dad as a young couple sitting around a room choking on candle smoke while arguing if they were reading each other's tarot cards properly or not. Great Aunt Gertrude, whom she had never seen wear anything other than floral patterned muumuus and cartoonishly large hair curlers, dancing around to perform spells. Grandpa with his inch-thick reading glasses and ever-quaking hands holding a parchment of ancient magics, reading aloud without his dentures, his dry lips curling over his gums. Grandma complaining about the smell of incense. Uncle Chuck itching from misplaced herbal powders. "No. I'm sorry. I can't imagine anyone in my family practicing *any* kind of magic."

"It's not uncommon for the gifts to be passed on by a family member who is unaware," Miss Harkins said.

Bree shook her head. "Everyone else here has parents who know. As you mentioned, some are on the institute's council."

"Mine don't know," Ryoku said. Back to leaning against a column with her arms crossed over her chest, her irritated gaze softened from shooting lasers to tossing daggers. "My grandparents moved from Japan when my father was a teenager. He met my mom ten years later when he was visiting relatives in Japan and she came back to the States with him. I was born over there when they were on vacation. I don't know which side of my family I inherited my gifts from, and neither of them know I have them."

"Oh," Bree said. "So, I guess we have something in common."

Smiling the way a shark would smile at a guppy, Ryoku said, "Don't push it." She then walked toward the exit, passing by Miss Harkins along the way. "I think I'm done with exercises for today. I'm going to grab a snack and then head home."

Willem followed Ryoku out the door.

Miss Harkins turned to the rest of the class and said, "That's not a bad idea. Why don't we call it a day and pick up tomorrow."

Strongbow slid from the windowsill and strode from the room. Lucien offered a subtle smile and a slight bow to Bree. "Until tomorrow."

"Okay," was all she could muster as she felt her cheeks catch fire from a blush and wiggled her fingers in a coy wave. As soon as Lucien turned to leave, Bree rolled her eyes and silently admonished herself for being so lame.

Siobhan put her arm around Bree's shoulders and joined her in watching Lucien walk away. She leaned close and whispered, "Don't worry. You'll do better next time."

Javier turned to leave, but Rumiel did not. Javier gestured for Rumiel to follow, but Rumiel jerked his head toward the remaining girls. Trying to be as subtle as possible, Javier and Rumiel wordlessly exchanged gestures, conveying their intent. Javier left. Rumiel stayed.

Siobhan turned to Bree, still gazing at the door Lucien left through, and said, "Come on up to my room. We'll listen to some Dead Kennedys."

Scrunching her nose, Bree jerked her head back and blinked rapidly as if a unicorn appeared out of nowhere and belched in her face. "What did you say?"

"The Dead Kennedys," Siobhan chuckled. "They're a classic American punk band. You're wearing their shirt."

Bree looked down at the stylized "DK" emblazoned in white on the black tee shirt and mumbled, "Oh. I thought it stood for 'Donna Karan'."

"Actually, I did too," Siza said from behind Bree and Siobhan, startling them both.

Siobhan said, "Girl, I swear to God, I'm gonna tie a bell around your neck like a cat. Now, come on up to my room. I have to educate you two in music."

As they started toward the exit, Rumiel cut them off. Hands in his pockets, he stood straight with locks of his dark hair falling over his face, past his cheeks. A weak smile etched across his face. "I like punk music."

"Umm," Siobhan said, glancing to Bree.

"Cool. But I think this is more of a … girl talk … sort of thing …." Bree said.

"Oh. Cool. Yeah. Cool." His poture deflated into a slouch and he trudged away, limp hair hanging in front of his face.

The girls waited for him to leave before they exchanged confused glances and shoulder shrugs. Not letting it bother them, they continued on their way. As they meandered to Siobhan's room, Bree asked, "So, what's it like growing up with magic? In your families?"

"Magic has been a part of my everyday life since I was born," Siza said. "My parents respect it and have taught me to respect it as well."

"My family is a little different," Siobhan shared. "Only my mother practices magic, and she barely dabbles in it. I've known about it for a few years now, but recently wanted to learn more. My mom only knows what has been passed down to her, but that's enough to keep her satisfied. My parents decided to send me here so I can learn more about it properly. My brothers dabble with it, but nowhere as seriously as I do."

"I'm just having a hard time imagining what that'd be like. To come from a family that has magic."

"It is very rare for an individual to possess such magics, especially a strong as you have demonstrated, without them coming from a family that has magic in it," Siza said. "You live with your mother, right?"

"Yeah. But—"

"What does she do for a career?"

"She's a real estate attorney. But—."

"Is she a successful real estate attorney?"

"Very. After my dad left when I was four, she put herself through school while single handedly raising me. She worked very hard to get to where she is."

Siza and Siobhan looked at each other and back to Bree. Siobhan said, "Bree, it sounds like your mom could be using magic."

"What?"

"Think about it. In about eleven years or so, she put herself through school, passed the bar, got whatever real estate licenses she needed, and is successful? As a single mother? That's a lot to do with no help."

"I agree," Siza added. "Her magic usage does not need to be grand or done with flourish. A well-placed luck spell now and again. Charms and potions are rather innocuous. Symbols of good fortune could be hidden anywhere in your house."

"Anywhere?" Bree's mind raced.

"Anywhere."

Bree followed the girls in silence, her thoughts now preoccupied with ransacking her own house.

CHAPTER 8

OVERWHELMED. The whirlwind of new ideas and experiences swirling around in Bree's brain was simply overwhelming. In fact, it seemed to be getting worse! Just as she'd started to wrap her mind around being a powerful conduit for magic, she'd learned that she'd inherited her abilities. But from whom? A parent? A grandparent? How far back did the magic go? Logic dictated she'd inherited the gift from her mother, and Bree was already concocting plans to search the house for evidence. But she'd have to wait. Because of all her new extra-curricular activities and time she spent at the Institute, she had forgotten to study for her English test.

Hurrying, she entered the school and went straight for her locker. In a way, she felt special, unique. How many other sophomore girls had a 17th century book about potions in their backpack next to their trig book? Okay, there was a fine line between "freak" and "unique," but Bree knew it was all contextual. At the institute with her newly found peers, she was unique. Here, a freak. And never more so than right now as she opened her locker and an avalanche of dry dirt spilled out onto her shirt and jeans, piling up around her shoes. A reddish brown cloud enveloped her as she stood stock still, wondering how so much dirt could fit in one locker. Then she felt a twist inside her chest as the hood and sleeve of her favorite hoodie lay limp on top of the pile, the rest of the sweatshirt buried. Pages from books and notes poked out from the mound as well, reaching for escape from a wrongful grave, including her English book.

She was so utterly surprised, she remained frozen even after the dirt stopped pouring out, not able to register what had just happened. No coherent thoughts formed. No logical questions starting with "why" or "when" or "who" could illuminate the darkness of her confused mind. Until she heard the laughing.

She turned to see Brittany and four other cheerleaders pointing from across the hall. "She loves her plants so much that she brings her own dirt to school with her," Brittany said with a laugh. "Including her very own snakes." Her comment elicited loud and overly enthusiastic laughter from her friends.

Bree looked to her feet, both lost within the pile of dirt, and then noticed the rubber snakes and clumps of philodendron leaves poking up from the pile. Realization slowly crept into her mind, and once the shock faded, anger billowed. Bree stared at Brittany, her wide-mouthed laugh, and her glistening pink lips splitting like a shark's over straight, gleaming teeth. The girl had everything she could want. She commanded a small army of mindless drones who followed her around and did her bidding. Half the boys in school were in love with her. Yet, for some reason, she hated Bree. It made no sense, but it was time for Bree to hate back.

"Bree!" A voice snapped her from her tunnel vision. Blinking, Bree looked at Miss Harkins standing next to her, and felt the teacher's hand squeezing her shoulder. Miss Harkins cast a quick glance downward and whispered, "You need to be aware of your surroundings."

Bree looked down again to see that the philodendron leaves had multiplied; the vine stems had elongated and were now snaking from the dirt toward the cheerleaders. Even though Bree felt as if her heart were a chunk of ice, it still pumped fire to her cheeks. She stepped out of the dirt pile and kicked the leaves back before anyone could notice.

Still keeping a hand on Bree's shoulder, Miss Harkins scowled at the cheerleaders and said, "I think you girls have done enough. You'll be hearing from the principal, but for now I suggest you get to your classes. None of you can afford another tardy."

Fists clenched, Bree turned away and tried to regain control of her emotions, fighting back the tears. Damn it, she was *not* going to cry! Standing with her back to the movements in the hall, she couldn't stop herself from turning her head just enough to watch the rest of the world move around her. Most students walked by swaddled in apathy, either not noticing a locker full of spilled dirt in the hallway or not believing the image to be spectacular enough to take notice. Bree was thankful for them the most. A few took photos with their phones, so she reminded herself not to do anything too dramatic. On occasion, a student or two would look over at Bree, pity in their eyes. Some chuckled and pointed. Then Amanda and Chelsea walked by, saying nothing as they passed. Amanda, now wearing contacts and sporting a cute long-sleeved T-shirt, laughed through glistening pink lips while Chelsea, wearing her favorite bulky sweatshirt and her wiry hair pulled into an untamed ponytail, offered a look of pained sympathy behind her too-big-for-her-face glasses.

Then the hall was empty. "Breathe, Bree," Miss Harkins said. "Just breathe through it."

Now that everyone was gone, and she was alone with just Miss Harkins, Bree's emotions threatened to overwhelm her. Her heartbeat consumed her whole body, pulsing all the way down through her ankles, rattling her ribs, rushing through her ears, and rippling her vision.

Bree closed her eyes, trying to think of anything other than vines strangling Brittany and her minions. She needed to calm herself, to push away her anger. She remembered the meditation class and how she lost herself in her thoughts. How Lucien helped her. How comforting his hand on her forearm was. How warm his skin felt on hers.

"Don't worry, honey, I'll get this all cleaned up," a different voice said. Bree opened her eyes to see one of the school's cleaning ladies. Even though the older woman smiled, it was one of pity. Bree allowed Miss Harkins to escort her from the mess while the cleaning woman used her dustpan as a makeshift shovel, scooping small mounds of dirt into the waist-high trashcan on wheels.

"I hate her," Bree growled.

"The cleaning lady?" Miss Harkins asked.

Bree glared at Miss Harkins.

Miss Harkins offered a soft smile in return. "I'm sorry. I thought a little humor might help."

Bree wanted to tell her that it didn't. Wanted to *yell* that it didn't help. Wanted to scream and holler and gnash her teeth and … and Bree knew deep in her heart that all Miss Harkins wanted to do was help. "Thank you," she whispered, but was uncertain if any words came out of her mouth.

Miss Harkins guided Bree to her science classroom, empty for the first period of the day. She then retrieved a towel from one of the supply drawers and a lint roller from her desk drawer. Bree took the towel and lethargically brushed the dirt off her shirt. Eyes welling with tears, Bree asked, "Did this kind of thing ever happen to you?"

Using the lint roller on Bree's sleeve, the sticky pad quickly turning brown, Miss Harkins sighed. "It happens to a lot more people than I care to think about. The good news is as adults Brittany will be a mean, unhappy woman with few friends while you will have earned everything you want."

Bree smirked and gave a huff of derision. "You make it sound so easy."

Miss Harkins shook her head. "I'm sorry. I sometimes forget that you're still watching a movie I've already seen."

Bree sighed again. She wished she could hit the fast forward button on the remote to Miss Harkins' movie analogy. Miss Harkins was at a point in life where Bree wanted to be—in control, accepted, self-assured. "How did you do it?"

"Survive high school?"

"All of it. School. Magic. Parents. Old friends and new friends. Bitchy cheerleaders."

Miss Harkins chuckled. "Yeah, there is a lot going on in life isn't there?"

"Sometimes I feel like it's too much."

"Well, you certainly have every right to feel that way."

"How did *you* do it? How did you get through?"

Miss Harkins walked to behind her desk and sat down in her chair. She leaned back, and gazed out the window, her eyebrows curled inward, her mind rifling through a file cabinet full of memories. "My teen years were a bit different. Sure, I lived in a suburb and went to regular school and had regular friends. But both of my parents knew about and were involved with helping me learn about my abilities. They both possessed magic and were involved in the council for our style of magic."

"The 'new' North American magic. Like what I possess."

"Yes, but I didn't go to a special school like the institute. My family wanted me to go to regular school and they chose to live mostly in non-magic society."

"So, there are people with magic who aren't a part of non-magic society?"

"Yes. When you involve more than two people with *anything*, you're going to get conflicting opinions. There are all kinds of different branches and factions within the society of magic users, each with their own agendas."

"Like the Mesos?"

Miss Harkins sighed and picked up a pen from her desk and turned it over and over in her fingers. "Unfortunately, sometimes extreme opinions and agendas are found within one magic type, like the Mesos. All Mesos are Mesoamerican magic users, but not all Mesoamerican magic users are Mesos. That situation is not unique to just Mesoamerican magic. That's why the different magic councils of the world decided to start a few experimental institutes like the one we're involved with."

"Kind of like an exchange program?"

Miss Harkins paused and looked down for a moment. "Yeah. Something like that."

"Your family helped you with your magic?"

"They did. But I, too, felt different from my fellow students. I always felt like an outcast because I had magic and no one else in my regular school did. But my parents and I were close, so I had them to turn to."

"Is magic always passed down by parent or can it skip a generation?"

"It's rare, but it can skip a generation or even more. I've also heard of people manifesting magic even though no one in their family is known to have had it. That's so rare, I've never met anyone like that. Those are special people, indeed."

A chill ran through Bree. She didn't want to be any more "special" than she already was and refused to entertain that thought. Someone in her family had magic. A quick climb of her family tree revealed to her that there was only one branch that could bear the fruit of magic – her mother.

"Bree? Are you okay?" Miss Harkins asked.

"I'm just wondering about my family. But, yeah, I'll be okay."

"Do I need to tell you not to seek revenge against Brittany? And not to use your magic here at school?"

Bree chuckled, her first of the morning. So enthralled with solving the mystery of magic within her family, Bree almost forgot about Brittany's bullying. And her former best friends' reaction to it. She brushed her hands over her sleeves and jeans one final time. "No. I'll be fine."

"Good. If you need anything, you have my cell phone number," Miss Harkins said. She wrote a quick note and signed it. "In the meantime, take this to class. You'll need an excuse for being tardy."

"Thanks." Bree accepted the note and headed toward her English class, mind occupied not by her upcoming test, but by thoughts of finding evidence that her mother was responsible for the magic.

CHAPTER 9

TWO WEEKS. Bree had been ransacking her own house for two weeks. Nothing. No arcane items, no mysterious symbols, no creepy charms. Every night that her mother had been away working late, Bree scoured a different room. She checked everything—lifted rugs, opened drawers, flipped cushions and mattresses, thumbed through every book in the house. She even raided her mother's underwear drawer! If there were one place she would hide something, it would be in the one place no one wanted to venture. Unfortunately, that expedition yielded nothing more than a case of the heebie-jeebies.

Last weekend her mother was gone part of Saturday, so Bree searched the attic. Hopes of discovering secret heirlooms linking her mother to magic disappeared as she uncovered unwanted junk. Boxes of old clothes, styles from decades long gone. Tacky knick-knacks with unknown purpose or appeal. Hope glimmered within her when she found a rogue jewelry box, but once she opened it she realized the only shine came from the gaudy baubles encased in tarnished metals. She examined every wall stud, looked at every ceiling joist and studied every exposed piece of plywood. No writing. No scrawled sigils. No hidden doors. Just a normal attic.

Today was a bit different than last Saturday. Her mother spent the morning and afternoon with Bree, a nice breakfast at the house followed by shoe shopping and lunch out. Bree so wanted to discuss magic with her, ask her about her lineage and if she had ever practiced. However, Bree realized that would be a desperate act and it would cause more harm than good. Plus, she still hadn't snooped through the basement yet. Although, that would have to wait.

Like last Saturday, her mother had a business social to attend. Despite wanting to use the time to explore the dark recesses of the basement, Bree had other plans. Her mother was thrilled to learn that she was going to go out with some of her new friends for the evening.

Now that her mom was gone, Bree added cherry red lipstick as the finishing touch to her makeup. She stepped back to regard herself in the mirror. Stylish top that either hid or playfully accentuated her breasts, depending on how she turned or twisted, and jeans tighter than she was accustomed to. She thought about trying her new pair of boots, but decided the heels were too high to be comfortable. Instead, she wore simple black flats that somehow seemed both dressy and casual.

Even though the ensemble was simple, she realized it all came together and made her look ... good. Really good. She never would have looked like this if she were going to hang out with Chelsea and Amanda. Then again, she never would have an opportunity to do something like this with those two.

With a couple minutes to spare before she had to leave, she thought about getting a head start on searching downstairs. She headed toward her bedroom door, but then stopped. Nah. She would barely get started before she'd have to leave. Maybe there was someplace she'd already looked that she should double check. There was her mom's room again—and her underwear drawer. A shudder raced down her spine. No, nothing but white cotton inhabited that drawer, which could only mean … did her mother have no social life? No reason to wear anything more than high-waisted, white cotton underwear? Her mother was successful and beautiful, and she deserved … The leap in logic from boring underwear to no social life suddenly made Bree explore other ideas regarding her mother and magic.

Bree had been sneaking off to meet with her own private cabal for almost three weeks now, so why not her mother? A normal person, even a driven person, didn't work as hard as her mother. Maybe she had her own group of magic-using friends? Maybe she stored all her implements of magic elsewhere? This was something she would have to talk to her friends about. No sooner than she thought about them, they appeared.

A door-port appeared in her bedroom and through it stepped Siobhan, Siza, Ryoku, and Willem. Willem scanned the room, a lecherous smirk across his face. He then noticed Bree and his smile widened. He slowly looked her up and down, from head to toe and back up, over every curve, stopping just below her face. With an inflection as obvious as his leer, he said, "Why, 'ello, beautiful!"

"Eeeeww!" Ryoku squealed. Slapping the back of his head, she said, "Give me a dollar!"

Willem whined. "What? Why?"

"For being a pig!"

"I told her she was beautiful!"

"No. You didn't. You were being a pig."

"But—"

"No. No 'but.' Pay your tax. Pay your pig tax."

Willem reached into his pocket and huffed, "Fine!"

Ryoku handed the crumpled dollar to Bree and said, "It's not much, but I have a feeling this is the only way we can train him."

Taller, Siobhan crossed her arms and looked down to Willem. "English dogs are the hardest to train."

Before Willem could reply, Ryoku wagged a finger at Siobhan. "No. We talked about this before we left. We're going to a place filled with English people and we can't have you turning into Michael Collins."

Siobhan smirked. "Michael Collins? I'm impressed."

"I'm Asian, remember? Gene of intelligence, plus ten."

"Nerd."

"Bitch."

Siobhan laughed. "Sorry. You're right. Do I owe you a dollar too?"

"No. That's just for our lapdog."

"Hey!" Willem shouted. "Don't forget, you need me for navigation for our little skip across the pond!"

"Then apologize to Bree."

Willem looked into Bree's eyes and said, "I apologize. Sometimes I become too overwhelmed by your devastating beauty that I lose control of my mental faculties."

"Devastating beauty? You are full of shit, but apology accepted," Bree replied.

However, Willem's gaze flicked back down her face, her chin, her neck as if he fought a losing battle with his eyes. Once they stopped moving, Bree crossed her arms over her chest and all four girls screamed, *"Willem!"*

"Bullocks!" William reached into his pocket and handed another crumpled dollar to Bree.

As Willem cowered under a barrage of Ryoku slaps, Siza turned to Bree. "It is impossible to condone his behavior, but you do look beautiful."

Bree smiled. "Thank you, Siza. You do, too."

Siza mumbled a thank you and tugged at her emerald-green top, shimmering with the same ornate design as her cloak. Bree wondered if Siza had simply used a spell to transform her cloak into a blouse.

"In fact," Bree went on, "everyone looks wonderful, like we're ready to party and have a great time. But I have to confess that I'm nervous. I've never done anything like this."

"As am I," Siza whispered. "For the same reason."

"No need to be nervous," Siobhan said. "Let's just have a good time! Are we ready?"

"As long as Captain Pervert can keep his eyes from popping out of his head, we should be good to go," Ryoku said, grabbing a hold of Willem's hand.

"I said I was sorry like a hundred times!" Willem said after an eye-rolling groan.

The other girls joined hands as well, no one else wanting to touch Willem. Everyone closed their eyes.

"Okay," Willem said, "You four concentrate on opening the door-port. I'll concentrate on the alleyway we want to go to. I've been there before. Nice secluded location in the city. No one should see us."

Siobhan chuckled. "The rat is familiar with an alley. How fitting."

"Quiet!" Ryoku scolded. "Now concentrate."

Bree and Siobhan we're still novices at creating door-ports, but both had shown an aptitude for it. Bree had again discovered how easily magic came to her while Siobhan's experience with magic before arriving at the institute gave her an advantage over other first-timers. However, on her best door-port, Bree was able to get from the institute to her house but was tired and shaky for hours after the trip. Now, as she concentrated, she felt the magic of her friends next to her, swirling around her, their energies stacking up and stretching out around the planet. She couldn't explain it, but Bree felt the Earth, felt her energy travel over the ocean to London. Even with eyes closed, she knew the door-port had opened into an alleyway, just as Willem promised.

Once Bree felt her feet on solid ground, she opened her eyes to see a dirty brick wall in front of her and smelled the sour stench of old trash all around her. Still holding hands, she and her friends walked through the doorway, from her clean, warm bedroom into the dank and chilly alley. The door-port vanished, and Willem gestured as if presenting a prized treasure. "Welcome to London, ladies!"

Accustomed to the magic involved, Willem, Ryoku, and Siza exited the alley with ease. Bree and Siobhan wobbled and leaned on each other to fight the disorientation. However, by the time they caught up with their friends, the feelings of nausea and fatigue had faded, and Willem was holding open the door to a nightclub.

The music punched Bree in the gut like a fist as loud, thumping, electronic beats designed thrummed through her whole body. She grabbed Siobhan's arm, needing assistance while her eyes adjusted to the darkness. Down a set of stairs, strobe lights flashed over the dance floor on the right while neon outlined the bar on the left. Small tables with two to four chairs were clustered around the walls. As soon as the five stepped off the stairs, Willem scanned the room like a hunter looking for prey. Finding what he wanted, he said, "Well, have fun. Let me know when it's time to leave," and headed straight for a table of two young women.

Bree watched in wonder as he sat down with the women. At first, they looked bemused by his intrusion, but as he talked to them, their expressions changed and soon the girls were giggling and looking absolutely charmed. Bree shook her head and turned her attention to her friends.

Watching the same scene, Ryoku shouted over the music, "Yeah, I don't get it either. Either they're dumber than we are, or he has two distinct personalities."

"I'd like to think it's the first choice," Siobhan said. "I can't stand the thought of him actually being charming. I'm gonna go get drinks. I'll meet you on the floor."

Bree and Siza looked at each other with a blend of fear and excitement. They didn't need to say a single word to let each other know that even though they shouldn't be here, they were thrilled that they were. Not knowing what to do next, they followed Ryoku to the dance floor. Because it was early, the floor wasn't too crowded, and they found a spot and began to move with the music. Bree danced to a song she never heard before, repetitive beat and flowing tempo. Timid movements at first, but she gradually became more comfortable when she saw that the strobe lights and colorful lasers made everyone on the floor look good. Siobhan showed up and handed a bottle of beer to her, and Bree let herself move more freely.

Even though the club was trendy and drew a younger crowd, Bree assumed that she was the youngest person in there. She knew that with her makeup and outfit she might be able to pull off early-twenties, but she didn't want to try. She wanted the night to be a bonding moment with her new friends, so she paid little attention to the other patrons—until she felt someone watching her. Through the flashing lights, she could tell he had dark eyes, thick, dark hair and a complexion darker than hers. Spanish, maybe? Italian or Greek? Definitely Mediterranean. She laughed at herself. What did she know about how people from far away looked? He could be from anywhere. Or he could be from right here in England. *Oh my god*, she thought. *I'm in England!* Every time that notion crept into her head, she quickly shooed it away, afraid she might freak-out if she dwelled on it too much.

Still dancing, she turned her back to the young man, waited a few minutes, then peeked over her shoulder. He was still staring at her. And then he smiled, dark eyes sparkling in the flashing lights. Feeling a rush from the flirting, something she was woefully inexperienced at, she smiled and turned away again. Letting herself enjoy the moment, she became much more liberal with her movements. She turned back and he was gone.

Giggling, a sense of liberation rushed through her. Had she seen a boy that handsome in school, she would have put her head down and fled as fast as humanly possible. Even though he disappeared, he had smiled at her. This energized her. Freed her. She tipped back her bottle and was surprised to discover that she had finished her beer, especially since she was not fond of the bitter taste.

"I'm heading to the bar. I'll be right back," Bree yelled over the music to Siobhan.

"Okay. Here. You'll need this," Siobhan yelled back, handing Bree some money.

The excitement of the situation overrode her nervousness of needing to pretend to be … Bree realized that she didn't even know how old she needed to be to buy a beer in England. Siobhan knew, of course. Siobhan the statuesque beauty. Strong. Confident. That was all Bree needed to be. Confident. *Just act like you know what you're doing*, she told herself.

Strolling to an empty spot along the bar, she set down her empty bottle and slid it forward toward the bartender. When she looked up at her, Bree decided to keep it simple and said, "Another one, please."

Without so much as a second look, the bartender set another beer in front of her. Bree paid and took a sip, relishing the moment. Not only was she doing things she never dreamed of, but she was good at it!

Then the guy to her right picked up his drink and headed back to the dance floor revealing the young man who had been watching her earlier. He was leaning on the bar, still staring at her, a charming smile on his lips. *He's really gorgeous*, she thought. She tried to study him without making it obvious that she was looking at him. She took another drink and noticed that the boy's features were a lot like Javier's, only everything seemed to fit together better. Like he had been sculpted to be an example of a particular kind of beauty.

She surprised herself again by lifting her beer in greeting and saying, "Hi."

Smile still fixed on his face, he replied, "Hi."

Embracing her newfound confidence, she kept going. "My name is Bree."

He looked her up and down as if appraising a piece of furniture. "I know."

Reeling back as if his words knocked her off balance, she frowned and sputtered. "Wait. How … how do you know my …?"

A forked tongue flickered from between bright, white teeth. "Because I am Talo, and I am here to kill you."

CHAPTER 10

BREE SWORE HER MUSCLES turned to stone, fear petrifying her body. She couldn't tell if Talo used a paralysis spell on her or not; he certainly didn't need to. Her thumping heart drowned out the music, the pulsing flow of blood from her chest to her fingers and toes all she could feel. Wide-eyed and unblinking, she could not pull her eyes away from Talo's, the color of powdered cinnamon flecked with gold, even as he transformed.

Talo's body pulled itself, elongating, his skin turning into scales. Forked tongue flicked toward her again and again as his features mutated into those of a snake. Everything about him changed and twisted. Everything except his eyes, which remained human and locked on Bree's.

Then, before her was a twenty-foot long snake, coiled, poised to strike, and swaying so his human eyes remained even with hers. The confidence she'd gained from the night was gone. The laughter, the flirting, the dancing, all shattered. The only thing left was pure fear. She thought of Lucien and how strong and confident he was, wishing he'd suddenly appear to her rescue. That was just a desperate fantasy. She was all alone when Talo struck.

Whether her strength came from her stray thought of Lucien's strength or from the instinct for self-preservation, she didn't know, but she jolted backward and fell to the floor as the snake lunged. One of the magics she had been practicing was a simple levitation spell, one everyone at the Institute learned. Panicked and on her back, she held her hands in front of her and called upon the spell, concentrating on the thoughts and energy involved. It worked! The snake floated four feet above her. However, before she could think of anything else, Talo thrashed against the spell and the serpent's weight became too much to keep aloft. Desperate, she used Talo's wriggling as momentum, and twisted her body, throwing the snake behind the bar.

Thoughts of how to escape through a panicked crowd of people consumed Bree as she jumped to her feet, but there was now panic, no crowd. No one was screaming or reacting at all to a boy transforming into a twenty-foot snake. All of the other patrons stood as still as statues— except for Siza, still on the dance floor with an emerald light radiating from her eyes. She held both hands out from her body, the fingers of her right hand wiggled while a soft nebula of shimmering powder drifted from her to the unmoving Siobhan and Ryoku. Palm out, she pointed her left hand at Bree, and with an authoritative tone, said, "Get down, Bree. Now."

Bree dropped to the floor, barely dodging a ball of swirling, sparkling light flying from Siza's hand. Hurrying back to her feet, Bree stumbled the rest of the way to Siza and looked back to Talo. The snake, now trying to slither up and over the bar, seemed to be unable to move past a ball of swirling, sparkling light, hanging in midair in front of the its face. When Talo darted right, the ball of light moved right. When Talo darted left, the ball moved left.

"Are Siobhan and Ryoku okay? Why is everyone frozen?"

"Time stop spell," Siza replied.

The explanation made no sense because the lights still flashed and the music still thumped, Bree asked, "Talo stopped time?"

"No. It is a spell that makes people 'think' time has stopped. It does not work on me. I've broken the spell with Ryoku and Siobhan. Go wake them up while I attend to Willem."

Still keeping the writhing snake at bay, Siza moved closer to Willem as Bree shook Ryoku and Siobhan free of the spell and held them up as they wobbled and moaned. Siobhan held her head as if she had a terrible headache and yelled over the music, "What happened?"

Ryoku understood immediately. She pointed toward the bar and yelled, "Meso attack!" All the bottles rattled and shook on the shelves behind the bar as she clenched her fists and gritted her teeth.

"No!" Bree grabbed Ryoku's arm and pointed to the bartender, frozen mid-pour at the left side of the bar. "You'll hurt her!"

Ryoku glanced from the bartender to the snake and back. The serpent still squirmed as it tried to find a way of escaping Siza's ball of crackling light. The bottles on the shelves by the bartender stopped moving while the ones behind the snake quaked and shook harder. Then they exploded in a spray of flying glass and colorful liquor. Glass shards pierced the snake's back and green, blue, and red liquid dripped from its scales. Trickles of blood leaked from cuts along the bartender's arm and cheek. Bree's stomach twisted and her fingers tingled, a flurry of electricity danced along her arms and chest. She wanted to help, to heal the bartender or fight the snake, but she lacked the training and feared she would just make things worse if she tried.

But Willem didn't hesitate.

Awakened by Siza from the time stop spell, Willem immediately realized what was happening. Without hesitating, he looked up at the ceiling over the dance floor, found the nearest light bulb, used a spell to shatter it, and molded the sparks into a raging fireball that he hurled toward the snake.

Even before Willem's fireball hit Talo, the electrical sparks from Ryoku's ball of light and the splashing alcohol combusted sending a flash of fire spreading over the bar. The bright conflagration disoriented Siza, breaking her spell. Talo slithered from the bar top, rolling and spinning on the floor to extinguish the flames along his body and scrape away the superficial pieces of glass. Now it was Talo's turn to retaliate.

The snake coiled itself again and lifted its head. Slowly, it started to sway as rich amber rays glowed from its eyes. Grabbing Ryoku's arm, Bree yelled, "What's he doing?"

"I don't know," Ryoku replied. "I don't recognize the spell!"

"I do!" Willem yelled over the still thumping beat of the electronic music. "It's not good!"

Breathing faster, Bree tried to prepare herself for anything. She concentrated on the only helpful spell she knew, ready to levitate whatever surprise Talo had in store for her. Her eyes darted from the snake to her friends to the snake to … she noticed something odd about one of the men on the dance floor. Standing soldier straight, arms by his sides, the man just stood there. Staring at Bree. Bright amber rays, like those emanating from Talo, glowed from his eyes.

Startled, she stumbled backward and ran into another person. She spun to see a woman staring at her with the same glowing eyes. Panicking, Bree looked for her friends and found them scattered among the other patrons. Over fifty men and women stood like duplicated statues—legs stiff, arms down, eyes glowing. Then in one split second, all of their arms sprung forward, hands reaching.

Being taller than most of the women and even some of the men, Siobhan punched the two people closest to her. Her action felled them with ease, but four more took their place, surging closer.

Ryoku called forth water from stray glasses and in the alcohol, and swirled the liquids together into whips. But there just wasn't enough. She didn't have the volume necessary to halt their progress, merely slow it.

Not wanting to hurt innocent people under Talo's spell, Willem stopped using sparks or fire. Instead he called forth illusion after illusion of snarling beasts and terrifying monsters. Still, the mind-controlled people marched closer. Then Willem gave up on the illusions and started flinging tables and chairs at the drones' legs in an effort to trip them.

Meanwhile, Siza was still twirling around, wriggling her arms, eyes glowing green. Three other patrons shared the same green glow in their eyes as they tussled with those with glowing yellow eyes. So Siza could turn people into drones just like Talo. Unfortunately, Bree realized, Siza's drones were outnumbered. Bree decided that was her best option was to get back to Siza and maybe levitate some tables and chairs to hinder the attackers and give Siza time to gain control of more patrons.

As soon as she headed across the dance floor, two patrons trundled toward her. Then three. Four. Five. Focusing, she levitated the one closest to her. Concentrating as best she could, she floated him into the other four and dropped him. Trying not to feel guilty for potentially hurting innocent people, Bree ran past the pile of fallen people. She'd almost reached Siza when, from the squirming pile, a hand reached out and grabbed her ankle. The grip was loose enough to escape from, but tight enough to make her stumble. Losing her balance, she tumbled into two golden-eyed women, both grasping for her. Swinging wildly, Bree tried to push herself away. Groping fingers buried themselves into a clump of her hair. Screaming, she kicked the woman's hip and jerked away. Wincing in pain, she freed herself, but realized the woman had pulled out a clump of her hair. She escaped, again falling backward.

Landing on the floor with a slap, Bree tried to scramble to her feet. She tripped over tables and chairs as she tried to run, but then tripped again. On the ground, a forest of legs appeared every which way she turned. She stayed low to avoid the reaching hands and slapped away grabbing fingers. She wrenched her arm away from one grip only to be caught by another. Pushing, kicking, punching, she managed somehow to get to her feet and plowed forward, driving her shoulders into chests until she fell back to the floor. Still kicking and screaming, she pulled herself along the floor, but there were too many hands gripping her legs.

The horde of people started to drag her toward Talo. Tears flowed as her fingernails scraped across the floor, searching for anything to grab on to. Because the club was still dark and the strobe lights still blinking, she didn't notice the swirls of black mist floating along the floor until a hand reached down and clasped hers. Suddenly the pulling stopped. Her legs were free. Bree looked at the hand that held onto hers and followed the arm all the way up to Lucien's face.

Miss Harkins and four other instructors were in the club and flashes of light and bolts of color danced from their fingertips as they fended off the attacking drones and released the innocent patrons from Talo's mind control. As the instructors advanced, Talo created a door port of his own and disappeared. And then it was over.

Lucien helped Bree to her feet, and, without thinking, she threw her arms around his neck and buried her face against his chest. She tried not to cry but wasn't successful and when the sobs came Lucien wrapped his arms around her.

She was safe. Alive. It was over. Against Lucien's muscled body, she felt comfortable and protected. But still, the horror of the Talo's attempt on her life left her stunned. She took a deep breath, pulled back, and looked into Lucien's dark eyes. "You ... you came?"

"You called." The reply was simple, matter of fact. He wiped a stray tear from her cheek with his thumb.

"I called?"

"Yes. I knew you were in danger, so I contacted the instructors." Concern was drawn upon his face.

"Thank you," Bree said just as the music stopped and the lights came on.

"I think you all need to thank Lucien," Miss Harkins said with a tone that made all the students drop their eyes to the floor. She and the other instructors milled about the woozy patrons, most sitting on the floor and confused by what happened. Creating a door port to the institute, Miss Harkins ordered them through it. "Go back to the institute and clean yourselves up." With a sweep of her arm, she took in the wrecked club and the disoriented patrons. "We will take care of all this and we will discuss what happened when we're finished."

Siza walked through first followed by Siobhan. Willem went next with Ryoku close behind, pausing only to turn and glare at Bree before she went through. Confused, Bree wondered what she could have possibly done to make Ryoku mad at her. It wasn't her fault Talo had shown up, turned into a snake, and tried to kill her. She didn't even know who Talo was! But as she and Lucien walked through the door port, she realized why Ryoku had been glaring. It wasn't about Talo. It was about Lucien ... and the fact that he still held Bree's hand in his.

CHAPTER 11

"BLOODY TRAITOR!" Willem yelled as he grabbed two fistfuls of Javier's shirt and shoved him against the wall of the game room.

Even though Javier was a couple inches taller and more than thirty pounds heavier, Willem had a wiry strength earned from hours on the soccer field that he was all too eager to recount, while the closest Javier got to a soccer field were the many hours of gaming on the couch. Willem, Bree had learned, also grew up with a much larger, older brother to roughhouse with for his first sixteen years while Javier was an only child who had mastered the art of conflict avoidance. The fear in Javier's eyes told as much as did his quaking voice, "Wha … what … why …?"

"I should be the one asking 'why,' but I think I already know the answer. Meso!"

Strongbow, Lucien, and Rumiel ran toward the fray, although Bree wasn't entirely sure what Rumiel thought he was going to do. Even though he was a head taller than Willem, Rumiel couldn't have weighed as much. Lucien stepped between Willem and Javier as Strongbow wrapped his left arm around Willem's chest, escorting him to the other end of the room. Rumiel shuffled Javier to the far corner of the wall like he needed to calm down, as if either of them had the means to survive if the situation had deteriorated into fisticuffs.

Not knowing what else to do and feeling sorry for him, Bree went to check on Javier, clearly shaken by the incident. Luckily, Ryoku knew how to address the situation. "Willem! Settle the hell down!"

Once far enough away, Strongbow relinquished his grip on Willem as Ryoku stormed her way over to him. Lucien and Siobhan stood their ground in the middle of the room while Siza sat at one of the tables, retreating into the confines of her suddenly re-appearing hood. Bree and Rumiel stood by Javier. All eyes were on Ryoku as she continued to admonish Willem.

"Look, we got reamed out by the instructors for sneaking out to a nightclub. It sucks. I get it. But they let us off easy. Very easy, considering what happened the last time a group of students snuck away. Don't blow it by starting a fight with someone who had nothing to do with the incident."

Ryoku was right about suffering no punishment, but Bree didn't think of it that way until now. During the scolding, Bree felt terrible, scared, and worried she would be kicked out of the institute. The five students involved got lectured about the dangers of using magic in public, especially being so inexperienced. Ashamed, Bree hadn't looked up from the table. Neither did the other students as they sat there while the teachers circled behind them, taking turns airing their grievances. Head hanging low, Siza's face had been completely hidden by her hood while

Willem's tight, furrowed expression gave away his silent fury. During a lull in the berating, he reminded the teachers that Talo attacked them. That didn't help.

If anything, Willem's comment gave the teachers more reasons to scold, more reason to explain why the world was a dangerous place, why they had rules about sneaking away from the institute. The teachers reminded the students about the fateful night that the institute lost Tierney, Cassidy, and Nicholas. Mr. St. Martin, Lucien's father, suggested the rule-breakers be expelled, but the sentiment in the room changed upon that suggestion. Most of the other teachers immediately disagreed. The yelling stopped. Other suggestions were made and compromises were reached. More work with the students was necessary. Those who lived at the institute would still receive regular schooling during the day, but the after-school magic curriculum would include more information about the potential dangers that lurked from using magic "out there" in the real world. Finally, the teachers dismissed the students to the game room, and that's when Willem charged Javier.

Now that Bree replayed the scolding in her mind, she focused on the change in teacher attitude, including Miss Harkins. She was adamant in her stance that the students not be expelled. *Almost like she needs us*, Bree thought. *But why? And why had Talo focus his attack on her?*

Bree's attention turned back to the situation at hand when Ryoku asked Willem, "Why do you think Javier is a traitor?"

"Because he knew *exactly* where we were going and when we were going to be there."

"I didn't tell anyone!" Javier protested, his voice cracking and wavering like he was on the verge of tears. "I don't know any Mesos! I don't know this … this Talo person!"

"You *are* a Meso!" Willem fired back.

"No! No I'm not!"

"Willem!" Ryoku yelled. Once his attention returned to her, she reminded him, "We invited him to come along just like we invited you. We invited everyone."

"Right. He said 'no.' He said 'no' so he wouldn't be there when Talo attacked."

"Rumiel, Lucien and Strongbow said 'no,' too."

Willem shifted his inflammatory gaze to Rumiel. "Strongbow is no traitor, I know that for sure. You, Rumiel? Rumiel with that dark, gypsy eastern European magic. Twitchy face, shifty eyes. Both Mesos and Gypsies use curses in their core magics. It wouldn't surprise me if Rumiel was the traitor. Are you the traitor, Captain Emo?"

"Willem!" Ryoku snapped.

"You're getting crazy," Siobhan added.

Dark eyes widening, Rumiel's pale skin turned pink. A rim of sweat beaded along his hairline. A slight tremor touched his fingers. "I … I … I don't … I don't …."

"I don't, I don't, I don't think an innocent person would have such a hard time defending himself."

Bree knew Willem was angry and frustrated, maybe even scared, but that certainly didn't give him the right to lash out at everyone else around him. She jumped to Rumiel's defense. "Just because he's not as strong as Lucien or Strongbow, doesn't mean he's a traitor!"

"You're right, Bree," Willem sneered, slowly turning to look at Lucien. "He's not as strong as Lucien. Another newbie. Another one we know nothing about. Another one who practices curses and plays with snakes. Who do you do with that voodoo you do?"

Fire blazed behind Lucien's normally calm eyes. Scowling, he strode from the center of the room to confront Willem face to face. "Me? Let's not forget, *you* were at the club. *You* knew exactly which club you were going to. It stands to reason that *you* could be the traitor as well!"

"What?" Willem yelled, the reddening of his face surpassing the color of his hair. "That makes no sense! I was attacked at the club! I was on the beach the night we lost Cassidy and Nicholas and *your brother!*"

Lucien's eyes widened. He clenched his fists so hard Bree swore she heard his muscles tighten. "I assure you, I wish nothing but the worst to those who hurt my brother. It would be wise if you do not speak of him again." He uncurled his fingers and gave one last glare to Willem and stormed out of the room.

Bree wanted to run after him, calm him, ask him about his brother and their childhood together. She wanted to comfort him, the way he comforted her during meditation, rescue him the way he rescued her at the club. But Willem was still on a rampage, still wanting to blame someone for Talo attacking them at the club. She turned back to him. "Why do you think it was one of us?"

"I'm just being logical. Strongbow and I were *attacked* at the beach. You girls and I were *attacked* at the club. We were ambushed. That means someone knew where we would be and when. That means someone gave Talo that information. The three that weren't attacked are, *conveniently*, three newbies. And one of the three newbies is a bloody Meso!"

Willem turned his ire back to Javier and stormed across the room to him. Ryoku waved her hand at the sink, turning the faucet on, and then commanded the flowing stream of water to splash Willem.

Soaked, he turned to Ryoku with a surprised look. Shaking his head, he huffed and growled, then ran his hands over his wet face and through his sopping hair. Glancing around the room, he pointed to Javier. "Okay. I get it. You're all a bunch of sodding Meso lovers. I read you loud and clear. I promise you this, though, I am not talking to him and I am not ever saying anything important in front of him."

Willem left the room and Ryoku ran after him.

Standing as straight as a totem pole, his face as expressionless as wood, Strongbow walked over to Javier. "I am sorry Willem accused you of treason. We have lost a great deal because of my quest to find my sister. His passion can be a great attribute and he is an ally. I hope someday you will see that."

Before Javier could formulate a response, Strongbow left the room.

Seeing the volatility of the situation diffuse, Bree looked at Rumiel and Javier. "Do you two need any help?"

Frowning, Rumiel mumbled, "We may not be as strong as Strongbow or Lucien, but we're strong enough to walk back to our rooms without any help." He shifted to his usual slump-shoulder posture, hair hiding the pain etched upon his face, and he slunk away. Javier followed, looking back to Bree. Emotions swirled within a single look: gratitude, confusion, hurt, anger, fear.

The situation had been tense, but Bree didn't believe she deserved any hostility from Rumiel. She said to Siobhan,

"Why'd Rumiel act like I was the one who attacked him? I came to his defense!"

"Because he's a guy," Siobhan muttered.

"I'll never understand guys," Bree sighed, images of all five of the young men she called fellow students swirled through her mind.

"Amen, sister. How about you, Siza?" Siobhan asked. Siza had been sitting at the table in the center of the room with her face completely hidden by her hood. So quiet, Bree had forgotten she was even there.

Without a word, Siza stood and waved her hand. Noiselessly, a door-port opened to her bedroom and she stepped through. It closed behind her, leaving only Siobhan and Bree in the game room.

Siobhan sighed and shook her head. "What a past few hours, huh?"

The weight of Siobhan's words slammed Bree in the chest. She mentally added up exactly how much had happened in the past four hours. She jumped across the Atlantic ocean to go to a night club, drank beer, flirted with a young man who tried to kill her and her friends by turning into a snake and using a mind-controlled army, discovered she had some kind of connection with a very attractive young man she had met mere weeks ago, got scolded by her high school science teacher who happened to recruit her into joining another school to learn about her magic, and all of that culminated in having to protect one of her fellow students from the wrath of another. Her vision blurred as her legs turned to taffy. Siobhan grabbed Bree's arm and said, "Bree? You okay, girl? You're a bit pale. And I'm from Ireland, a whole country of pale people."

Swallowing hard, her throat dry, Bree said, "Yeah. Sorry. Just … a lot happened. I guess it's just all catching up to me."

"You wanna talk about it?"

Bree looked at the clock. "I can't right now. I have to get home."

"How about tomorrow? Let's do a little Sunday shopping. I'll come to your place. Noon."

A smile swept across Bree's face as she said, "I'd like that. But I gotta go now. Can you help me with my door-port?"

Hard enough to shake and sweat, both girls concentrated on Bree's room. A doorway opened and Bree stepped through. As soon as she did, the door-port closed and she flopped onto her bed. Exhausted, she passed out, and was immediately greeted to dreams involving snakes and voodoo.

CHAPTER 12

"YOUR FATHER IS A LOSER."

Bree's eyes widened, shocked that the words came out of her mother's mouth.

Disappointment and frustration washed over Allyson's face as she ran a hand through her short hair. Frowning, she heaved a sigh. "I'm sorry. I didn't mean it to sound so...."

"Harsh?" Bree whispered, still stunned.

Allyson sighed again, her eyes shimmering from the beginnings of tears. "Yes. Harsh. I'm sorry. Your father is, or at least was when I knew him, a very well-meaning man."

"But a *loser*." Bree made sure her mother knew exactly how harsh the word sounded.

Allyson turned away and stared off into the distance, watching events that Bree couldn't see. "He and I met in high school. I was lost, confused, looking for an identity. Then along came your father, free and unaffected by society's norms. Education was in the world around us, not in books. Art, music, poetry, philosophy. These were the things he valued."

"Not you?" Bree asked.

Allyson wiped away a stray tear and looked at her daughter. "Oh, Sweety, I did. I do. After high school, that was our major in college. Art. Music. Writing. Philosophy. We changed each semester, your father never happy with the rules of the establishment. Never happy with what the teachers had to say about him. Blaming them for not seeing his talent, when the reality was he didn't want to work for success, didn't want to put forth the extra effort to be exceptional. Then sophomore year, I got pregnant."

Bree knew how old her parents were, knew they were young, but she never knew the whole story. Her throat constricted as she squeaked out the words, "I'm … I'm an accident?"

Silent tears rolled faster down Allyson's face. "No, Sweety. No, no, no, no. We got married against our parents' will freshman year of college. We wanted to start a family to learn responsibility, as if that would magically make us adults. As if it would magically give him the drive to succeed."

Speechless, Bree couldn't form a question, even though a hundred swarmed through her brain like angry bees. She couldn't recall her father, other than frozen images from photographs, so she could only stare at her mother.

Allyson pulled a tissue from a nearby box and dabbed at her eyes and nose. "I didn't mean to use such a nasty word like 'loser,' Bree. I swear I didn't. But life with him was not easy. Especially for two … kids, really … with no education, no marketable skills, trying to raise a baby. Your father couldn't—more accurately, *wouldn't*—hold a job. I took part-time temp work when I could. My mother snuck me money when she could, just so we could afford a rat-trap apartment. We couldn't even make that work. Then—"

Gut twisting, Bree watched a dozen emotions play across her mother's face. Unable to bear the torment any longer, she asked, "Then what happened?"

Within a few fluttered blinks, more tears streamed down Allyson's cheeks. "Then I had to rescue you."

Her mother's words shocked Bree into sitting up straight. "Rescue me? From … from … Dad?" Had her "loser" father put her in harm's way?

Allyson took a cleansing breath, eyes still wet, as she wiped her cheeks with the tissue. She adjusted herself in her chair, tall and proud, finding the resolve to finish her unpleasant story. "Sort of. He wanted us to move into a commune. Shacks. Literal shacks, Bree. Some were just sheets of metal siding welded together. Two dozen people all living together, sharing everything, which was *nothing*. Shoeless children ran about with dirt-streaked faces and clumped hair. I couldn't do it anymore. I couldn't be with a man who so willingly led his wife and four year-old daughter down a path of pure squalor due to his own laziness. That's when I divorced him and turned my life around. Turned *our lives* around."

"I'm so sorry, Mom. I … I didn't know. I just knew you'd get so angry any time I brought up Dad. I didn't know why."

"I'm sorry I didn't tell you the truth before. I just know that my high school and college self would not like who I am today. And now *you* are in high school, and … and I worry that you—" Allyson choked on the final words, but Bree understood the sentiment behind the fat tears sliding down her mother's cheeks.

Tearing up as well, Bree leapt from her chair and ran to her mother for a hug, slobbering, "I love you, Mom."

Allyson jumped up from her chair as well and wrapped her arms around Bree. "I love you so much, Bree. You are the world to me."

Separating from their embrace, they regarded each other and started to laugh at the messy state of their faces. They each reached for the nearby box of tissues to wipe away the remains of their emotional outburst.

Pulling out a compact, Allyson checked her appearance. "I'm so sorry to do this, especially after the moment we just shared, but I have a meeting."

Bree chuckled. "That's okay. I'm meeting a friend at the mall."

Smiling, Allyson snapped her compact shut and returned it to her clutch purse. "A new friend from your after-school, multi-national club?"

"Yeah."

"Good!" Allyson kissed her daughter on the forehead. "I'm so proud of you. Okay, I'm off. Wish me luck."

"Luck," Bree said as her mom walked out the door. She, too, took a moment to clean up, walking to the sink to give her face a quick wash. When satisfied, she sent a text to Siobhan, and then concentrated, reaching out to her for help with the door-port. In seconds, one appeared and Siobhan strode through.

As always, Siobhan entered the room like a silent hurricane, making her presence known without even needing to say a word. Even in a black concert tee shirt of a punk band that Bree had never heard of and jeans. Even with no make-up, she looked stunning, sure to turn the head of every guy at the mall. With just the words, "Hi. Ready to go?" she exuded strength and confidence.

The intensity of her ice blue eyes made Bree's heart beat faster. Even without magic Siobhan had power, and Bree so desperately wanted to be like her.

They walked to the mall and shopped. Even though they laughed and talked and bonded over good clothing styles and bad, Bree couldn't shake the conversation with her mother. Bree had learned a lot about her family, potentially herself, in the matter of minutes. She tried to process what she had learned while trying to stay in the moment with her new friend. After three hours and two full bags each, the girls took a late lunch break at the food court.

Bree pushed around the lettuce in her salad with her fork. Piercing a small leaf and a cherry tomato, she took a bite, then went right back to absently rearranging the vegetables.

"You seem distracted, girl. Everything okay?" Siobhan asked, chomping away at a triple patty burger.

Bree looked to Siobhan and wondered what to say. She enjoyed being around her, shopping and talking, but did she want to barf out her family problems on her? Images of Siobhan yawning and then leaving from sheer boredom danced through Bree's head. Yet she didn't want to appear too aloof and uninviting. Trying to find the right balance, she smirked, shrugged a shoulder and went with, "Yeah. Just lots of stuff all at once, I guess."

"You mean the incident at the dance club? Look, I am soooooooo sorry that I dragged you into that." For the first time since meeting her, Siobhan wore an expression other than unshakable confidence.

Bree pointed her plastic fast-food fork at Siobhan. "Trust me, you have *nothing* to apologize for. Before almost getting eaten by a mutant snake boy or being crushed by a zombified mob, I was having a *great* time!"

The girls shared a giggle, and Siobhan took another bite of her burger. "I do feel bad," she managed to mumble through a mouthful of burger.

"Don't. It kinda helped with some of my thoughts."

"Almost getting killed helped?"

Bree sighed. "My mother always says that you become an adult once you realize how dangerous the world really is."

"I guess that's true. You handled yourself pretty well, by the way."

"Me? I ran, fell down, and prayed that Lucien would come rescue us."

"At least you were in control of your magic. I forgot everything I learned."

"Yeah, but you were totally kicking ass! Where'd you learn to fight?"

Siobhan flexed her right arm, showing off defined muscles. "Irish, remember? Brothers galore. Gene of fighting, plus ten."

"I guess I got the feet of clumsiness, plus twenty. I just wish I'd done better."

"Don't forget, it really wasn't supposed to be a fight for our lives. I just wanted us girls to get out and bond a little."

"And then Willem invited himself along with the excuse that we needed him to door-port into London and that he knew the best clubs."

Siobhan shoved the last of her burger in her mouth and moaned, "Ugh. Don't remind me. Thanks to him we had to invite everyone else. I'm glad they said 'no.' But we still had to deal with that English dog. Willem is the embodiment of everything wrong with boys."

Bree chuckled. "I don't think I can disagree with that. Especially since Lucien is the embodiment of everything right with boys."

"Meh. I guess," Siobhan shrugged a shoulder while wiping her fingers in a balled-up wad of napkins.

Bree dropped her fork, shocked that Siobhan showed so little enthusiasm about Lucien. "You don't think he's … gorgeous?"

"There's no denying he's attractive. He's just not my type."

"Oh. Then someone like Strongbow?"

Siobhan squinted and cocked her head. "Noooooooo."

Bree crunched her face as if she smelled rotten eggs. "You can't mean someone like Rumiel or Javier?"

"Noooooooo."

"I'm confused. Who *is* your type?"

Siobhan looked Bree in the eyes and heaved a soul-cleansing sigh. The silence lengthened to the point where Bree felt herself blush, embarrassed by not understanding what Siobhan was trying to tell her. Finally, Siobhan said, "I saw a couple pictures of Strongbow's sister, Lila. If she's even half as intelligent as he is, then *she* would definitely be my type."

Bree's world screeched to a halt. All movement in the mall stopped, all sound muted. She felt stupid for not understanding, ashamed for not making the connections. She wanted nothing more than to forge a strong friendship with one of the most interesting people she had ever met in her life and she had just blatantly insulted her. Gut twisting, she didn't even know how to react or what to say. Luckily for her, Siobhan demonstrated why Bree thought she was so amazing by asking, "Are you … okay … with … that…?"

Realizing that she hadn't ruined everything with her own ignorance, she jumped at a chance to respond. "Yeah! Yes! Yes, I am."

"Are you sure? You blanked out."

"God, I'm so sorry. I just … I don't know anyone who's, well, gay."

Siobhan smiled. "Yeah. That's pretty obvious. I'm sorry I didn't tell you sooner."

"No. That's perfectly fine. This is … this is good."

"You sure?"

"Seriously. It's awesome that you're gay."

Siobhan laughed. "Really? Awesome?"

Bree huffed a flustered sigh. "I mean it's awesome that you know so much about yourself, that you have such control over your life."

Siobhan laughed again. "Bree, are you hetero?"

"Umm, yeah."

"There you go. You know as much about yourself as I know about myself."

"But you're so … so … strong! And confident."

"Bree. I'm strong because I had to beat the crap out of my brothers for sixteen plus years. I'm confident because I know I'll be seventeen in December. I'm confused and I don't know much about the world around me and that's right where I *should be* at sixteen. I don't have anything figured out, but that's exactly the stage of life that I should be in. I'm confident because I'm where I should be."

"*You* feel like *you* don't have it together?"

"Bree. I was so nervous to tell you that I'm gay that I didn't tell you until … well, until I had to."

"Really? Why?"

"I was afraid of how you'd react. You're one of the coolest people I know. You're really freakin' smart, funny, and fun to be with. That's rare for a regular human being, let alone people like us. We're becoming … oh, God, I hate this term … BFFs. I didn't want to ruin that."

Bree slapped the table and barked out a loud laugh. "I can't believe you said 'BFF'."

"Shut up or I'll take it back."

"You can't. The second 'F' means 'forever'."

"Jerk," Siobhan laughed and threw a French fry at Bree.

"So, gay best friend forever, shall we continue shopping?"

"You know Irish people have bad tempers, right? I started with ten brothers, now I'm down to three. That's because I ate them. They teased me and made me mad and I ate them."

The girls shared another laugh as they disposed of their trash, grabbed their shopping bags, and left, completely unaware that Amanda had been sitting behind them, just one table away, listening the whole conversation.

CHAPTER 13

A WOBBLING FOOTBALL arced toward Strongbow. He caught it with ease and with just as much grace threw a perfect spiral to Rumiel. Even though he concentrated on the ball, it slipped right through his hands. Grumbling to himself, Rumiel chased after the football, the frustration obvious in the way he snatched it from the grass. Putting his whole body into it, he threw it with all his might, spotlighting his lankiness. The football twisted through the air like a plane being shot down from the sky, its trajectory in the direction of Lucien, but ten feet out of his reach. Lucien wiggled his fingers to cast a simple spell; the ball changed direction, flying right to him.

Bree smiled as she watched Lucien catch the football. She assumed that he used his magic so Rumiel wouldn't feel bad about not being very skilled at throwing a football. However, when she glanced to Rumiel, he seemed to be scowling, upset by what Lucien just did.

She went back to watching Lucien as he tossed a low velocity perfect spiral right to Javier. Using both hands, arms, and his whole chest, Javier caught it. Unable to stop his smile of pride, he threw a wobbling pass back to Strongbow.

A sense of relief washed through Bree as Strongbow repeated the whole process by throwing the football to Rumiel, who subsequently missed it again, swore to himself and chased after it. She had worried about how Strongbow was going to react when Rumiel and Javier first asked him and Lucien to join in. Sure, Rumiel was the one who did the talking, but Strongbow continued to wear an expression of stone-cold stoicism on his face. If the direction of tossing the football were reversed, Strongbow would undoubtedly throw bullets right into Javier's chest. Bree was *very* happy to see them interacting without incident. Now, if she could only do something about the Siobhan/Willem feud.

"I can't believe we're trusting Willem to cook our food," Siobhan said.

"Who better than someone whose talisman is fire?" Siza asked, a genuine earnestness to her statement.

"Someone more mature? Who knows what he's doing to our food? We could end up with a spit sausage or booger burger."

Bree laughed. Siza laughed too, but it was forced, as if guessing Siobhan had made a joke.

Barefooted, the three girls sat in the grass behind the institute, relishing the simple joy of thick grass on a warm, spring day. Even though Bree had been coming to the institute for over a month now, she still marveled at its beauty. Built of red brick, it possessed the sophistication of a mansion without any of the gaudiness. Behind the enormous building was the expansive lawn, dotted with gardens so intricate that walkways were needed to admire the many statues, and leading to a lush forest beyond. Bree enjoyed the gardens, and had spent more than a few hours reading in the gazebos. What amazed her most was that this, the whole estate, was hidden from the rest of the world with spells designed to make the place look like nothing more than overgrown, inhospitable brush and woods to anyone who happened to pass by.

On the picnic table sat the standard accoutrements of a cookout: a stack of paper plates, condiments, plastic cups filled with either soda or water from the three full pitchers all along the table. To the right of the picnic table, Willem manned the grill and Ryoku supervised, collecting an easily earned dollar every few minutes. The other four tossed the football on the lawn.

"Ryoku is keeping him in line, I'm sure. I've seen her collect at least three dollars from him so far, so I'm confident that our lunch will turn out just fine. Let's sit back and enjoy the grass between our fingers and toes," Bree said, smiling.

"Speaking of.... I've been practicing something. You know how earth is my talisman? Watch." Siobhan rolled over into a kneeling position, facing away from the game of catch and the cooking. Closing her eyes, she took a deep breath. Again. And again. Each time, slower and deeper than before. Leaning forward slightly, she whispered an incantation and placed both palms on the ground, blades of grass unevenly poking around her fingers. Her eyes snapped open and her hands sunk into the ground, up to her elbows.

Bree and Siza gasped at Siobhan plunging her hands into the earth as easily as if reaching into pool of water. They could only offer stunned silence as two hands grew from the ground in front of Siobhan. Fingertips first, hands emerged, growing like tiny trees and stopping at the elbows. Grass coated the forearms and backs of the hands while the palms were moist, dark brown dirt.

"Amazing," Siza whispered.

"So very, very cool," Bree agreed.

Siobhan bit her bottom lip and nodded her head as she continued to control the fingers of grass and dirt, making them wiggle. They moved along the ground like shark fins through a green ocean as Siobhan shifted her weight, guiding them. She finally had them stop and give themselves a high five before she pulled her arms from the ground, the simulated hands retreating back into the earth, the patches of ground completely undisturbed as if nothing happened.

"I don't know if there's any practical purpose, but it feels nice to have that connection to my talisman," Siobhan said.

"I know what you mean," Bree replied, skimming her hand over the soft blanket of grass, nurturing the feelings of comfort deep within her.

The girls turned back to watch the boys tossing the football: Rumiel dropping it and swearing, Lucien doing the best he could to help out who he received it from and who he threw it to, Javier grinning and unable to hide his enthusiasm, Strongbow expressionless. Stretching out on the grass, the girls glanced over at Ryoku who had her hand held out for another dollar. She critiqued every move Willem made while he defended his cooking skills and his manhood. They seemed to be enjoying themselves.

"I am very happy we did this," Siza said, a soft smile on her face.

"Me too," Bree replied. She was content. Then her contentedness exploded into a chest-rending burst of happiness when Lucien looked over and flashed her a broad smile. The lingering look was broken when Rumiel swore again, and Lucien turned back to catch a poorly thrown incoming pass.

It had been two weeks since Bree learned about Siobhan's sexuality. During those two weeks, they had grown closer while everyone else seemed satisfied to learn about magic alongside each other, but not by really working together. Bree managed to set up a few study sessions with Lucien, even though Rumiel repeatedly asked her to study with him. "Our magics really have nothing in common," Bree would tell him, and he would slink away, pouting. Why did that upset him so? She didn't understand. She did try to find other ways to hang out with Rumiel, and all of the other students as well. But as a whole, they weren't working together, weren't bonding in a way she thought they would, or should. This was a group of special people who weren't celebrating what made them special, weren't realizing how unique they were.

A few days earlier, Bree brought it up to Siobhan, who agreed. "So, what do you want to do?"

"How about a cookout out on Saturday. Here. At the institute, so none of the instructors object."

"Love it! Do we have to invite Willem?"

"Yes."

"Damn! Do I have to be nice to him?"

"You have to at least try."

"Damn!"

Since they'd all gathered on the lawn, Siobhan had barely said a word to Willem. Bree knew that Siobhan honestly felt she was being nice by ignoring him. But after a while, she noticed a sly smile on Siobhan's face as her friend's index fingers sunk into the ground. Bree turned to check on Willem.

She felt bad being suspicious of Siobhan, but she knew just how much Willem got under her skin. He seemed fine, though, still arguing with Ryoku. Then he reached down and swatted at his right foot. By his bare feet, Bree could see two small patches of grass rippling, like underground sharks circling their prey. A grassy finger poked up and stroked his foot and quickly disappeared before Willem swatted again at the sudden tickle. The other grassy finger tickled his toes and disappeared. He yelped and jumped, looking down.

And then Bree and Siobhan were doused with a ball of flying water. Open-mouthed, Bree stared at Ryoku who stood next to Willem, her arms planted on her hips, and her lips twisted into a sneer. That's when Bree noticed that all of the water pitchers were empty. Siza, who had not completely escaped the deluge, wiped her face with her scarf and looked up as both Bree and Siobhan got to their feet. The two girls looked at each other—rivulets ran from hair plastered to their faces, drenched shirts clung to their bodies, and their pants were soaked and dripping. Bree pulled her wet shirt out to look at it as Siobhan pushed her hair out of her eyes. They burst into giggles and then full-on belly laughs.

Bree wiped the water from her face, gave a thumbs up to Ryoku, and swatted Siobhan in the arm. "I think you deserve that for making me collateral damage." She pulled her hair to one side and twisted it to ring it out and then held a hand out to pull Siza to her feet. "Blame Siobhan the troublemaker for the shower."

Siobhan smiled and shrugged. "I just can't help myself sometimes."

"You are definitely my new hero!" Willem held his hand up to give Ryoku a high five.

"Don't you forget it," she replied as she slapped his hand. She then glanced at the grill. "Perfect timing. Looks like the food's ready!"

Everyone congregated around the picnic table. Willem placed hamburgers and chicken breasts and Portobello mushrooms onto a large serving plate while Ryoku opened a package of buns and jars of condiments. Smiling, Javier handed out paper plates and Siza arranged sliced tomatoes and onions on one plate, sliced carrots and peppers on another, and opened containers of hummus and baba ghanoush.

Bree pulled at her wet shirt and tried to shake it out. Wearing a disarming smile, Lucien approached with his hands behind his back. "Need help?"

Bree smiled, embracing the ridiculousness of the situation. "Very much so."

"Here," Lucien said, offering her a paper napkin. One lone napkin.

Arching an eyebrow, Bree said, "This? This is you helping."

"It is."

"It is?"

"Very much so." His thick accent added sincerity to his words, the glint in his eye added mirth.

"Please forgive me if I fail to see how this helps."

"I'll show you." Lucien dabbed the napkin against her cheek, twice against her forehead, three times against her chin, and once more against her other cheek. "There. Just like that. It is like you were never splashed."

"Just like that?"

"Yes."

"Never splashed?"

"Dry as a desert."

"Hmm. That's some powerful magic you've got there." She held up her index finger, her eyes widening as if she just remembered something important. "Hold that thought."

"Consider it held," he said, crossing his arms over his chest, waiting.

Using both hands, Bree gathered her shirt tight around her waist and leaned forward, twisting and twisting and twisting as water cascaded onto Lucien's right foot, soaking his sneaker. With exaggerated movement, they both tilted their heads downward to observe his sneaker as if it would mutate into something else. Simultaneously, they lifted their heads back up, meeting eye-to-eye. With fake surprise, Lucien said, "I guess my napkin was not as magical as I thought."

"No. Not really," Bree answered.

Before either could say another word, Javier appeared next to them with an empty paper plate in each hand and asked, "Plates?"

Lucien accepted both plates, never taking his eyes off Bree. "Since you deemed my last efforts ineffective, please allow me to make restitution."

Fighting to keep from swooning, Bree took a seat at the picnic table and said, "Chicken, please."

Bree planted her elbow on the table and leaned her chin on her hand, her fingers covering her mouth to keep from laughing as she watched Lucien. As he walked around the table, he drew out the step of his right foot, creating a squish from his newly saturated shoe. Step. *Squish*. Step *Squiiiiish*. All the way around the table, he made those squishing noises. After loading the plates, he returned, the noises even more emphasized. Step. *Squiiiiiiiiiiish*. Step. *Squiiiiiiiiiiiiiiiiiiish*. Straight faced throughout the whole act, he sat shoulder-to-shoulder next to Bree.

After accepting the plate and thanking him, she savored being so close to him, loving the idea that *he* chose to sit next to her, and not the other way around. She didn't want to seem creepy sitting next to him in silence, so she cleared her throat and said, "I'll get you new pair of sneakers for Christmas. Or your birthday. Whichever comes first. So, when is your birthday?"

Lucien stopped, his burger inches from his open mouth. Befuddled, he placed the burger on his plate and regarded Bree in quizzical silence. That was when she realized that everyone had gone quiet. No chewing. No drinking. No gulping. Just the sounds of Bree's embarrassment raging around inside of her; heart slamming her chest and throat and ears and arms and feet. She *thought* she was doing so well at flirting with Lucien! What did she do wrong? What did she say? Did she cross the line asking about his birthday? That made no sense, though, especially after he showed *zero* concern for her getting his shoes wet. But it was definitely *something* she said or did! In front of *everybody!*

"It's ... December 21st. The same as yours."

Embarrassment mutated quickly into bewilderment. Before she could react to any of those emotions, Siobhan sat down across from her and said, "It's mine as well."

"That date belongs to everyone at this table," Siza added.

Bree's lips quivered, trying to form the words "what" or "how" or "why" but finding it too difficult. Focusing on one question at a time, she grabbed it tightly and pulled it from her own mouth, "Why didn't anyone tell me?"

Being as earnest as ever, Siza answered for them all. "We thought you already knew."

"Why? Why would I possibly think that we would all have the same birthday?"

"Because it is the same as Talo's," Lucien said. "We are all exactly the same age."

Bree's mind seized again. All her questions exploded into a jumble of falling words, an avalanche clogging the way out of her mouth. Wide-eyed and panicked, she stared at Lucien. His smile might have been gone and his eyes no longer danced to the songs of flirtation, but he was there for her, strong and willing to support her, willing to be an ambassador to this crazy new experience.

"There are many different beliefs in the world of magic," he said. "Different groups sharing similar ideals within themselves, but different from others. The Mesos are one of those groups and can be quite dangerous. December 21st is a special day for them, a magical day. They believe that on that day—no one knows what year—Talo will be the conduit for one of their gods, Tláloc, to reappear on earth."

Bree wanted to ask more, but could only choke out, "Why … does it matter that our birthdays are the same as Talo's?"

Keeping his voice smooth and steady, Lucien continued, "It is like a cosmic equalizer. All of us were brought into this world under the same moon and stars, the same position around the sun, the same numerology and astrology and Earth energy. Imagine two runners eating the exact same meal the day before a race, thusly taking away one potentially competitive variable between the two."

Equalizer. Competitive. Surprise and confusion had their turn, now it was time for them to step aside for anger. Frowning, Bree asked, "So, we're all here to be trained to … what? Fight Talo? Stop the Mesos?"

"It's not that simple," Siza said. "Or at least that's not the only reason."

Lucien took Bree's left hand into both of his to pull her attention back to him. "According to my father, the purpose of the institute has been debated since before it opened. The skills we will learn here are like … well, my father says they are like swimming. It is important to learn in case of emergency, yet the skills can be used for recreation or competition."

Bree blinked, hard and fast, as she tried to process what she had just learned. To herself, she whispered, "I can't believe Miss Harkins didn't tell me. *None* of the instructors did." She looked up at her peers, all wearing expressions of pity or concern. She leaned forward. "So, what do you all think? Are we here to learn about our magics or are we just tools? Soldiers groomed to stop Talo from channeling this Tláloc guy?"

Eight pairs of eyes held the same silent answer: they weren't sure. There were shrugged shoulders. Arched eyebrows. Shaking heads. Even the stone-faced, determined

Strongbow had no answer. But he was the first one to speak.

"When I was first recruited, I decided to come to learn more about my magic and about other magics and cultures. My parents had concerns about the school being a target because it's the first of its kind and they were uncertain why the different councils felt the need to create it to begin with. Almost immediately after arriving, though, my sister was kidnapped by the Mesos and finding her became my sole focus. It didn't occur to me then that the instructors might be using us for their own agenda. Now that we're talking about it? I don't know."

Lucien cleared his throat. "After my brother was murdered, my father told me about Talo and Tláloc. He lost one son and does not want to lose another, yet here we are. I don't fully understand what the dangers are or what lies ahead, but I knew that everyone here shared a birthday and I believe that, together, we will be more powerful because of it. I hope to learn other things, too." He looked around the table. "I hope to learn from each one of you—about your magic and about your cultures. But I am here because of my brother. I am here to learn how to defend against Talo."

"We now know why Lucien's here," Willem chimed in. "But we don't know what the adults want from us. Just like we don't know why the Mesos took Strongbow's sister or where she is."

Strongbow's face darkened as Rumiel cast him a glance and then spoke up. "I came to the institute to be around other students like me," Rumiel said. "I don't remember how I found out about the birthdays, but I thought it was simply an astrological quirk of some kind, perhaps something about having special magics. It was only once I got here and talked to Javier did I realized the significance of the date to the Mesos."

"I knew because my family told me," Javier said. "They're concerned that there might be members of the Meso cult in our council of Mesoamerican magic users. My family sent me here because they wanted me to learn about other magics and thought I would be safer surrounded by teachers and students like me. I wanted to come so I can show people that the Mesos do not speak for us, they do not represent me. I want to show that I am good and want to help my friends and family."

"Then *that* is our answer," Bree said. Again, she was greeted with silent confusion. "Like Rumiel, I came here because Miss Harkins said I would be learning about my magic and magics from around the world right alongside kids just like me. At my regular school, I was ... different. Here, I'm surrounded by ... well, you. None of us came here expecting to fight some cosmic battle. None of us knows what the adults' agenda is or why they even created this institute. From what Lucien says, they don't even agree on an agenda. Let's say, 'Screw their agenda,' and make our own. This is ours. This is our ... club! *Our* after-school club. Where *we* choose what *we* do with what *we* learn."

Ryoku nodded and a crooked smile cracked Willem's face. "I like it," he said. "Our own little Apocalypse Club."

Siobhan slapped the table and Siza beamed. In unison, they said, "I'm in!"

"I'm in, too, Bree," Lucien said.

Bree squeezed his hand and everyone nodded and murmured with a sort of grim determination. For once, there was no bickering. Everyone at the table agreed and was on the same side. They were a club. A team. Even Siobhan and Willem. Even Strongbow and Javier. They would control their own destiny.

Then Javier asked, "So, now what?"

All eyes turned back to Bree. Her heart lurched, not expecting that question, not knowing what to say next. She scanned the table, looking at faces ready for the next step. She stopped at Strongbow's. "I don't care about the Mesos. I don't care if the adults want us to fight them or defend ourselves against them or whatever. I care about us, and I think we should help each other. I say we find Strongbow's sister."

Smiles disappeared. Mouths dropped open, everyone looked to everyone else, again looking for the right answer. This time, Siobhan had it. "Hell, yeah!"

With that, the group erupted with conversation, questions, and debate. Everyone participated, asking Strongbow to give as many details as possible about his sister, while Ryoku encouraged everyone to dig in, attesting that the food was free from Willem's sweat, spit, and/or snot.

And, for the first time since she arrived at the institute, Strongbow smiled at Bree.

CHAPTER 14

MONDAY MORNING, turmoil knotted Bree's stomach. Ever since the cookout two days ago, she obsessed over why Miss Harkins withheld information from her. When she told Bree of the institute, Bree felt worthy, deserving. Now? Now Bree felt like a necessary piece of a puzzle, only chosen to make the puzzle complete. In fact, she was merely a *back-up* puzzle piece, Cassidy being the original "New American" magic user at the institute with the necessary birthdate. Bree only took her place because Cassidy died fighting Talo alongside Lucien's brother, trying to help Strongbow find his sister.

Why, *oh why*, did Bree open her big mouth about the "club" needing to find Strongbow's sister? Stupid. *Stupid!* She felt stupid for saying it on Saturday, and now she felt even *more* stupid today! A few ideas were discussed at the cookout, but the conversations quickly changed, bouncing from one topic to the next. Bree was grateful for that since she had zero ideas about how to find Strongbow's sister. Now the one person she had to turn to she was mad at. Bree's stomach churned, wondering how she'd react when seeing Miss Harkins today.

"Good morning, Bree," she heard from behind her as she aimed for her locker.

"Good morning, Sam," she replied as Sci-Fi Sam caught up to her. For almost two weeks this had been her new routine. Walking through the school's front doors, Sci-Fi Sam greeting her, and walking with her to her locker. A friendly chat and then he walked with her to her first class. Random times throughout the school day, they'd run into each other and he'd walk with her, occasionally even escorting her home after school. During the same two weeks, though, she had also noticed more looks from people, more whispered asides from strangers to other strangers. But now ... now it didn't bother her as much, assuming it was harmless gossip about Sam and her. She knew the friends she made at the other institute—her new, exclusive club—were more substantial, meaningful. She had always wanted to be normal, but now that she knew she was unique, she wondered if she'd ever have anything in common with the people in these halls again?

Chuckling to herself, Bree realized that over the past school year she had lost a "Chelsea" and an "Amanda", but gained a "Sci-Fi Sam", even though she heard rumors that she had originally lost the Sam because of the same reasons why she recently lost the Chelsea and the Amanda. Then again, how solid was the information from the beginning of the year about Sam's motivations when the same information flow was now wrong about Sam and her being involved? It was nice to have him back in her life, even though that led to more questions about why he truly distanced himself from her at the beginning of the year and why all of the sudden he showed renewed interest.

"How was your weekend?" he asked.

Bree noticed that she slowed her step, to spend another minute or two in conversation. "Nice. Had a cookout with some friends. Funny mishap with water, but nothing too crazy. You?"

"Yeah, nothing crazy either. Family stuff Friday night and Sunday. Nerd stuff on Saturday."

Bree smiled. "Nerd stuff?"

Sam glanced around as a blush dabbed his cheeks. "Yeah. Video games. Watched *Star Wars* for the thousandth time."

Bree giggled. "That's not nerdy, Sam."

Sam reddened. "Sure, it is."

"So, did you blog about it?"

"No."

"Update your Facebook status that you were watching it?"

"No."

"Tweet every scene? Did you type, 'OMG, Luke is so lost and alone! Hash-tag the force is with me'?"

Sam laughed. "Umm, definitely not."

"Then there was nothing nerdy about your weekend, Sam."

Looking back to Bree, Sam smiled. She thought she noticed something different about him, truly realizing that people sometimes didn't observe the things they saw every day. She had known Sci-Fi Sam since the beginning of middle school and, in her mind, he had not changed one iota. Logic dictated that he had, of course. He got taller over the years, added proportional weight. So what was it she noticed now? Was it his hair? A mop of shaggy muss, a style he possessed for as long as she could remember, but it was always just … there. Now, it looked like it was on purpose? Styled that way? She then wondered how many locks of misplaced hair separated "out of style" from "in style?" With a smile that she swore hadn't changed in years— or had it?—Sam said, "Well, that's very nice of you to say. Hey, I have to run. I gotta meet with my lab partner about a chemistry experiment. I'll meet you after school and we can walk home together."

Before he left, he ran his hand through his hair to push loose curls from his eyes, Bree noticed a ripple under his long sleeve. Was that a muscle? Had he been working out? How could she ask him if he worked out? "Do you work out?" was a cousin to "Do you come here often?" and "What's your sign?" From the recent wave a secretive glances, it seemed like people already thought that they were a couple. The last thing she wanted to do was fan those flames by tossing lame pick-up lines at him. She resigned herself to being patient; her curiosity would just have to wait. Instead, after Sam left, she just went about her routine and opened her locker. Immediately, she wished she had just stayed home.

Just like the last time it was defiled, she heard overzealous laughter from behind her. However, this time the prank was far less destructive. A red flannel shirt, a faded pair of men's jeans, and a green, wide-billed trucker's cap hung from the coat hooks in her locker. Angry that once again Brittany had broken into her locker, but confused as to what the "joke" was supposed to be, Bree snatched the articles from the hooks and turned. Shocked, her eyes went wide.

Standing next to Brittany was Amanda. They both wore their hair the same way and had similar makeup schemes, including the exact same shade of vampire red lipstick. They even laughed the same fake belly laugh. She was suddenly surprised that they weren't dressed alike. Bree dismissed the growing number of hallway eyes on her as she walked over to the duo of laughing girls.

Ignoring Brittany, Bree asked Amanda, "Where's Chelsea?"

Amanda stopped laughing and gave a lip-curled sneer—another of Brittany's influences—and snapped, "How should I know?"

"What's happened to you?"

Smile oozing across her face like spilled paint, Amanda answered, "Jealous? I did what you couldn't do."

"Be like Brittany? I *never* wanted to do that!"

"I know," Brittany said, her snide words crackling like a whip. "That's why I got you new clothes."

Almost forgetting she was holding them, Bree looked at them, then back to Brittany. "Yeah, okay. What are these supposed to mean?"

"For your new lifestyle. Since you came out of the closet recently."

"Came out? What are you even talking about?"

Amanda answered, her angry words punching Bree in the chest, "I saw you and your new girlfriend at the mall. I heard you two talking about being gay."

Realization rearranged Bree's insides, flipping her burning stomach to the top of her chest, flopping her thumping heart to the bottom of her gut. For the past two weeks, people weren't gossiping about her and Sam. They were just gossiping about *her*. People weren't eyeing a new couple, they were looking at the school's newest lesbian. That still didn't explain Sam's renewed interest in her or why her one-time best friend betrayed her. How did Brittany do it? How did she get Amanda on her side? Motivate her to spread false rumors? Bree didn't care about the rumors, because she no longer cared about the people who spread them. She did care that somehow Brittany had brainwashed Amanda, the same girl Bree doted on when sick, stayed up late with to quell silly fears, studied with so her parents wouldn't be disappointed in her grades. That girl was gone, and in her place was poorly replicated clone who now smiled with bright red lips and gleaming white teeth, who looked Bree right in the eye and said, "Dyke."

In a burst of fury, Bree pushed Amanda, slamming her against the lockers. Face contorted in an amalgam of shock and pain, Bree's once friend fell, hitting the floor hard.

She didn't know why she did it. She knew—*knew*—it wasn't Amanda's fault. Knew Brittany had manipulated this betrayal. And Brittany stood right there, right next to Amanda. Yet, Bree took her frustration out on Amanda. As always, Brittany eluded justice. Bree's hatred wore Brittany's face like a cheap Halloween mask, yet Amanda paid the price. In one burst, one half-second of misplaced aggression, Bree ruined her friendship with Amanda. It had been strained, but Bree always held hope that they could repair it, turning this "bad patch" into a vague blip in time when she reminisced about high school decades from now. Not anymore. No chance of repairing this.

Of course, as instantly as the action, came the reactions of gasps and laughs and ooohs and aaahs and a wall of cellphones ready to capture whatever happened next. And Miss Harkins' sharp voice. "Bree!"

The fight ended before it even began, before any form of "cat-fight!" chant could begin. Bystanders closest to the situation hastened their pace to get out of the way. Gawkers farther away tried to be subtle by pretending their attention was on something else before being interrupted. A faint curiosity flickered through her mind as she saw the smartphones in hands—how many times would this get posted to the internet?

Bree stood straight and turned her head slightly to acknowledge Miss Harkins, but she just couldn't bring herself to look at her mentor. "My classroom. Now."

Showing zero concern for her new friend struggling to get up off the floor, Brittany crossed her arms and cocked her hip, glaring at Bree. Desires and consequences buzzed through Bree's head like stirred-up hornets, but all she did was toss the jeans, flannel shirt, and hat at Brittany's feet.

Hallway activity returned to normal, albeit abuzz with the most recent happenings, while Miss Harkins held the door to the science classroom open for Bree. Glaring at nothing, Bree stomped into the room and plopped herself down at a desk in front of Miss Harkins'.

Heaving a sigh, Miss Harkins sat on her desk. "What was that all about, Bree?"

Cheek muscles rippling as she clenched her jaw, Bree looked to her left, anger radiating from her whole body.

"Bree? You *attacked* one of your best friends," Miss Harkins said.

Bree's head snapped around, eyes burning into Miss Harkins like molten steel. "Isn't that what you want? Isn't that why we're at the institute? To fight? To attack the Mesos?"

Miss Harkins jerked back, her face shifting from frustration to surprise. "Fight the Mesos?"

"Isn't that why all of our birthdays are the same? The same as Talo's? To remove a competitive variable?"

Miss Harkins leaned forward, her expression softening to show that she understood what Bree was talking about. "Bree, the institute is for learning. It's like learning to swim—"

"Yeah, I heard. It's good to know for emergencies, but you can also do it for fun or competition. I got the secondhand brochure." To punctuate her mood, Bree crossed her arms over her chest and threw herself against the back of her chair, right into a typical teenager slouch. Her lips twisted into a soured pucker, eyes holding the glare of indignation from not having her sense of entitlement stroked. Miss Harkins' eyes were stern, a blend of disappointment and anger. After a minute of silence, she said, "You know, Bree, Brittany does the exact same thing when I try to talk to her like an adult."

Her words worked. Bree's icy righteousness melted into a puddle. She slouched even more, this time from shame. Voice barely a squeak, she asked, "Why didn't you tell me?"

Miss Harkins shifted her gaze to an indiscriminant spot on her desk. "Honestly, I don't know. I'm sure you've learned by now that adults are not infallible. I don't know why I didn't tell you. Maybe I thought it would scare you. You have such amazing potential that I really, really wanted you to come to the institute and learn about what you have to offer. I wanted you to discover yourself *for* yourself. I didn't want you to worry about Mesos or ulterior motives or agendas. In fact, we instructors, as well as the councils, are *still* debating about what we should be teaching you.

It's … it's complicated. And, Bree? I'm sorry. I'm sorry I didn't tell you sooner."

Shifting in her seat, Bree processed Miss Harkins' words, trying to determine truth from lies. She decided that she would research to see if there was any spell or potion or charm that could do that. For now, she just mumbled, "It's okay."

Miss Harkins' tone changed again, concerned. "So, Bree. What was all that about in the hall? I thought you and Amanda…?"

The bitterness came back in Bree's voice. "Not anymore."

"What happened?"

Her throat tighten again, too many constricting emotions. "I … I can't. I just can't … talk about it yet."

"Okay," Miss Harkins replied. "One thing that helps … people like us … clear our heads is spending quality alone time with our talismans. As you know, the institute has some amazing gardens, an expansive green house, and a rich forest along the perimeter. Maybe next time you're there, immerse yourself in your talisman. Collect your thoughts."

Anger still close to the surface, Bree did appreciate the advice. "Yeah. I'd … I'd like that."

Miss Harkins moved on to the incident in the hallway, letting Bree know that her mother would be called and that she didn't think Bree would get into real trouble since the girls had broken into Bree's locker and it was "just" a push. Bree couldn't focus on Miss Harkins' jumbled words. It was just another thing on Bree's plate. Another stress to worry about, obstacle to overcome. Even though Miss Harkins spoke said she wanted to help in any way she could, Bree still wasn't sure if she could trust her again.

CHAPTER 15

BREE DOOR-PORTED to the institute and headed right for the greenhouse. Today was an open day on the curriculum—no exercises, no lessons. A day off. She didn't have to come in, but now that she'd mastered door-porting, she could come and go without anyone's help, and today she wanted to visit the greenhouse without anyone else knowing. She'd told her mom that she'd be going to her after school club, and after the awkward conversation from the night before, her mother offered no resistance.

Allyson had received a call from the principal's office to come in about "an incident"—every school's euphemism they used when telling a parent that their child screwed up—involving Bree and Amanda. Throughout the meeting, Bree noticed that her mother looked more confused than angry, then relieved that there would be no suspension or detention.

The car ride home was uncomfortably quiet, but when they returned home, things got weird. Bree started off by telling her mother she was grateful that she wasn't in trouble. Her mother tossed her keys in the small, decorative bowl on her kitchen counter and immediately took a seat on the table. "Well, Bree," she started, "I have to confess that I am not unhappy that you stood up for yourself. Although, I'm sure you can guess, I would have preferred a different course of action to solve your differences."

Knowing that a discussion was to ensue, Bree pulled out a chair across from her mother. Not wanting to say the wrong thing, Bree went with, "I know I shouldn't have been so physical. I'm sorry."

"These things happen. Sometimes the situation calls for it."

Confused, Bree wondered why her mother couldn't make eye contact. Why she was making the "I understand" face that usually came with a heavy talk. But about what? *Oh no!* Allyson looked up at her daughter and said, "I also heard *why* you pushed Amanda. Heard what she said about you…."

"Mom." Bree tried to stop her mom from starting a conversation that wasn't necessary, but like a runaway train, Allyson chugged forth with her words.

"And I don't know if what she said is true or not, but…."

"Mom! I'm not gay."

"It's okay if you are. I know my negative views and comments about men don't help…."

"Not gay, Mom." Bree leaned forward in her chair. "Seriously. Not gay."

"And just because I voice my frustrations about men doesn't mean they're all bad and I understand thoughts of experimenting…."

"Experimenting? Eww! Mom!" Bree buried her face in her hands, hoping if she hid her eyes, she could stop the images of her mom making out with a room full of men and women. Working long hours and weekends gave her mother plenty of time for clandestine meetings with people she would rather others not find out about. Digging the heels of her palms into her eyes, to the point of random burst of color exploding in the blackness, Bree found solace in her mom's underwear drawer—white cotton means no social life, with men or women! Feeling a little queasy that she needed to recall images of her mother's underwear, Bree finally looked up. "Mom! Please! Please stop talking."

Allyson sighed. A blush welled up in her cheeks. "I'm sorry, Bree. It's … it's just a lot to deal with."

"There is *nothing* to deal with, Mom. One of my new friends from the club is a lesbian. Amanda—I don't know why—but Amanda overheard us talking at the mall and started rumors about me."

"I just wanted to let you know that I understand. I know people say that about me behind my back. I have short hair and say 'no' to inappropriate advances from men and have barracuda-like aggressiveness at work. But our situations are different, and I just … I just want to make sure that you're okay, and that you know you can talk to me. And I want you to be happy, no matter who you are or what your lifestyle is. And I want you to know that I love you."

"I love you, too, Mom," Bree said, face burning from embarrassment, mind buzzing with images of her mom that she'd rather never, *ever* think about. Shifting in her chair, she readied herself to sprint away at the first chance she got.

"Good. I just wanted to make sure that you know it's okay if you are—"

"Mom!"

"Okay. Okay. Okay?"

"Okay."

"Okay."

"Okay."

Mother and daughter sat, staring at each other, the same awkward look of concern, the air around them stewing with anxiety. Simultaneously, they both stood and left the room, each giving one last, "Okay."

Now, as Bree scurried through the halls of the institute to the greenhouse, she shuddered as she replayed that moment in her mind. Trying to push those images out of her head, she focused on her goal. She had been to the greenhouse only once, but the memory of that visit was intense. It was before she had a true understanding of what her talisman was or what it meant to her. That first time, she'd walked in only to stop on the threshold as all five of her senses seemed to shift into hyper-spastic mode. The beauty engulfed her, the scents overwhelmed her, the colors threatened to drown her. From flowers to ferns, trees and cactuses, mosses and even fungi—they infiltrated her feelings, penetrated her psyche, and overdosed her with happiness and feelings of intense contentment. Her heart had raced as electricity pulsed through her body. It was so different from the forests and gardens she'd grown up with. The greenhouse held species of flora she never knew existed, all grown *from* magic, *for* magic.

This time, Bree prepared herself for the experience, readied her mind and body for how the greenhouse would affect her. She was confident, until she turned the last corner. Heading toward her from the other end of the hall was Ryoku, looking as fussy as ever. A vice threatened to crush

Bree's heart as she and Ryoku stopped at the greenhouse's door.

"Today's a free day," Ryoku said. "Surprised that you're here."

Offering a sheepish smile, Bree said, "There's a lot going on at home, so I just wanted clear my head. Miss Harkins suggested that I spend more time with my talisman, and I figured today's a good day to start."

Ryoku frowned. "There's a really nice garden on the west side of the property. Why don't you go meditate there?"

Taken aback, Bree voiced her own curiosity. "So, why are you here? I thought water was your talisman?"

Ryoku's expression shifted, although Bree could hardly tell since most of Ryoku's expressions consisted of big frowns, medium frowns, and small frowns. Bree thought it shifted from a medium frown to a small frown. "Cherry blossoms, remember? You're not the only one with special plant mutant super powers, you know."

"Sorry," Bree replied in earnest. Wondering if Ryoku would eventually see the similarities in their respective lives, Bree hoped that this might be an opportunity for them to bond. Opening the door to the greenhouse, Bree gestured for Ryoku to enter. "After you."

Ryoku's small frown wavered, her hard eyes drilling into Bree's. "Very well," she said as she stepped inside.

Bree followed, sensory overload almost knocking her over. First the hot, humid air slapped her, then every color of the rainbow assaulted her, fighting for her attention. Intoxicating, the aromas wafted around her, and she inhaled each and every one of them. The flowers and plants closest to her twitched and shook, aware of her presence just as she was of theirs. She was instantly and intimately connected to the flora she was familiar with, and those foreign to her called out in a thousand whispers in a thousand different languages. She heard them all. She heard … "Is that music?"

Ryoku seemed a bit jittery, and her face went to medium frown. "How about you go back to swooning?"

Still under the spell of every plant and tree and bush and vine, Bree slowly became aware of her surroundings, her tunnel vision widening until it disappeared. In a patch of heaven she thought had to be the size of a football field, Bree could not even see the walls. Aisles of green with bursts of purples, blasts of reds, explosions of orange and yellow, waves of whites and swirls of pinks spread out before her. She wanted to get to know each and every one of them, lose herself in what they had to offer. That had to wait, though, because of the music. It didn't belong here. She needed to find where it was coming from. "Come on," she said, walking straight ahead, deeper into the greenhouse's embrace. "I think the music is this way."

"Why are you interested in music?" Ryoku said, her brow furrowed in one of her usual frowns. "I thought you said you wanted to come here to clear your mind. Music would be a distraction."

Ignoring Ryoku, Bree kept moving deeper into the greenhouse while waves of sensations and feelings flowed around and through her as she passed different plants and trees and flowers.

"This isn't a good idea," Ryoku hissed from behind Bree.

Bree ignored her and kept going. At the end of the aisle stood three small sakura trees, in full bloom, thick with cherry blossoms, supple white petals, tinged pink toward the stem. Her view was blocked, but she saw movement on the other side of the aisle from the cherry blossoms and could tell that's where the music, now a soft rhythmic drumming, came from. She crept closer and stepped around a row of thick bushes of honeysuckle, cascading with fragrant orange flowers.

Sitting cross-legged on the floor, and swaying with the music, sat Lucien. Shirtless. Eyes closed, a thin sheen of sweat on his skin, he moved with the simple rhythm, three echoing thumps, then a fourth heavier one. Forward, right, back, left, forward again on the forth beat, his movement embodied the music and Bree couldn't take her eyes of him. Or the black mist swirling above him. Wispy clouds of ink looped and pooled, danced in spirals with Lucien and the music. It was like watching a work of art, a moving masterpiece, something so essential and elemental that Bree wondered if she'd stopped breathing. *He was shirtless.* Her eyes traced his strong jaw, his tapered neck, his rounded shoulders, chest, and arms with every muscle relaxed yet defined as if poised to move in an instant. A bead of sweat meandered down his neck, and she had a difficult time reconciling that he was her age – her *exact* age to the day – because no boy in her high school, even the most popular athletes, looked like this. Her eyes lingered so long that she felt the need to apologize to Willem for getting mad about him leering at her chest.

Blinking rapidly, she tried to break herself of the spell, reminding herself that Ryoku was standing right next to her, probably preparing a snarky comment. No comment came because Ryoku was all but hiding behind a cherry blossom tree, watching Lucien just as intently. Bree finally put two and two together – Ryoku knew about this. She knew Lucien would be here listening to music that's why she had her "medium frown" face on this whole time and had tried to shoo Bree away. Angry about Ryoku's little game, Bree blurted, "Lucien?"

Lucien's eyes snapped open and his body stopped swaying as the swirls of black mist faded to nothingness. He pressed "stop" on the mp3 player, attached to two small speakers, and smiled up at them. "I apologize. I didn't realize anyone else would be using the greenhouse today. I hope I wasn't disturbing either of you."

Bree swallowed hard, internally screaming reminders to *look at his eyes, look at his eyes, don't look down, look at his eyes*, and said, "No. Not at all. I just … I just needed to clear my mind and thought what better place than a room full of my talisman?"

"Me too," Ryoku said meekly, "Well, not my talisman, but sakura trees. I love the cherry blossoms."

"So you meditate and practice your magic in the greenhouse?" Bree asked Lucien.

A soft smile slid across his face, almost with a bashful tone, he said, "I like the aromas in here. Today I found the honeysuckles exceptionally appealing."

Both girls gave polite smiles. Ryoku said, "Very nice. Well, we'll let you get back to…."

"You're both welcome to stay. The drums help me relax, so if you don't mind my music, you're welcome to join me."

A blush swept over both girls' cheeks. Bree blamed the sweat matting locks of her hair on the sultry greenhouse air, overly warm and excessively moist. "Okay," they said in tandem.

Sitting cross-legged, the girls sat equidistant from each other and Lucien. Bree got comfortable and tried to relax while Lucien tapped away at his mp3 player. When he hit "play" the speakers came alive with the sounds of drums, similar to what Bree heard when she first walked in, but the beat much slower.

"The drums help put me in a trance-like state. They start slow, but become faster," Lucien explained.

The three closed their eyes, but Bree was too curious to keep hers shut. She did relax, and the drums did help, but she watched as Lucien started to sway to the music again. Like when she first arrived, swirls of black mist formed around him. It started faintly at first, nothing more than dark steam, but after a few minutes, streaks of black clouds flowed around his body, his magic moving with him. And he wasn't the only one.

Ryoku sat in front of the sakura trees and as the speed of the drumbeats increased, the cherry blossoms across the aisle began to vibrate. Then one released itself from the tree. Then another. And another. Then a snowfall of white and pink. They didn't fall to the ground, though. Instead, like Lucien's smoky swirls, they floated in the air around Ryoku.

Bree felt her magic course through her, flowing like the blood in her veins. It was a part of her, it *was* her. She embraced and nurtured it, explored it as she allowed herself to get lost in the quickening rhythm of the drums. The honeysuckle vines from behind her grew, creeping forth to her, over her shoulders and legs.

Drums thumping faster, Bree breathed heavier. More vines flowed over her body. More mist spiraled around Lucien. More cherry blossoms swarmed around Ryoku.

Then they all began to meet in the middle, the space in between the three students.

Honeysuckle vines crept along the floor, twisting and wriggling, rising upward like curious snakes. The flowery cherry blossoms danced around the vines, floating upward along with them. The streams of black mist wove in and out of the vines and cherry blossoms, adding inky veins to both.

The drums beat faster. Getting lost in the moment, Bree felt Lucien's and Ryoku's magics around her, as palpable as the hot breath of a secret whisper against her ear. She felt their magics and added hers to them. Her body tingled, electricity skating across her skin, her very soul ready to burst, she released her magic. Honey suckles burst from the vines, popping up inside of the cherry blossoms while the mist created swirling tribal markings on the petals of both sets of flowers.

Bree's lids narrowed, predatory. The more she felt the music, the more the mist-laced vines and flowers enveloped her, the more she primal she felt. Skin burning, tingling, the feeling inside of her begged for release. Watching. Watching the black mist dance with the green vines and mingle with the narrow orange petals and full white ones. Mingling. Merging. Joining together.

That was it!

"I got it!" Bree yelled, snapping wide-awake from her dreamlike state. As quick as her exclamation, the vines and flowers went limp and fell to the floor, the black mist dissipated.

Eyes opened wide in disoriented panic as if awoken abruptly from a deep sleep, Lucien and Ryoku looked to Bree as honeysuckle and cherry blossom petals floated languidly to the floor, some landing softly in the trio's hair.

Beads of sweat tickled their way over Bree's face. "I know how to find Strongbow's sister!"

CHAPTER 16

WILLEM WAS THE LAST to arrive, sauntering into the game room, smiling as if everyone's gaze was a spotlight and he owned center stage. "How courteous of you to wait for me, my minions."

As he sat on the barstool next to Ryoku, she grimaced and said, "You know, for someone who comes from the country where the language was invented, you sure don't speak it well."

"Hey, it's Wednesday evening, our day off, and I find myself jostled from my studies to join everyone in a last minute, hush-hush meeting. I'm a bit off my game at the moment, so if you'd like, I can leave and re-enter with a wittier statement?"

"No. And no one here believes you were working on your 'studies.' But please, please, please do not tell us what 'studies' is a euphemism for. Anyway, Bree had an idea on how to find Lila."

"Oh, does she now? This ought to be good," Willem said. "So, let's hear it."

All eyes turned to Bree. A lump formed at the back of her throat as she tried to think of the best way to explain her idea, feeling the pressure of everyone looking at her. Especially Willem and Ryoku since they sat by the juice bar, looking down at her from barstools. Everyone else sat in their usual spots—Siobhan next to Bree at the table in the center of the room with Siza across from them, Javier and Rumiel at one end, Lucien and Strongbow at the other. Bree looked around and swallowed hard. "I think … I think if we combine some of our magics, we might be able to find Lila."

Silent, everyone looked at each other, exchanging expressions of confusion. Bree's mouth went dry, but she continued. "Earlier this evening, Lucien, Ryoku, and I were meditating and focusing on our magics in the greenhouse."

Willem smirked and elbowed Ryoku. "Sound like a fun time."

Ryoku was having none of it. She turned and hissed, "You are dangerously close to paying a jerk tax."

Reeling back as if her words were acid, Willem lost his smirk and whispered, "Whoa."

"Some time during our meditation, our magics … combined. We each had our eyes shut, so we didn't see it happen," she lied, feeling uneasy about the idea of Ryoku and Lucien knowing she had watched the events unfold, "but we could *feel* it."

"When you say 'combined' what do mean?" Siobhan asked. "Like when we joined together to open the door-port to London?"

"Not exactly," Bree started, desperately trying to unjumble her emotions from her words, forcing her brain to talk and not her heart. "For the door-port, we used our magics together, like layering them or using them to build momentum. I'm talking about *joining* them. Fusing them. I don't know how to explain it, but there's a difference."

No one was making fun of her, so she continued. "In the greenhouse, each of us were using our magics on what we were comfortable with: me with honeysuckle, Ryoku with cherry blossoms, and Lucien with darkness, and the music, too. Anyway, as we went deeper into our meditations, we went deeper into our magics." *And deeper into our souls*, Bree thought as she glanced to Lucien, warm tingles skittering up and down her spine. "The three of us bonded and combined our magics to make the honeysuckles and cherry blossoms and darkness fuse and … and … dance together. It was kinda like the difference between pressing your palm against someone else's and *really* holding hands, fingers intertwined."

Ryoku rolled her eyes and sucked her teeth. "I was there, remember? It was nowhere as *romantic* as that! It was like making chocolate milk—add syrup and stir."

At first, Bree thought that was how Ryoku perceived the experience, just a formula, but her lack of eye contact showed that it affected her more than she let on.

Willem looked around the room, posing his question to everyone. "Are you sure? I mean can that even happen? It doesn't make sense."

"Of course, it happened," Ryoku huffed. "You think we're making it up?"

"It does make sense that magics can be combined to create something unique," Siza offered. "If this were not the case, then, logically, the world would only have one magic."

"Exactly what I was thinking," Bree added. "My magic, the so-called New American magic, is the 'newest' style of magic. It was influenced by Western European settlers. It has a heavy influence of Celtic, like Siobhan's, and even some hints of Willem's. Mix those with the Native American magics that have been on this continent longer and then after a few generations, it became its own unique magic with its own talismans and spells and beliefs and rituals."

"Are you sure it was 'combining' magic?" Willem challenged again. "I think it'd be rather easy for the three of you to make honeysuckles and cherry blossoms and 'darkness'—whatever the bloody hell you mean by that—to 'dance' together."

"I hate to agree with Willem, but it doesn't seem like your three magics are all that compatible," Rumiel said. "It just seems like you were just using your magics together, at the same time. No big deal."

"See?" Willem gestured toward Rumiel. "He gets what I'm saying."

Rumiel shook his head. "Did you miss my preface where I said I hated to agree with you?"

Javier chuckled, but quickly stopped himself and blushed.

"Our magics aren't that dissimilar," Bree countered. "It was *more* than just doing magic at the same time. Our magics *joined*." Emphasizing her point, Bree slapped her hands together and clasped her fingers.

Rumiel crossed his arms over his chest and slouched in his chair. Shaking his head, he looked away from the group.

Willem continued to voice his disbelief. "Then how come none of us ever heard of that before? Why haven't the instructors told us about this?"

"None of us are exactly experts here," Siobhan said. "Even those of us who grew up with families who use magic barely know the tip of the iceberg."

"Remember, we don't know all the motivations of the instructors," Lucien added. "Even the instructors don't know the motivations of the instructors or the purpose of gathering us all together at this institute."

"Maybe this is one of their goals for us?" Siza added. "Maybe they brought us together not only to learn *about* each other's magics, but maybe *to learn* each other's magics? Learn how to combine magics?"

Bree frowned, still feeling the sting of Miss Harkins' betrayal. "Well, it doesn't really matter what the instructors want for us. Right now, it's about what *we* want, what *we* need, and I think we need to at least explore how we can combine magics to find Lila."

Strongbow drew in a deep breath but said nothing.

Willem pursed his lips in a skeptical scowl. "I just don't see how this could work."

"That's okay," Bree said with a smirk. "We aren't going to use your magic anyway."

"What? Why not? What's wrong with my magic? Why don't you want my magic?"

"Needy much?" Ryoku asked.

"Because I think we'd need magics that have a spirit core."

"I got spirit!"

Ryoku rolled her eyes. "Only if you're a cheerleader."

Bree crossed her arms and gave Willem a flat expression. "Seriously? You have spirit?"

Willem crossed his arms in defiance. "I do!"

"So, you have spells to touch a person's soul?"

"Umm … no …"

"Charms? Potions? Medallions? Incantations to reach inside an individual and see who they *really* are?"

Willem's posture deflated. "Okay. Okay. I'm out. I get it. But you're out too, then."

"I know. Not only that, I just don't think I'm experienced enough or have the strength. I still get woozy door-porting from home to here and can't do another spell for like an hour. I think that means Javier and Rumiel and Siobhan are out too."

Javier twisted his face and tilted his head, a quizzical look upon his face as if trying to solve a puzzle. Bree stifled a giggle while watching him, watching his pursed lips and wispy mustache tussle for control of his face.

Siobhan sighed and looked at Strongbow. "She's right. I don't think I'm strong enough. But I'll certainly help out any way I can."

"Me, too," Javier blurted out.

Rumiel remained steadfast in his silence, offering only his profile to his peers. He didn't shun the group, but his posture didn't indicate he was a part of it either. Disappointed in his behavior, Bree audibly sighed and continued, "So, that leaves Strongbow, Siza, Lucien and Ryoku—"

"I'm out," Ryoku said. Even though her voice held her usual caustic tone, she didn't possess her usual poise. She, too, turned sideways from the group, discomfort etched across her face.

Confused, Bree started, "I thought that spirit was—"

"Different kind of spirit," Ryoku snipped.

Willem looked at her like as if she had spoken a foreign language. "Different spirit? How can it be a 'different spirit'? I thought Eastern philosophies focus on the spirit. Yin and yang? Aligning your chi?"

"Right," Ryoku glared at Willem. "*My* chi. *My* center of being. *My* spirit. There is a lot of 'knowing one's self' in Japanese philosophy. It's about how the individual moves with nature. If I tried to combine magics with Siza or Lucien, I don't think it would help."

Bree wondered if anyone else noticed Ryoku's voice catch on Lucien's name. A stray thought flickered through her head, wondering how long Ryoku had been sneaking off to the greenhouse to watch Lucien meditate. "Okay. So Lucien? Siza? Strongbow? Do you have any ideas for spells that could track Lila?"

All three furrowed their brows, but it was Siza who spoke first, "I cannot think of a spell, but we do have an item, one enchanted by our ancient gods. It is called The Eye of Ra, and I have seen reference to it having the ability to find what the user seeks. As with many enchanted items, the ability to use it with any form of accuracy is difficult, but …."

"Do you think that the accuracy would improve if Lucien and Strongbow joined their magic with yours while using similar spells from their magics?" Bree asked.

Siza smiled. "I certainly believe it would."

Strongbow sat forward, now clearly encouraged—until Siza's smile evaporated. "Unfortunately, it is kept in Egypt, in a school similar to this one; the one I was attending before coming here."

Deflated sighs filled the room.

But Bree wouldn't let that stop her. "No, that's okay! I already have an idea for that." She turned to Lucien and Strongbow. "Can you think of a spell or totem or … well, anything that we could combine with the Eye of Ra that could help?"

Strongbow frowned. "I don't have an object or particular spell, but our focus on communing with the spirit world could amplify Siza's magic."

Fingers folded together, elbows on the table, Lucien leaned in and rested his face in his hands. Only his eyes remained exposed, darting from left to right as if reading something only he could see. After a few minutes of silence, Bree whispered, "How did you hear me call for help in the night club?"

With a jolt, he sat upright, half the room jumping in response. As if he didn't hear Bree's question, he said, "There is something that might help. It is called the Web of Anansi, the spider god. But like Siza's Eye of Ra, it, too, is difficult to obtain."

"How difficult?" Bree asked.

His jaw muscles worked, and he exhaled slowly. "It is held by the Voice of the Loa, a cult. Although they are not as extreme as the Mesos, they share a similar belief in the primacy of their own magic. They believe voodoo should dominant all the magics."

"Loa?" Siobhan asked.

"The Loa are the spirits we serve, intermediaries between the creator and humanity."

"But you believe this Web of Anansi could help find Lila? If used with Siza's Eye of Ra," Bree said.

"I do." Lucien turned toward Strongbow. "We would

need one of Lila's personal items, but I think this idea could work."

"Okay, smart-guy," Willem said. "Even if it works, how are we gonna get these items?"

Bree put her hands on the table and leaned forward. Her smile lit up the room. "Who wants to go on a field trip? Miss Harkins told me coming to the institute would give me an opportunity to learn about the magics of other cultures as well as my own, so I think it's time for a trip to Egypt. The Eye of Ra is waiting for us."

CHAPTER 17

STARES. GOSSIP. FINGERS POINTED and heads nodded toward Bree. The crowded school halls were still alive with rumors of Bree being gay and her fight with Amanda. She didn't care. She knew who she was and didn't need to justify it to anyone. What she didn't know about herself, she was learning *outside* this school's walls and the petty problems they contained.

Bree walked to class with confidence, a smile on her face. She now knew that high school was temporary, as fleeting as a falling flower petal. Uncle Ross, her mother's younger brother, once told her when she was in middle school that high school was a joke and any adult who referred to that time as the best years of their life was a loser. Was he right? Was her time in school really that unimportant to her future life? Her mother emphasized grades first; socialization was healthy, but never a priority. In fact, her mother had never gone to a single class reunion, and to the best of Bree's knowledge, had zero interaction with anyone she went to school with. This realization made Bree feel above it all, as if this time wasn't as critical as she used to think. Outside of school was the real world. Outside of school was Siobhan and Siza and … and Lucien. Outside of school, she and her friends were trying to save another human being's life. What could be more important than that? But, even so, her mind kept drifting back to her early morning conversation with Sci-Fi Sam.

Sci-Fi Sam had caught up with her on her walk to school. This had become a regular routine, and Bree enjoyed the newfound comfort in their banter.

"So, what'd you do last night?" she asked.

"Watched *Lord of the Rings* for the seven hundredth time," he replied, his tone self-deprecating.

Bree examined him as they walked, still trying to pinpoint specific physical changes. He was bigger, she was certain, but she couldn't find the proof. Even though he wore a tee shirt with a robot on it, it was over a formless long sleeve shirt. "I don't get *Lord of the Rings*."

"What's not to get?"

"How they made three movies about two friends having to toss a piece of jewelry into a volcano."

"Well, there is a bit more to it than just that. Did you miss the big adventures along the way?"

Bree waved her hand dismissively, "Yeah, yeah, yeah. I get that. But why was the ring so powerful?"

"Because it controlled the other rings."

Bree tried to glance down to see if his legs looked bigger, but his baggy jeans offered no hints. She did notice that he walked with more confidence, his slouched shoulders a thing of the past. "Yeah, great call with that," she said. "Give rings to the different species and then make one to 'rule' them all. Who did that and why? The elves only got three, while the humans got nine? And the poor hobbits get zero?"

"It was the committee."

"The what?"

"The ring committee. They're the ones who decided all of that."

Bree wrinkled her nose, confused. "I don't remember that in any of the movies."

"It's in the special edition version that was only released in Japan with ten extra minutes of ring committee deliberation."

"The what? What are you—?" Bree stopped when she saw his smirk. She laughed and jabbed her elbow into his arm. "Jerk."

Sam mimicked her action. "You made it too easy."

As they ascended the school's stairs to the main door, a distant rumble grew louder. Before entering the building, they stopped and looked back at the busy parking lot to see a large red motorcycle, gleaming in the morning sun, with two occupants. The motorcycle pulled up to the curb to drop off the passenger, a girl in short shorts to accentuate her long legs, smooth enough to glimmer in the sunlight. Her helmet hid her face, but her tank top did little to hide her torso, her cleavage primed to strike at any moment.

"Whoa," Sam whispered. "Who is *that?*"

"We have plenty of skanks in this school, Sam. It could be any one of them." Bree turned to enter the building, but Sam didn't move. Bree rolled her eyes and stifled a pang of disappointment that Sci-Fi Sam wasn't so different from the other guys at school. She pushed her ogling of Lucien's bare torso out of her mind and watched as the girl removed her helmet.

Bree's world screeched to a halt.

It was Amanda.

"Whoa," Sam whispered.

"Who is she with?" Bree asked, more to herself.

"Whoa," Sam said again.

The rider set the kickstand and got off, but kept the motorcycle running. He removed his helmet as well to reveal a broad, chiseled face, deep-set eyes, and thick black hair pulled back in a sleek ponytail. Looking at Amanda with hungry eyes, he wrapped his right arm around her waist and pulled her close. She squealed before she threw her arms around him and went in for a deep kiss.

Wearing a sleeveless shirt, he had a Dia de los Muertos sugar skull tattoo on his left shoulder, and it seemed to stare at Bree. As she stared back, one thought ricocheted through her mind—*Meso.*

Breaking from their kiss, they both noticed Bree staring at them. Amanda laughed and whispered into his ear. He looked right at Bree and smiled knowingly. *What the hell?* Bree wondered. *Is he REALLY a Meso?* She made an assumption just based on the way he looked. A chill skittered down her spine when she realized she had jumped to conclusions just like Willem would have done. The boy's eyes seemed to mock her, but maybe that was just him. Maybe that was how he *always* looked?

With a wink and a smile, he put his helmet back on and jumped on his motorcycle. Revving the engine three times, he gunned it and sped away, leaving teenaged speculation in his wake. Brittany and two other cheerleaders ran to meet Amanda, giggling and hugging each other.

"O! M! G! How hot was that?" Brittany declared, loud enough for half the school to hear.

"Where'd you meet *him?*" one of the other girls squeeled.

Before Amanda could answer, Brittany jumped in. "At dinner, over the weekend. He was our waiter and he couldn't take his eyes off of her. Amanda was sooooooo smooth, too! The way he flirted with her in that sexy accent of his...."

Bree chuckled to herself. Brittany told a story about a handsome boy choosing Amanda over her, yet she derived all the attention from manipulating the situation so well. However, Sam continued to stare. Frustrated, Bree opened the front door and pushed Sam into school.

Bree brushed it off as silly drama, unworthy of her attention, even though she couldn't quite shake the memory of the boy's tattoo. She used her new attitude as a shield—a problem at school was a problem not worth focusing on. Although, she now needed to address an institute problem and so as soon as she had a free period, she went to Miss Harkins' classroom. It was Miss Harkins' prep period, so she knocked and stuck her head in. "Hi. Do you have a second?"

Looking up from grading papers, Miss Harkins smiled. "Of course, Bree. Come in. Is everything okay?"

Bree knew Miss Harkins recognized that the circumstances had been less than spectacular the last few times they had met one-on-one. She also knew that Miss Harkins liked her and sympathized with her, which was why her stomach knotted as she put on a happy face and said, "Oh yes. Everything is fine."

Taking a seat in front of Miss Harkins' desk and pushing down all her guilty feelings, Bree continued, "I have a question ... well, request ... regarding the institute."

Miss Harkins put her pencil down and gave Bree her full attention. "Request? Okay, what is it?"

"I … well, all the students actually … were wondering if you could take us on a field trip?"

"A field trip certainly sounds interesting. Do you have anyplace specific in mind?"

"We were thinking one of the other institutes. Since we're supposed to be learning about other cultures and other magics, we thought we could tour another school…"

"Well, there are only three others like ours and they are newer with fewer students—"

"Exactly," Bree interrupted. "Which is why we were thinking about one more established. We were thinking the one in Egypt."

"Whoa," Miss Harkins jerked back as her smile disappeared. "Egypt? That's—"

"We know it's a lot to ask, but you said yourself that the instructors and councils don't have a set idea as to what to do with the new institutes. Well, we were all taking and thought taking us to visit one so *we* can see how a traditional institute is run and what those students are learning."

Miss Harkins stared into the distance as if she was peeling through the many layers of Bree's idea. "That's … that's … not too bad of an idea. But Egypt is—"

"Not far away with door-ports. No travel plans, no passports needed, no customs. And Siza has been very lethargic ever since the … incident … in England. I think it would really help if she could go home for a weekend."

"A weekend?" Miss Harkins asked, looking back to Bree.

Bree blushed and shrugged a shoulder. "Why not? We're all hoping you'll say yes. Ever since the idea came up we've all been really excited about it. How 'bout this weekend?"

"This weekend?" Miss Harkins put her pen down on the stack of papers. "And your mother will…?"

"Sign a permission slip. I'll tell her it's a trip to the Egyptian Embassy."

Miss Harkins frowned. "I don't condone lying, Bree."

"More like truth stretching."

"Same thing."

Bree dropped her gaze. She knew Miss Harkins felt guilty for not being upfront about the institute's motivations, and she preyed on this. It made her feel guilty, too, and she used that as well. "Miss Harkins, I can't tell my mom the whole truth, the *real* truth. I promise you that I will some day. Right now, I'm trying to figure out if she's the family member I got my magic from or if she's not, then who is, and if she knows or not and if she does, then why she hasn't said anything to me. I don't like lying to her, I really don't, but if she's not willing to volunteer information to me, I need to find out about my magics, more about me, on my own."

Miss Harkins shook her head and frowned. "So, I'm guessing all the students are on board for this field trip?"

Bree looked up, hopeful. "Yes."

"And it's one hundred percent unanimous that the institute in Egypt is the place you'd like to visit this weekend?"

"Yes."

Miss Harkins heaved a sigh. "Well, before I say yes, let me check in with the rest of the instructors."

"Really?" Bree could hardly believe her plan was working. It was only the first part of the plan, but the rest would crumble if this part failed.

"Yes, really. You're right about a lot of things, Bree. I think this trip would be good for everybody. So, if they're okay with it—and I suspect they will be—then I guess we'll be spending the weekend in Egypt."

"I can't wait to tell the other students!"

Miss Harkins laughed. "Give me until the end of the day. I'll work out the details with the other instructors and the councils, and then I'll let you know."

Almost giddy, Bree bounced out of her chair and headed toward the door. Then she stopped and back to Miss Harkins.

"Is there something else?"

"How can you tell a Meso?" The question fell out of Bree's mouth before she could even think about it.

"Excuse me?"

"I know … I know you told me that there is still some debate as to the direction of the institute. Well, if the direction is more … aggressive … then I was just curious if there is any way of figuring out if someone is a Meso or not."

Miss Harkins offered a sympathetic smile. "Unfortunately, not. Unless you're Willem, then you just assume *everyone* who uses Mesoamerican magic is a Meso."

"Are there any ways to determine if someone uses magic or not?"

"There are, but they're very complex. Is this about trying to figure out if your mother uses magic?"

It wasn't, but Bree went with it. "Umm, yeah. Just trying to figure things out."

"I understand. Sorry, but you'll have to do good ol' fashion research to solve that mystery I've got to get back to grading papers, but if you want help or to talk more about this, you know where to find me."

"Okay. Thanks."

During the next two classes, she couldn't stop thinking about the young man who dropped Amanda off to school. So, he looked Hispanic. That didn't mean he was a Meso. There was no way for her to tell if he even used magic. Pure coincidence. How could she find out? Maybe Siobhan or Siza or Lucien knew how to find out if someone used magic. No, that would have to wait—one problem at a time and Bree still basked in the success of taking the first step to solving the problem of getting them to Egypt.

After her last class, she met up with Sci-fi Sam for the walk home. Unfortunately, he kept going on about Amanda's dramatic entrance. He couldn't get over how much she had changed and how amazing she looked while Bree couldn't stop wondering about her ex-friend's motivations. What changed within her? Was she tired of all the late-night slumber-party talk about empowerment and boys and decided to make those fantasies a reality? Was she doing this to spite Bree? What about Chelsea? Where was she in all of this? Bree didn't have any classes with her and usually only saw her once a day in the hallway. She looked so lonely. Bree sighed. She knew she should reach out to Chelsea and that there were some problems within the school walls that couldn't be ignored.

CHAPTER 18

SIOBHAN HELD UP A SHIRT. "How about this one?"

Siza closed one eye and held out her hand then wobbled it back and forth, the universal sign for *average*. "I like the pockets and it is practical, but it's nowhere near as cute as the other one."

Sitting in the swivel chair at Bree's desk, Lucien flashed a playful smile. "Girls are the only creatures on the planet who choose form over function."

"Don't forget, most boys choose a girl's form over her brain function," Bree countered, flipping through the collection of tops hanging in her closet.

Leaning back in mock offense, Lucien said, "Perhaps most, but certainly not all. I know I don't," Lucien replied. "Although form *and* function …"

Siobhan paused from the task of selecting which shirts to pack for the weekend so she could roll her eyes at Siza and stick her finger in her mouth to pantomime a gag. Cross-legged on Bree's bed, Siza laughed at Siobhan's antic.

"Please accept my deepest apologies for offending your sensibilities," Lucien said to Siobhan. "I know aficionados of *punk music* have terribly discerning tastes."

Siobhan responded by looking at Lucien and repeating her gag gesture, this time adding retching noises.

Lucien laughed. "All I meant was that while I'm stunned by the inner and outer beauty of each of my classmates, I'm particularly taken with the fact that Bree came up such an excellent idea to help find Lila."

"Bree, you have a shovel in your garage? Lucien needs one to keep digging his way out of his sexist hole."

"Before anyone gets too impressed, let's see if my idea works," Bree said, ignoring their jests.

"It was also your idea to convince Miss Harkins to take us on a field trip to the institute in Egypt."

A small bloom of pride tickled Bree. "All I did was tell her that not only would it help the other students get a better understanding of how an institute with a longer history is run, but it would help snap Siza out of her funk that's she's been in since the night club incident."

Still cross-legged, Siza bounced up and down on the bed while quietly clapping her hands. Bree had never seen Siza so animated. Even the hood of her omnipresent silk cloak was down. "It was an excellent idea. I can't wait to be back home."

"Yeah, our little Bree is a smart one," Siobhan said. "This bit today, though, was risky, no? Bringing us to your house to meet your mum could've gone all sorts of wrong."

Siobhan was right. It was potentially opening Pandora's Box, but Bree knew she had to show her mother *something* regarding her after school club. She made up a fake permission slip for a two-night field trip to an Egyptian embassy, knowing her mother would assume that it was in Washington, D.C. Bree also knew that she had to introduce at least a few of the other students from the club to add to the authenticity. Siobhan was an obvious choice. She was so strong and confident, Bree knew her mother would respond well to her. Siza was charming and disarming, and kind enough to enchant the permission slip with a little spell to make her mother more agreeable than common sense should allow. As courteous as expected, Lucien never missed a "please" or "thank you." It didn't hurt that his handsomeness was a spell all of its own, no incantation necessary. Allyson signed off, gave her daughter a hug, wished everyone a safe trip, and left for a business meeting.

Bree felt bad about deceiving her mom, but it was a necessary means to an end. She looked at her friends and said, "Thanks for helping out, guys."

"No problem. Although, I thought it was impressive that Siza was able to help out," Siobhan replied.

Siza tilted her head in confusion. "What do you mean?"

Holding one of Bree's shirts by the shoulders to get a better look at it, Siobhan offered a casual, "Well, with all the astral projections and door-porting you do, I'm surprised you actually know how to *walk* through a *regular* door."

Bree and Lucien laughed while Siobhan continued to consider the shirt. Siza, however, tucked her feet under her crossed legs, closed her eyes and took a deep breath. Within a second, her astral form flew from her body, lunging for Siobhan. Jerking backward, Siobhan screamed and threw the shirt at the image of Siza. It passed through the apparition, ending up draped over Siza's real face.

"Damn it, girl!" Siobhan gasped, wide-eyed. "You creep me out when you do that!"

Laughing, Siza removed the shirt from her face and handed it to Bree. Her astral projection dissipated. "I know, and I must confess, it gives me a certain level of satisfaction."

Siobhan gave a playful sneer as she said, "Ha, ha."

Bree laughed as she placed the shirt in her overnight bag, but froze when Siobhan blurted, "You can't wear that now!"

"Why not? It's a cute top."

"It passed through astral goo!"

Siza snapped to attention and said, "It is *not* goo. It's a visual manifestation of my soul."

Siobhan's expression fell flat as she looked at Bree. "So, do you *still* want to wear a shirt that passed through *her soul?*"

Bree crinkled her nose. With pitying eyes, she looked to Siza. "Sorry. I know Siobhan is making it sound way more gross than it really is, but...." She tossed the shirt into her clothes hamper.

Siza responded by sticking her tongue out at Siobhan, then giggled.

"This slumber party talk is simply riveting," Lucien remarked. "When do we start considering shoes? Don't most girls have an obsession with shoes?"

"You didn't have to come along, you know," Siobhan said, holding up another shirt.

"I'm a nice guy. I wanted to help Bree pack."

"Well, Mr. Nice Guy," Bree said. "Are you going to help, or what?"

"Absolutely," Lucien said with an all-business look on his face. "You should bring an extra pair of sneakers."

"What? Why?"

"Just in case you find yourself in a situation with one wet sneaker."

"In Egypt? It's mostly desert."

"With a very large river, remember? Besides, I once went to a cookout and suddenly found myself with one wet sneaker. I was uncomfortable for the rest of the day." Bree, Siobhan, and Siza stared at him. He shrugged. "I just wanted to pass along my knowledge, that's all."

"Knowledge?" Bree asked as she went to her jewelry box and picked out a necklace and matching bracelet. "Any knowledge you want to share about *how* you got one wet sneaker?"

"Nope. Not at all."

"I bet it had to do with being a smart ass?" Siobhan said with a laugh. "Besides I have fewer shoes than my brothers. Talk about obsessed. My parents have practically gone to the poor house keeping those boys in shoes. Those boats you call shoes look like they cost an arm and a leg."

Lucien ignored the jibe. He pointed to Bree's jewelry box. "Jewelry?"

"Why not?"

"We're going on a dangerous mission. It's highly impractical to have pretty little baubles bouncing around."

"It's still a field trip! We will be meeting and mingling with people from another school."

"There's going to be snakes and scorpions and sphinxes that may very well come to life and attack us."

"Maybe these are charms against snakes and scorpions and sphinxes!"

"Well, *are they* charms against snakes and scorpions and sphinxes?"

"No! But the snakes and scorpions and sphinxes didn't know that until you opened your big mouth." Bree returned both pieces to her jewelry box and walked back to her closet, still not quite believing that Lucien was sitting at her desk in her bedroom in her house joking with her like they'd known each other for years. Sometimes she couldn't even look at him without blushing or feeling her pulse start to race. She pulled out a drawer, grabbed a sweater, and folded it. She then went to her bed and placed the sweater in her overnight bag.

"You're packing a sweater?" Lucien asked.

"Umm, yeah?"

"*Why* are you packing a sweater?"

"In case it gets cold?"

"In Egypt? Do you know *nothing* about Egypt? The average temperature is three-hundred degrees."

"It's the desert. The temperature has to go down at night."

"By two degrees. You should pack a swimsuit."

"Ugh!" Siobhan moaned. "Get a room!"

"We're already in a room," Bree said, then immediately froze. Even though she meant it as a joke, she knew exactly how Siobhan would interpret it.

With a devious smile, Siobhan turned to Siza and purred. "Well, Siza? You heard the woman."

Displaying a rare playfulness, Siza answered with a wicked smile of her own. "I most certainly did."

Before Bree could explain or even change the topic, the two girls created separate door-ports and disappeared. Bree stood statue still, not even breathing.

She was alone.

In her room.

With a boy.

No, not *a* boy, *the* boy of her dreams. Gorgeous. Intelligent. Sexy. Well-spoken. Handsome. Exotic. Quick-witted. Had things in common with her. *Or did_he?* Their magic was unique and somehow connected, but was that it? What kind of music did he like? Movies? Television shows? Did he even *watch* television? Did he read for fun? What was his family like? How did he cope after his twin was killed? What motivated him? What made him want to be here … here in her bedroom?

Lucien smiled, eyes twinkling. Bree melted. Cheeks burning, she prayed she would stop blushing and hoped that she didn't look as ridiculous as she thought she did. Before an awkward silence could emerge, she stammered, "I … I didn't mean … I didn't mean for them to go," while admonishing herself, *Why can't I ever say the right thing? Just once?*

"I know," Lucien said, standing.

"What I said … I just kind of barfed words out of my mouth." *Did I REALLY just say I "barfed words" to the most gorgeous guy in the world? What the hell is WRONG with me?*

Lucien glided over to Bree's hamper and plucked out the shirt that Siobhan had thrown at Siza. "It's okay."

"I … I didn't mean for them to leave." *Work, brain! Work!*

After folding her shirt nicely, he held it with both hands and offered it to her. "Here. You should pack this one. Siobhan was only teasing about the astral goo."

Bree laughed and accepted the shirt. When she did, her hands touched his, her fingers and toes tingling the same way they did when they'd worked magic together in the greenhouse. She realized this, too, was magic, just a different kind reserved for movies involving overly pretty Hollywood darlings fawning over each other in contrived situations.

In a daze, she moved her arm and dropped the shirt into her overnight bag, but she couldn't pull her eyes away from his. Their fingers intertwined as he moved closer. He smelled of mint. She tried to breathe normally. Failed. He took a step closer. She looked up at him. He looked down at her. Their fingers tightened. Then, too nervous to continue, Bree snapped out of her stupor and began babbling. "It's hot. Are you hot? Maybe I should open a window. Or check the air conditioning. I'm thirsty. Are you thirsty? I need a drink. Do you need a drink?"

As if waking from a dream, Lucien blinked and took a step back. He pulled his hand from hers and chuckled. "Umm, yeah. I mean, yes. Yes, I think a drink would be a great idea."

"Okay. This way." Bree led the way, trying to use her hair to hide her face. She imagined her cheeks were the color of a clown nose and felt just as silly. The walk didn't calm her at all as she had hoped it would, very aware of his presence right behind her. A slight squeak from each stair from behind her as they descended, until she reached the bottom of the steps. Suddenly, the burning from her cheeks disappeared and her spine turned to ice. Someone was in the kitchen.

Through the doorway, she saw movement. Heard footsteps. Was it Talo? Did the Mesos find out where she lived? Or was this yet another threat that Miss Harkins failed to disclose? With her fingers ready and the words on her lips, she prepared a levitation spell as she crept from the stairs to the kitchen. She burst into the kitchen, spell ready, but stopped herself when she saw a startled Chelsea standing there, eyes glassy and nose red from crying.

Before Bree could say a word, Chelsea's emotional dam burst as words flooded from her mouth. "Bree! I'm so sorry I let myself in! I knocked and rang the doorbell and knocked again, but I saw lights on and thought maybe no one heard me and I have the key you gave me, so I let myself in. I'm sorry I've been ignoring you, but Amanda said so and I don't know why she said so and I don't know why I listened to her, but now she's ignoring me too, and I don't know why she's doing that either. She accused you of trying to be popular and now *she* is popular by being a Brittany clone and—"

Chelsea cut herself short when Lucien appeared behind Bree. She blushed and whispered, "I'm sorry. I didn't know you had company."

Lucien stayed in the doorway. "Is everything okay? I can head back up to your room if you need privacy?"

"No, that's okay! I'm just gonna get going!" Chelsea blurted as she turned to leave.

Despite talking faster than the speed of sound, Bree understood Chelsea. She always spoke quickly when upset, like when she broke her mother's vase and was afraid to confess or after watching a scary movie, convinced that the monsters were real. Bree realized this was the same old Chelsea, unchanged.

With all the major happenings in her life, the way Sci-Fi Sam seemed different, and the abrupt changes with Amanda, it struck Bree that Chelsea hadn't changed in years. Maybe it was the way her nose turned red every time she cried, or the way she had to struggle with the natural curve of her upper lip to cover her braces, or the freckles on her cheeks refusing to fade away. This was the same girl who used Barbies and Kens to act out her ideas of romance just three years ago. Bree remembered the stilted language Chelsea used every time the dolls went on a date, too young to know any better, awkward from lack of experience. Standing before Bree was that same girl. Bree reached out and grabbed her friend's hand. "Chelsea, wait."

Chelsea stopped and looked back to Bree with pleading doe eyes, silent tears rolling from under her glasses and over her cheeks. Bree knew what it was like to feel alone and abandoned. Even though Chelsea was one of the reasons why she had felt that way, Bree didn't have the meanness in her to hold it against her. She released her friend and put a reassuring hand on her shoulder. "I have a field trip this weekend, but I'll call you when I get back."

"Yeah?" Chelsea asked, fingers folded together as she rocked back and forth on her tiptoes.

"Yes. Promise."

Without warning, Chelsea pounced on Bree and gave her a bone-cracking hug. "I missed you."

Bree returned the hug, finding comfort in getting back something she had lost. "I missed you, too."

Wiping her nose with the back of her hand, Chelsea let go. She looked at Lucien, then back to Bree. A smile twitched across her lips as she giggled. "I knew Amanda was lying."

Eyes widening, Bree blushed and changed the subject. "Okay, Chelsea, I gotta get back to packing for my field trip."

"Okay." Another awkward giggle tumbled from Chelsea's mouth as she turned to leave. "Bye!"

Bree waved as her lifelong friend pulled the kitchen door closed behind her. So wrapped up in the excitement of her new life that she forgot there were plenty of good things about her old one. Could she keep parts of her old life while leading a new one? She could feel Lucien's presence behind her. She desperately hoped she could.

CHAPTER 19

"SIZA, WHERE IS YOUR NIQAB?"

"Mother! I told you I am not going to wear the veil."

"Don't you 'mother' me! You are home now, not in the West!"

"I am who I am. That does not change with the time zone."

Amina's eyes narrowed, as if trying to transfer her thoughts to her daughter through sheer concentration. Unwavering as a long-held ideal, Amina's straight posture was evidence of her strong will to everyone who knew her. After a long moment, she sighed and reached for her daughter's cloak, straightening the hood. "That much is true. I guess this hood is passable, almost like a hijab, no?"

A familiar warmth washed through Bree. Mothers and daughters shared similar relationships, no matter the culture. She looked around at Siza's peers. A few wore veils, but most of the girls had their hair covered with fashionable scarves, accentuating their dark eyes and curious gazes.

"My dear, Amina," Siza's father said, "I care little about current fashion trends. I am more concerned—as you well know—that my daughter is getting the education she needs and deserves with regards to our culture's magics. I know, I know," he said, putting his hands up to stop anyone from interrupting, "Siza was chosen to attend this new *fledgling* institute because she was the best student in Cairo, but I am still not convinced it was the best decision." He looked from his wife to his daughter to Miss Harkins and back to his wife. "Now this sudden trip home … with more advance notice, we could have prepared a feast for the visitors and demonstrated true Cairene hospitality. But, no. This was last minute. Hodge podge. Is that how this new American school is being run? Hodge podge?"

Ouch. Bree could see why Siza pulled the hood of her cloak over her face to hide. Her parents were like—what did her mom say?—forces of nature. Larger than life. Bree felt her own face flush, a pang of embarrassment stinging within her chest. Even though she had no control over the education available at the institute, she had found home there and felt like she was a representative, an ambassador. To think that Siza's father did not think it was a good school hurt.

Wondering how everyone else reacted, Bree tried to be as inconspicuous as possible while peeking down the table. The long table was reserved for girls, except for Siza's father, Aman, who, as head of school, sat at the head of the table. Amina sat on his right and Siza sat across from her. Even though it was suggested that the guests be intermingled with the hosting students to encourage more social contact, Siza insisted that Bree sit next to her. Miss Harkins sat across from Bree.

Bree looked down the table to Siobhan, a few seats away. The flat-browed, pursed lip gaze from Siobhan showed that she heard the comment and didn't appreciate it. Looking past her, even farther, she saw Ryoku frowning, also obviously annoyed. Since they'd arrived, a few inquisitive girls had latched onto Ryoku and hadn't stopped asking her about Japan. Finally, Bree turned to Miss Harkins to see how she'd react. With a confident smile, Miss Harkins glanced over to one of the boy's tables where the magics teacher in question was sitting. "Now, Aman, you know very well that our Egyptian magics instructor came from your institute. He is one of the best instructors we have, if not the best."

With a huff, Siza's father said, "Even though he may be the best instructor at your institute, he had only been here a few years. He does not have enough experience to be the only instructor tasked with imparting the intricacies of our magics to novices."

"Aman," Amina said with a mildly scolding tone. "Be civil to our guests."

Offering a deep sigh, Aman's pinched face expression relaxed. "I apologize. I miss my daughter and am naturally concerned about her education. It is a dangerous world, she is far away, and … and I am afraid my emotions have manifested themselves in less than flattering ways."

Head down, but eyes glancing about the table, Siza mumbled, "I miss you, too, Father."

Amina put a hand on her husband's arm. "We agreed the new school would be a good opportunity for Siza. We also agreed to leave her alone so she could learn and make friends without our interference, but remember that she is, after all, only a door-port away. If necessary, you could be there in an instant." She held up her hand and snapped her fingers for dramatic effect.

Siza went back to eating, focusing only on her plate. Miss Harkins changed the topic, and Bree attended to her own meal, wondering if Siza was truly the best student in the school or if Aman's statement was based on fatherly pride. Until the girl next to her, Eshe, leaned over and whispered, "She was."

Not entirely sure the girl was even talking to her, Bree turned and said, "Excuse me?"

"Siza's father stated that she was the best student in the school. Ever since he made that proclamation, you have been curious if it was true. It is," Eshe said, offering the slightest upward turn of her lips, the same way Siza did after giving useful information.

"How … how did you know?"

Eshe took a bite, swallowed, and then turned back to Bree. "She always had the highest marks and learned the spells and potions faster than any other student I know of. Her abilities are quite impressive."

Bree scrunched her nose and shook her head. "No. I meant, how did you know I was curious about that statement?"

Just like Siza would do, Eshe shifted her smile, broader with just with a hint of condescension. "By the change in your expression, it was obvious that was what you were thinking."

Bree sat straighter. Eshe was just being honest, but a part of Bree felt like an unsophisticated simpleton. *Am I that easy to read? Were my thoughts written so clearly on my face?*

Eshe turned her attention back to her plate. "I apologize. I've offended you."

Is it really that obvious? Bree wondered. *Or does she have the ability to read my mind. Wait! Is there some kind of thought reading, telepathy spell? Or potion? Maybe she slipped it into my food? Oh, no! If she can read my thoughts, then does she know about what we're planning tonight at the dance? Probably not until now when I JUST thought about it! Gah! I suck so bad at espionage!*

Bree forced a smile and placed her hand on the Eshe's. "Don't be sorry. I'm new to the institute and to magics and this is all so amazing and beautiful. And very, very overwhelming."

Eshe perked up, excitement sparkling within her eyes. "I understand. I believe I would be just as overwhelmed to visit America. Lush forests. Blankets of snow. Cute boys."

Bree and Eshe shared a giggle, and unable to stop herself, Bree glanced over her shoulder to the boys' table where Lucien sat. Even though conversation buzzed at all of the tables in the dining room, Bree could pick out parts from the table behind her if she focused. The school had internet access, and allowed smart phones, so the boys talked about which games were better, which actress was the hottest and which sport was superior—soccer or American football. Lucien joined in, laughing and keeping it lighthearted. While someone took a turn in the conversation, Lucian stole a moment to glance around. He looked right at Bree. Pausing, his smile grew, bright and warm. Four boys around Lucien turned to look at Bree.

Blushing, Bree turned back to her plate. Eshe asked, "Is he yours?"

"Who?" Bree asked even though she knew very well that she didn't have the skill set to play coy.

"The tall handsome one who looks like an athlete."

With those words, Bree peeked back over her shoulder. The boys had gone back to comparing something to something else, as boys always do. Lucien was certainly handsome and built like an athlete. "No."

"But you wish him to be."

So set in her ways, Bree couldn't stop herself from turning to Eshe and saying, "Why would you say that?"

Eshe tilted her head. Even though she didn't say a word, the look on her face screamed, *Either you're stupid for not realizing I told you that you're easy to read, or you're stupid for thinking I'm stupid by not seeing how easy you are to read.*

Cheeks heating up from the growing blush, Bree chuckled. "Yeah, I guess you're right."

"Well, he seems to be taken with you, too, because he's looking at you again."

"Really?" Bree squeaked, turning too conspicuously. Lucien was, indeed, looking at her. He winked and grinned, then went back to his conversation.

So embarrassed, she felt her ears glow red, Bree refocused on her dinner. Eshe leaned closer and whispered, "I do not guess that I am right. I *know* that I am right."

Feeling like an open book, Bree whispered back, "Yeah, you're right," and finished her dinner in silence.

Dessert cheered her up. In between the exotic flavors and sticky sweetness, Bree remained mindful of her actions— no turning around, not even a backward glance, lest she be scrutinized by Eshe again. Much to Bree's relief, meal time ended soon after.

The dance was to follow, but there was free time to walk around and mingle, and Siza took the opportunity to steal a moment with Bree. She asked, "What did you think of the food?"

Bree smiled. "It was delicious. Although, I can see how hard it must be to have a father who is the head of the school."

"Like all fathers, he makes the choices he deems right."

Thoughts of her own father stumbled around the rooms of her mind. Clearly, Bree's father proved Siza's statement inaccurate. A stray question came to mind—what if he thought leaving her and her mother alone was the right thing? Sure, Bree's mother had spun the story so that she was the one who left him to brave a cruel and unexplored world. Even if that was the case, he had never once in the past decade tried to contact his own daughter. Why? If it was her mother who left, why hadn't her father stayed in her life? Where was he? What was he doing and—

"Bree? Are you okay?"

Bree blinked and looked at Siza. "Yeah, fine."

"And like all fathers," Siza continued, "he has his strengths and his flaws."

Bree chuckled. "Your father seems like he works hard to control or at least minimize his flaws."

"Minimize, yes, but not eliminate." With a wicked smile, Siza held up his access card.

Eyes bugging out, Bree looked over both shoulders and whispered, "Is that his swipe card?"

"Yes, it is his swipe card."

"Won't you get in trouble when he notices it's gone?"

"I will only get in trouble if I'm caught. We should be gone for less than an hour. He will be too busy being a doting chaperone to notice it missing." With the sleight of hand that would make a street magician jealous, Siza made it disappear within her emerald cloak.

Bree covered her mouth with her right hand and slowly slid it off her face, as if to drag away all the words she wanted to say like, *We need to stop. We can't do this. I quit. I'm too scared. We're going to get caught.* Instead, she saw a glimmer in Siza's eyes and a determined confidence in her smile. "Okay, then. We're doing this."

"Yes. Yes, we are."

"Okay," Bree said one last time, clutching her purse with both hands and trying to reassure herself that the squirming in her belly and the flutters in her chest were worth it.

CHAPTER 20

BREE ENTERED THE BALLROOM. As with everything else in this school, the act was done with rigidity. Boys first. Then the girls were allowed to enter. Bree and her fellow students gawked about the room, stunned by the ornate decorations. Siza's father stood upon the stage, raised only slightly off the floor, and made a few announcements.

The boys nodded to people and whispered amongst themselves, followed by smiles and elbowing. The girls actually talked about the décor, the residents explaining the meanings to the guests. Except for Bree. While mingling, she nodded and smiled when appropriate, but retained little of the information shared with her, too busy internally fretting over what was about to happen. Was she the only one concerned? Scared witless? So wrapped up in her gut-wrenching panic, she didn't even realize that the dance had officially begun until Siobhan approached and asked, "Are you gonna make it, girl?"

"What do you mean?" Bree asked, fingers working over her purse.

"I mean, you're fidgeting with your purse so much that it's gonna be shredded to ribbons before the night's over."

"Sorry. I don't usually carry one. It's so weird. Bulky. Awkward."

"Well, it's making you look awkward. And nervous. Like you're going to puke in it at any moment."

"Actually, that's a good idea. I'm going to go over to that corner over there and purse puke. Will you hold my hair for me?"

The girls laughed, and Bree relaxed for the first time since she'd stepped through the door-port into Egypt. "That felt good. Thanks." The feeling was too fleeting and she immediately went back to being nervous.

"Well, you needed it. You really do look like you're gonna puke, though."

"I know. I feel like I'm going to. How do you do it?"

"Do what?"

"Remain so cool and calm."

Siobhan chuckled. "First of all, I'm not going on 'the mission.' All I'm doing is running interference. Second of all, when you look this good, you can't help but be cool." To emphasize her point, she turned in a full circle, ending with a smoldering eye squint and a dramatic hair flip, her black hair now flowing over her right shoulder.

Siobhan was like a statue carved from strength and confidence. If Bree didn't love her as a best friend, she'd be incredibly jealous of her. "Diva," Bree said with a smirk.

The girls laughed again. Siobhan placed her hand on Bree's shoulder and asked, "Are you okay with this? Just say the word and we can switch places. I know a couple healing spells if we need them, you know, to be the designated healer-girl. I can be Bree for a few minutes. I do a fun impression of you behind your back."

Bree chuckled, and then took a deep breath. Exhaling through pursed lips, she said, "No. I'm good. I can do this."

"Good. Because even though I do a good impression of you, I don't think I'd be any good at flirting with Lucien. He's just not my type."

Bree's eyebrows knotted in confusion. "Excuse me?"

Siobhan leaned close enough to whisper into Bree's ear, "He's on his way over, genius, and I'm sure he doesn't want to talk mission strategy."

Bree spun on her heel. Siobhan was right. The boys were now allowed to mingle with the girls and Lucien was aiming right for Bree. Blushing, Bree turned back to Siobhan just as she started to walk away. Siobhan paused just long enough to wink and say, "I'm off to go see if anyone has spiked the punch yet."

Butterflies danced and fluttered in her stomach, for different reasons this time, Bree gripped her purse and attempted to look demure as Lucien approached. With a demeanor that far surpassed his years, he walked up and said, "Hi."

"Hi." She hoped she didn't sound squeaky.

"I came over to talk mission strategy."

Bree's eyes widened. "What?"

Lucien leaned in to whisper, "Siobhan is neither subtle nor quiet."

Glancing over to the punch bowl, Bree watched Siobhan pour a drink as she feigned innocence. Around her, a semi-circle of boys gathered to gawk, obviously trying to get up the confidence to say something. "Yeah, she's about as subtle as a brick through a window."

"Well, since we're both here ... shall we dance?"

Yes! Bree's mouth opened and closed and then she realized nothing had come out. She tried again. "Yes!" Her agitated nerves squirmed and twisted. She wanted to feel his arms around her, get lost in his eyes and his smile, but could she stop thinking of the mission long enough to enjoy herself? She imagined herself on the dance floor as stiff and unbending as a plank of wood and could almost see Lucien rolling his eyes, getting bored, and making a hasty escape. There was still the issue of her purse. Unaccustomed to carrying one, it seemed to grow from three, to five, to ten times it original size. Cumbersome as it was to hold, it would be impossible to try to dance with it. She looked around for someplace to stash it, and then, magically, it disappeared. Well, not real magic. Siobhan glided by and snatched the purse from Bree's fidgety hands. "Relax, girl," she said as she continued on her way.

"Again, not subtle," Lucien said as he took Bree's hand and led her onto the dance floor. She turned to face him and as he placed his hands on her waist a tingly *zing* shot from her toes to the top of her scalp and then cascaded down her spine like a waterfall. *Confident*, Bree told herself, *be confident. Don't be a giggly girl gushing ga-ga because the hot, cool stud is dancing with you. And stop using alliteration. That's what giggly girls do.* With her purse gone and her hands free, she reached up to rest her hands on his shoulders, hoping it wasn't obvious to everyone in the room that she had never danced with a boy before.

The music was slow, yet melodic, lending itself nicely for a slow dance. Siza's father had made the rules clear—there must be at least a foot between dance partners at all times. Despite the awkward distance, Bree felt like she and

Lucien moved together well. They were still close enough for her to feel his body heat.

Cheeks sore from smiling, she commanded herself to take it down a notch. He was looking down, watching her. Her peripheral vision blurred, the ballroom and everyone in it faded away. Only Lucien remained. She felt like she was in a silly rom-com. She realized if that were the case, her next lines would need to be witty or deep or endearing or pithy. What would a movie star say in this situation? Bree tried to recall all of the rom-coms she had ever seen, the scenes and actors and dialog piling up like a log-jam in her mind.

"Bree?" Lucien asked. "Are you okay?"

Wondering what she did to embarrass herself, Bree answered, "Yeah? Why?"

"You had a really strange smile. Like you were in pain."

Bree laughed. *Oh my god, I'm being so lame! Get a grip.* "Sorry. No, I'm fine. This trip has been overwhelming."

Lucien eyebrows knitted in concern. "What do you mean?"

"I mean, we're in Egypt!"

"Yes. Yes, we are."

"That is so *mind blowingly* cool!"

"Yes. Yes, it is."

"I mean, it's—" Bree paused from her rambling. Lucien's eyes sparkled with wonder, not of his surroundings, but of her. "You've been here before, haven't you?"

"Not to this school, no."

She drew her lips tight and lightly swatted his shoulder. "Not what I mean. Have you been to Egypt before?"

"Yes."

"Any other countries?"

He was quiet as he guided her around the dance floor, while he sought the right answer. She appreciated his humility when he said, "Yes. I have done some traveling."

A feeling of awe washed through Bree, amazed that at such a young age he had experienced different places and cultures while she'd barely been out of her hometown. That sensation then mutated into one of inadequacy and self-pity. He'd obviously done so many things and she'd done nothing. He'd had experiences she'd never get to share with him and she had nothing to share. Her smile faded and she looked away. "Oh."

"What's wrong?"

"Nothing."

"Bree. Seriously? I don't need voodoo to know that something I said affected your mood."

Bree heaved a defeated sigh. "It's ... it's ... just that I must be so boring to you."

Lucien jerked his head back as if she stung him with an insult. "First of all, no. Second of all, why would you even think that?"

"You've been to Egypt before. *Egypt*. Not to mention probably a bazillion other cool places. And you've been doing voodoo all of your life and I just learned that magic is real a couple of months ago. And I've never been to Egypt before. Or *any* of the places you've been. I've barely been out of my own yard. I went to Ohio a few times to visit my whackadoodle Uncle Ross, but even though he's my mom's brother, she doesn't like to visit him because she thinks he's a counterculture slacker, and, according to my mom, and she's afraid he might corrupt me or something, so—"

"Bree?"

"What?"

"Take a breath before you hyperventilate."

Feeling even smaller and more ridiculous, she whispered, "Sorry."

"Don't be. You're not boring."

"Compared to you, I am." *God, now I sound whiny!*

Lucien pulled her just a little bit closer and smiled down at her. "Bree, we've both had life experiences."

"Yours are so much better than mine."

"How do you know they're better? I'm sure we've both had joy and pain. Good times and hard times. A few months ago, after my brother—"

Bree stopped moving, forcing another couple to swerve around them. "Oh, Lucien! I didn't mean to… oh my God, I'm so stupid! Please forgive me, I'm being an idiot."

Lucien frowned and shook his head. "Bree, there's nothing to forgive. Honestly. You weren't at the institute then and had nothing to do with his death. No one likes to talk about what happened, so … really, it's okay. Don't be sorry for not being preoccupied with the past."

"Still, I feel terrible."

"Don't. I'm trying to live my life for the future, not the past. We're all just travelers upon this road of life that leads to the future. It's necessary to visit the past now and then, but it is no place to live. Our lives have been different, but mine hasn't been better than yours." He tugged her a bit closer and they continued to glide about the room.

"Okay," Bree said, "I get what you're saying, but coming from my background, you have to understand why I think your life has, at the very least, been more exciting. You get to go traipsing off to exotic lands in between your time at a cool voodoo school. I have to go to regular public school. My form of fun is either movie night with my friends or a wild, crazy time at the mall. If it's an *extreme* weekend, then it's a Sunday craft show with my grandmother!"

Lucien laughed. "Well, I have *never* been to a craft show."

Smirking, Bree cocked her head. "I'm sure it's at the top of your to-do list."

"I'm just saying that I might enjoy going to a craft show. You know, I could get into that. Knick-knacks. Wood carvings. Quilts."

"Quilts?"

"Quilts. I love me a good quilt, I do. Quilts."

"You do, huh?"

"Absolutely. Have an extensive collection of quilts. A quilt collection."

"Quilt collector? This is what you're going with?"

They paused to regard each other, their smiles growing with every heartbeat. Then they both laughed. Bree wanted to say something meaningful, but she couldn't focus on anything other than Lucien's laugh, so deep and rich, she swore she could feel it reverberating in her blood and her bones. Lucien drew in a breath and shook his head at her. "What I'm trying to say is no one who has made it to the age of sixteen is boring. Everyone goes through many, many life experiences to shape who they are. Some good and some bad. You and I have had different experiences. Just because we haven't experienced something yet, doesn't mean we won't. That's what life is all about."

"You're so cool," she whispered, awestruck.

In one fluid movement, he took one step backward, raised his right hand holding her left, twirled her twice, and then pulled her to him. Chest to chest, he placed his left hand on her back and held her close. His leaned down, lips in her hair, warm breath on her ear sending shivers down her spine. "Only when I'm with you," he whispered.

Bree would have swooned in Lucien's arms if Miss Harkins hadn't strolled by clearing her throat and directing a few fake coughs at them. Lucien stepped back and resumed proper stance and distance, Bree all but putty in his arms. And then the song ended, the lights dimmed, the music's tempo picked up, and the deejay shouted something in Arabic. A loud cheer went up and the students crowded the dance floor. Siza had said this would happen, and it was their cue to start the mission.

Weaving between the moving bodies, Siobhan joined Bree and Lucien. With a wink, she gave Bree her purse back. Then Willem and Ryoku appeared, and trying to be as inconspicuous as possible, they located the rest of their fellow students and found the stairwell access door toward the back of the ballroom. Since none of them had been to the room in question before, they decided that door-porting wasn't the best option and they had to break in the old-fashioned way.

Clutching her purse, Bree separated herself from her friends and slowly wound her way through the crowd, smiling as if her happy face were a mask and nodding to the students she'd met so far. She willed herself to think of anything other than the mission, just in case there was some kind of mind-reading spell being used. Failing miserably at her own mental subterfuge, she fixated on the events to come.

When they'd planned the mission, it was obvious Siza needed to be in the actual break-in group because she was the only one who had an idea of where the Eye of Ra was stored or even what it looked like. Willem was in because he had the skills to create illusions. Javier volunteered, a broad smile across his face, as soon as it was suggested he could be useful if there were any snakes. Plus, both Willem and Javier had a penchant for fire. Everyone wanted Bree to be the fourth, for her healing magics, in case something went awry. She had learned as much as she could and felt confident she could take care of minor cuts and bruises. Rumiel insisted there should be five in the group, and he should be the fifth because of his specialty with darkness and insects. However, the group decided that anything more than four would be too cumbersome and obvious when it was time to go. Consequently, he'd crossed his arms and pouted.

Now, still unhappy that he wasn't a part of the break-in crew, Rumiel took on the task of engaging with other boys from the host school and diverting their attention away from the others' disappearance. He even managed to crack a smile once in a while.

The four chosen for the mission meandered from different parts of the room toward the door as inconspicuously as possible. Siza met up with Bree and hooked their arms together. Aiming them toward their destination, Siza pointed to paintings on the wall along the way and explained the immortalized subjects. Javier joined in, strolling along next to them. By the time they reached the door, Bree fidgeted and prayed that the rest of her wasn't as sweaty as her clammy palms. She was jealous of Willem's calm demeanor as he sauntered over, hands in his pockets. Was he really that cool under pressure, or just a good actor? Did he even care about the mission?

Hovering by the door, they waited for the right moment. Blood rushing through her whole body, Bree swore her heart was a discontent prisoner hammering on her ribcage trying to escape. She gripped her purse with both hands to keep them from shaking and reminded herself to breathe. In through the nose. Out through the mouth. Trying not to hyperventilate and pass out, she focused so hard on not freaking out, she almost missed the opportunity.

Those not going on the mission were nearby. In a coordinated effort, each of them asked the people closest to them a question about something on the wall or someone in the room, all averting attention away from the door. Lucien quickly glanced back, though, and winked at Bree and that kept her from losing her dinner all over the floor. Then Siza swiped her father's key card in the lock, and Bree followed the other three through the door.

CHAPTER 21

THE DOOR LATCHED behind her with a soft click, and Bree released a cautious sigh of relief. She was far from calm, but nowhere near the brink of blind hysteria. The stairwell looked like any other institutional stairwell, bright lights illuminating walls of white-painted cinderblock. Siza led the way down the stairs. At the bottom, there was nothing. Nothing but an empty landing and four blank walls.

Bree clenched her teeth so hard that her jaw hurt. The panic of failing replaced the panic of getting caught then was quickly replaced by the panic of failing *then* getting caught.

"I do not understand," Siza whispered, looking at one of the walls. "There should be a door here."

"Can you astral project to the other side?" Javier asked.

Siza reached out to touch the empty wall. "Unfortunately, no. I can only project to where I have been before."

Hands clasped behind his back and a smirk on his face, Willem strolled over to the wall in question. "Oh, my pretty, pretty poppets. One of the many benefits that come with being a master of illusion is that I can detect them quite easily."

With flourish, he waved his hand back and forth over the wall as if washing it. With every movement, the wall rippled like water, exposing a standard stairwell door in between the waves. Of course, Willem continued, "I mean, this is why you wanted me along, right? To reveal the illusions, right? Unless it was a clever ploy to get me alone in the basement, you naughty minxes. Javier, you go stand lookout at the top of the stairs while—"

Filled to the brim with dread and in no mood for his antics, Bree snapped, "Just open the damn door."

Willem jumped away from the door as if it tried to bite him and raised his hands in the air. "Whoa, whoa, whoa. I'm not opening the hidden door of great mystery. I have no idea what's on the other side. Spiders. Snakes. Big rolling boulders. Floor tiles rigged to have darts shoot from the walls."

With a huff, Bree pushed on the door latch and opened it. "First of all, Indiana Jones, this isn't the Temple of Doom. It's the basement of a school. Second of all, you need to start watching movies that are more contemporary."

Standing behind Bree, making no pretense that he wasn't using her as a shield, Willem peered into the newly exposed hallway. Soft light emanated from wall mounts, thick wires between them. The hallway was long and crudely carved through dark brown stone. Willem muttered, "First of all, I do watch contemporary movies. I just don't like them. Second of all, I'm not convinced that this *isn't* the Temple of Doom."

Leading the way, Siza strode into the hallway. Javier followed, shrugging his shoulders as he passed Bree and Willem, implying, *Why not?* Trusting Siza, Bree stepped into the hallway as well, the unevenness of the cut-stone floor making her happy she opted to wear flats. Willem, however, clinging to her every move like dryer lint made her uneasy about the situation.

"Siza," he whispered, are you sure this is safe? No traps or spells that we might accidentally trip?"

"This is the sub-basement of a school, so there is security, but not in the way you think. Don't forget Egypt has a long history of hiding things in basements … and underground tombs."

"Tombs? Did she say tombs? Is this a tomb?"

"Not to the best of my knowledge." The lilt in Siza's voice was to goad Willem, but it unnerved Bree as well. Willem closing the gap between them didn't help either, all but stepping on her heels as they walked toward a steel door placed into the stone at the end of the hallway. "Okay, so let's say we get through the arcane magics of your Egyptian security. What then? How will the Eye not be missed?"

"According to my father, the room is only visited for inventorying purposes and that happens every two years. My father complains about it when it's going on, and that's how I know they just completed the most recent inventory over the last school break. The next break is in three weeks, so I've got plenty of time to return it."

"It's your head, not mine," Willem whispered.

"Unless a buzz saw blade pops from the wall and decapitates you," Javier quipped.

Willem frowned and glanced at the walls. Then he nudged Bree toward the center of the hallway and dogged her heels the rest of the way.

Taller and wider than a normal door, the metal slab seemed to have been shoved into the rock wall, the crags around it looking like ominous scars. Finally, Willem released Bree and approached the door. He cracked his knuckles and rolled his neck then snorted and swallowed, causing the girls to grimace in dismay. "Okay, so what kinds of mystical tethers are binding this door? What kinds of ancient magics are we dealing with?"

Siza walked up next to him and swiped the key card through the reader by the door's latch. A tiny light went from red to green, unlocking the door. Smugly, she held up the card while opening the door and said, "The ancient and arcane language of binary."

Dim lights flickered to life as the door opened. A labyrinth of artifacts on pedestals or in cases stretched out before the students. Clay pots and carved stone figures, gem encrusted ornaments and golden objects.

"Oh," Bree whispered. She'd never seen anything like this room or the amazing artifacts within it. One beautiful piece would catch her attention until the next, equally beautiful peace demanded her to look at it. She wanted to spend hours in this room, wanted to learn about every single piece, wanted to share it with Lucien, wanted—

"Are you *sure* there are no cameras in here?"

Leave it to Willem to snap her back to reality.

"Absolutely certain," Siza replied. "Ah, Here it is."

The other three joined Siza around a stone pedestal upon which rested the Eye of Ra. About the size of a fist. Bree thought it looked like a hieroglyphic eye, almond shaped with a lone eyebrow arching away, a curl at the tip, with emeralds inlaid on the center, surrounded by gleaming gold.

"Well, okay then," Willem said as he sidled up to the artifact. "No cameras means I can take this trinket with impunity."

As soon as Willem's fingers touched the Eye of Ra, bright blue arcs of electricity danced along his arms. Yanking his hands to his chest, he jumped backwards. "*Aaah!* Bullocks! Son of a …! That bloody hurt!"

With a delightfully satisfied smirk, Siza said, "Your statement prior to touching the Eye of Ra was wrong for very many reasons. But thank you, for your action was needed in activating the riddle."

Still nursing his hands, Willem asked, "Riddle?"

Siza pointed to the Eye of Ra. Translucent images of ancient hieroglyph symbols now floated in the air in front of it. "I did mention this was Egypt. We have been known to ask a riddle or two."

Running his hand over his chin, Javier approached the pedestal and the symbols rearranged themselves, some changing, others disappearing. He stepped back, so that Siza was the closest and the image changed back. He gestured to Bree to step closer. Doing so, the symbols again danced about, stopping in a configuration different than the prior two. "Interesting."

"What?" Bree asked.

"It's a word puzzle. Like the ones found in newspapers where one letter means another letter?"

"A cryptogram," Bree answered. "My mom loves those."

"*Si!* Yes. Cryptogram."

"Why is it changing?"

"I think it can … sense? … our native language. It rearranges for whoever is closer."

BRIAN KOSCIENSKI & CHRIS PISANO

"Fascinating," Siza said as she stepped closer to the Eye of Ra than Bree. The symbols shifted and changed. She stepped away and they changed back. "It is obvious that Bree or Willem should stand the closest since all four of us know English."

"I ain't goin' near that bloody thing!" Willem groaned.

"Yeah, we know," Bree said as she reached in her purse to pull out a pen and a small notebook. Writing down the different symbols and then blank lines for each letter, she said, "The trick is to focus on the smaller words. Maybe find a 'the' or 'and'."

Three of them concentrated on the puzzle while Willem alternated between looking at his hands for signs of injury and letting his eyes wander around the room from boredom. Javier whispered to himself and Bree scribbled different combinations on her pad while Siza stared intently. After a few minutes, Bree said, "If that word is 'the' then the second word is 'he' and the first word could be 'let'. That makes the word next to 'the' E blank E. Eve? Eye?"

"Eye," Siza replied. Pointing, she said, "These four words are 'the Eye of Ra'."

"I think you're right! Hold on," Bree said, writing frantically. "Let he who has betrayal in his heart use the Eye of Ra to find what he seeks."

With those words the images faded.

"Betrayal?" Willem asked. "That doesn't even make sense."

Slowly walking around the pedestal, never looking away from the Eye, Siza said, "In our mythology, the Eye is actually an entity. The Eye of Ra is the feminine side of the god Ra."

"How very metrosexual," Willem said with a chuckle. "I didn't know your ancient deities were so progressive."

Bree slapped Willem's shoulder and then held out her hand. "Dollar!"

"Ow! What? Why?"

"Just because Ryoku isn't here doesn't mean your filter comes off and you can make fun of Siza's culture. Now, give me a dollar so I can give it to her."

"Fine," Willem mumbled, reaching into his pocket.

"During creation," Siza continued, "Ra's children drifted away, flowing along the waters of Nu."

"Shu and Tefnut," Javier said. "Ra's children were Shu and Tefnut."

Siza paused in her pacing to reward Javier with a warm smile. "Yes. You are correct."

"Bullocks," Willem moaned, rolling his eyes. "Must you be a suck-up *all* the time at *every*thing? Or maybe this is part of your clever plan to lull us into a false sense of security."

Bree smacked Willem's shoulder again. And again, Willem retrieved a dollar. "No matter how many dollars I have to pay, it's not gonna change the fact that I think he's a bloody Meso."

Javier frowned and put his hands in his pockets and went back to studying the artifact.

Siza continued her story, "Ra sent the Eye of Ra to find the children. When she returned with the children, she found herself replaced by a new Eye of Ra."

"A betrayal," Bree said.

"So his mistress is in and the missus is out," Willem said. "Heartbreaking. So, who's gonna touch the Eye of Ra? Who has betrayal in their heart?"

"I will do it," Javier said, lifting his head.

"What?" Bree asked. "Why?"

"To prove to Willem. To prove to everyone. I am not a Meso. I do not have betrayal in my heart."

"That's the very reason not to touch it!"

"I must!"

Before Bree could argue any more, Javier stepped toward the Eye and snatched it from the pedestal. Holding it with both hands, he stared at it, then looked up to Bree as if his own actions surprised him.

Bree stared at the Eye sitting in Javier's palm. What did it mean? *Did* Javier have betrayal in his heart? Was he the Meso that Willem accused him of being? Or was the message just a meaningless answer to a puzzle to unlock the prize? Then Javier's jaw clenched shut and his eyes bulged. His hair and tie stuck out away from him as if pulled by magnets, and he began to tremble. Bright blue arcs of electricity appeared and danced around him, emitting a low hum as he moaned in pain.

Siza leapt forward and slapped the Eye from his hands. It clanked to the floor as Javier collapsed. His breath was rapid and shallow, and his face was twisted in pain. Siza and Bree dropped to their knees beside him, Bree squeezing his hand while Siza brushed his hair from his face.

"Can you speak?" Siza said. "Are you going to be okay?"

Willem stood over him and huffed, "Well, I'm glad he's not dead."

"Eloquently put, Sergeant Sensitivity," Bree said with a sneer.

In between ragged breaths, Javier huffed, "Means ... I'm ... not ... traitor ... Meso."

"Yeah?" Willem replied. "I guess that means we have to find the traitor so they can pick up the Eye of Ra laying there on the ground."

"No," Bree said. "I don't think that's what the riddle means. In Siza's story, the Eye of Ra was the one who was betrayed. Maybe that's what the riddle means. Maybe only someone who has been betrayed is allowed to touch the Eye of Ra?"

"That doesn't make sense," Willem argued. "We've all been betrayed. We're all *currently* being betrayed. Even if Javier is telling the truth, which I don't think he is, then he's being betrayed like the rest of us. So, why'd he get zapped?"

Even though she addressed Willem's question, Siza looked to Bree. "In my story, the Eye of Ra loved Ra and was betrayed by him. It is a story about lost love, not espionage."

"So," Willem snapped, crossing his arms and shaking his head. "Anyone been screwed over lately by someone they love?"

Bree thought of Amanda and knew how the Eye of Ra felt, or more accurately, the emotions that the myth was trying to convey. Disappointment and sadness added themselves to the mix of betrayal swirling around in Bree. She said, "I have."

"You?" Willem asked, not even attempting to hide his snide tone. "What kind of life could you possibly have where someone betrayed you? You have one of the most boring lives I have ever seen!"

"Not boring," Bree muttered as she walked over to the Eye of Ra and picked it up. "Just different."

Javier reached out and tried to say something, but only mustered a deflated wheeze. Willem cringed, ready to shield his face at any moment. Siza leapt to her feet and hurried to Bree.

Nothing happened.

Light glinting off the slight sheen of their sweat-glistened brows, the four looked at each other, gazes bouncing from one set of eyes to the other. Smiles tugged at their lips and quickly melted into laughs, including Javier.

"Whew!" Bree sighed, gently tucking the Eye of Ra in her purse. "Well, *that* happened."

"It most certainly did," Siza said as she knelt beside Javier. "Are you going to be able to walk?"

Willem extended a hand and helped Javier to his feet. Dusting him off, Willem said, "Oh, the ol' chap is fine. You Mesos are a tough lot, aren't you?"

Javier frowned and yanked himself away from Willem's grasp while both girls said in unison, "Shut up, Willem!"

"I'm okay," Javier said. "Let's get out of here."

Siza shut the vault door behind them as Bree sent a text to Siobhan, telling her to reply when it was clear to return. In less than two minutes, Bree received, "Now!"

Siza opened a doorport to the ballroom, right in front of the door that led to the stairwell. The foursome walked through and acted as nonchalant as possible. All was normal. Students mingled and formed a perimeter around those who decided to dance. Chaperones patrolled the room, smiling sentries making their rounds. Bree took a few pensive steps away from the door while scanning the room. No one seemed to notice. Success!

Willem quickly burrowed his way into the crowd, undoubtedly looking for Ryoku. Javier went off on his own as well, undoubtedly looking for Rumiel. Wide smile on her face, Siobhan strode to the girls. "It certainly looks like everyone is no worse for wear?"

"Indubitably," Siza said. With a mischievous smile on her lips, she flashed her father's I.D. badge. "Now it is time to return to my father what is rightfully his."

Siobhan hooked her arm with Bree's and they slowly aimed for one of the exits. "Good job, girl. Now, let's get you back to your room and hide our newly acquired package."

Bree liked the sound of that. The elation of completing a successful mission made her feel like she could float—or even fly!—even as the stress of the adventure made her want to crawl in bed and pull the covers over her head. She realized her hands were shaking and her knees felt like jelly. She wanted to celebrate, but she knew that of the two missions to get the items they needed to find Lila, this was the easy one.

CHAPTER 22

BREE TOOK A DEEP cleansing breath and exhaled. All morning her mind had been racing, reviewing the events of the weekend. All through her Monday morning classes, she'd relived their tour of Egypt, their time at the school, the dinner, the dance with Lucien, the mission, the riddle. The plan, *her plan*, was successful! Sitting in the crowded cafeteria, her lunch tray in front of her, Bree finally had a moment to decompress. Until Chelsea joined her.

"Hi!" Chelsea said, braces-filled smile beaming. "So, how was your field trip?"

"Good. Met some interesting people. Did some cool things," Bree said, her nonchalant tone indicating there was far more to the story. Luckily, Chelsea didn't pick up on that and Bree changed the topic. "So, what'd you do this weekend?"

That was all it took to activate Chatty Chelsea. Bree smiled as her friend talked. It was like the first ninety percent of the school year, like the shunning and ignoring never happened. Maybe that was true friendship? Forgiveness coming in the form of moving on and forgetting. Bree wondered if she and Amanda could do that. Bree then gained new appreciation for the phrase, "Speak of the devil" when Amanda entered the cafeteria with Brittany and her minions.

Brittany's over-the-top squeal of laughter led the way. Six girls entered, all laughing and talking over each other, so fast and so loud that Bree doubted that any of them heard anything the others were saying. Every move and gesture calibrated with such flare that the message to everyone else in the cafeteria was clear: our lives are so much cooler and more exciting than all you other people that you should just sit back and behold our beauty.

"Traitor," Chelsea growled as she watched the girls swarm toward the food line.

Bree huffed. "Surprised you didn't use stronger language."

Chelsea sat straight and folded her fingers together. "I choose not to stoop to her level."

"Good choice. Me either." She couldn't stop her thoughts from going back to her ex-friend's new boyfriend. "Do you know anything about the guy she's seeing?"

"No. I didn't know she was even seeing anyone until her highness pulled up on his royal red steed and Brittany trumpeted their arrival last week."

Bree chuckled at Chelsea's comment as she watched Amanda. Even though she couldn't hear the details, she could tell by the tone and theatrics that Brittany was bragging to the other girls about the weekend antics with her newest creation. She turned back to Chelsea quickly, not wanting *anyone* at that table to notice her attention. "I just don't understand."

"Neither do I," Chelsea replied shoveling french-fries into her mouth by the handful.

Bree watched Chelsea, afraid to ask the next question, afraid to hurt her feelings. "So, when you two were mad at me, what happened to Amanda?"

Keeping her eyes down, focusing on her food, Chelsea shrugged. "I don't know. She was mad when you went through your swan-like transformation. More like jealous, really, I guess."

Bree smiled. "Swan-like. Hardly. But, thanks."

"You were *always* the prettiest. And smartest. And coolest. Amanda has always been jealous of you."

Never thinking of herself as any of those things, Bree tried to process those words. When she spent time with Amanda and Chelsea over the years, she thought of herself as just Bree, just one of the trio. Even though she always had better grades, she never saw them as a measure of being more intelligent than either of her friends. "That's sweet, Chelsea, but—"

Chelsea looked up. Her exasperation tugged at the corners of her mouth, demonstrating both sadness and anger. "But, nothing, Bree. That's just the way it is. Or was. Or I don't know. I personally thought it was great, and I was happy that the three of us were best friends. Everything we did was fun even if it was just hanging out, talking about nothing. But Amanda has always been more competitive. Please tell me you at least knew that."

Bree stared off into the distance. Now that she thought about it, she could remember many times when Amanda was less than thrilled by Bree's successes and more than ready to exult any time she performed better, from grades to games. Bree never viewed it as competition, because *she* wasn't competing. *It can't be a race with only one runner*, she thought to herself. Realization was as cold as ice water flowing down her back. "I guess I never realized how much certain things meant to her."

"Well, they did," Chelsea said. "She was always jealous that she had to work harder than you just to stay even. Then when you went from one of us—braces and glasses and zits and all—to princess and then to, well, really beautiful, that was the breaking point for her."

"Was that the breaking point for you?" Bree asked, afraid that the question might tailspin her relationship with Chelsea back into a burning heap of wreckage.

"No. Yes? Maybe? No. It wasn't." Chelsea stopped and took three quick breaths to collect her thoughts. "I was scared you wouldn't be my friend anymore and that growing up together didn't mean as much to you as it did to me. You'd changed so much so fast, that I believed Amanda when she said that you were trying to ditch us to be popular. I'm sorry I did, but I did. Then you go and join some cool international club and what was I supposed to believe?"

"Sorry about that. That all happened really fast, and I tried to apologize, but—"

Chelsea shook her head and wiggled her fingers, dismissing Bree's apology. "It's all good. I get it, but Amanda didn't. She really thought *you* were trying to be popular, so that's why *she* wanted to be popular. I didn't even know she knew Brittany until she started cancelling our movie nights to hang out with her."

"I'm sorry about that, too."

"Don't be. I just felt so alone. I thought I lost two people I had known all my life."

Bree offered a sympathetic smile. "I know how it feels. I thought that, too."

Chelsea sat up straight, exuberance returning to her face as well as her big smile. With confidence, she said, "But we didn't. We lost one of our trio, who we both hope is just going through a sad phase, but you and I are still friends."

Bree displayed solidarity by mimicking Chelsea's posture and tone. "Exactly!"

Chelsea giggled. Then her face brightened even more. "Sam just came in!"

Not sure why Chelsea was so excited by his arrival, Bree turned to verify the proclamation. Hands in his pockets, Sci-Fi Sam entered the cafeteria and scanned the room. Once he saw Bree and Chelsea, he smiled and waved. The girls waved back, Chelsea with more enthusiasm than Bree thought the situation called for. Sam raised his eyebrows and repeatedly pointed between himself and the girls, wordlessly asking if he could join them. Chelsea replied by bouncing up and down and rapidly giving tiny claps of her hands while Bree nodded and mouthed the word, "Yes."

Laughing, Bree looked to Chelsea and said, "What is with you today?"

"I'm just so happy to see you and Sci-Fi Sam getting along."

Bree chuckled. "Umm, okay. Why?"

Leaning forward and giving an exaggerated whisper no quieter than her regular speaking voice, Chelsea said, "Because I think he likes you."

Reeling back from the notion, Bree said, "We're just friends."

Chelsea furrowed her brows and pursed her lips. "Oh, pah-*leez*!"

"I'm serious, Chelsea," Bree continued. "Don't forget, he and I went on a date last year and then he completely went off grid until a few weeks ago."

Chelsea looked at Bree as if she said she didn't understand two plus two. "That's because you intimidated him."

"Me?" Bree squeaked. Was Chelsea even talking about the right Bree and Sam. "Intimidate him?"

"Yeah. You went through your 'teen movie rom-com' transformation from regular duck to swan and scared him off. Although, I *always* knew you were a swan."

Bree couldn't have been more confused if Chelsea suddenly slapped her with a live fish. "What are you…? It's not like I tried to push him away. I was just trying to …."

"Oh, I know. But he didn't. He's been working out ever since. My dad sees him at the gym like all the time."

"So, he *has* been working out," Bree mumbled, more to herself.

"Yes. He has. Why do you think that is?"

Bree curled her lip and shrugged her shoulders. "I don't know. To get in shape?"

"Duh! For *you!*"

As much as she didn't want to believe her friend and tried to dismiss her theories as a feeble attempt to drag her girlish dreams into the real world, Bree couldn't help but wonder if there was any truth to them. "Did … did he tell you this? Or did you hear it from anyone?"

"No. Just my guess." Chelsea bopped her head from side to side, opened her milk, and stuck in her straw. "I'm observant, you know."

Bree felt more comfortable now. Obviously, Chelsea was just reporting what she saw in her fantasyland. Wondering how deep Chelsea's delusion went, Bree asked, "So why has he waited so long to start hanging out with me again?"

"Maybe he finally feels more comfortable with himself? Anyway, you can ask him yourself. Here he comes."

Bree greeted Sam as he approached the table with a tray of food. Nothing was out of the ordinary other than the new and crazy ideas buzzing around her head. She felt a mild flush tickle her cheeks as she thought Chelsea's theory.

"Hey," Sam said as he sat down.

"Hi," both girls replied in unison. Bree noticed the disparity between Sam's tray and theirs. Two burgers, two slices of pizza, a side of fries and a large bowl of pudding that almost didn't fit on his tray. A half-eaten slice of pizza and half-eaten salad was on hers, and Chelsea's was … empty? Bree looked up to see a smile so broad that the cafeteria's light gleamed off of every rivet of Chelsea's braces. Offering a wink to Bree, Chelsea stood and said, "I gotta go do some research in the library. Bye."

Both Sam and Bree replied with, "Bye," as Chelsea disappeared. Bree felt set-up by a master ninja.

Oblivious to being a pawn in Chelsea's gambit, Sam shoved half a pizza slice in his mouth and mumbled, "So, what'd I miss?"

Bree chuckled. "Not much. Just dishing about Amanda."

"Really?" Sam asked, way too excitedly, as he turned to glance over to where Amanda and her new friends sat.

Bree wondered how he could have possibly missed the cattiness in her tone. She hoped he wouldn't miss the irritation in her voice when she hissed, "Seriously, Sam?"

"What? She's hot!" The mouthful of half chewed food must have affected his tone, because he sounded confused.

Every theory Chelsea spouted was wrong. Sam shattered them all within ten seconds of sitting down. Bree knew little about boys, but she knew that if Sam had indeed liked her in *any* kind of romantic sense, he wouldn't have said what he did. "Why would you say that?"

Eyes wide, he finished his mouthful of food in one audible gulp, certainly catching Bree's tone this time, but displaying no understanding as to why it was there. Clearly not knowing what else to say, he blurted, "You don't think she is?"

"What kind of question is *that?*"

"I'm so confused. It sounds like you're … jealous?"

Cheeks burning from frustration, Bree almost turned to look behind her to see if there were any other people Sam could be talking to, because none of this conversation made any sense to her. Mind spinning too fast for anything else, all she could muster was, "What?"

Satisfied that he figured out what was going on, Sam took a chomp out of one of the burgers. "Don't be. You're way hotter than her."

Sam's comment just sent the swirling in her mind into tornado speed. Chelsea was now partially right, but the nonchalant, unromantic tone was so incongruent with his words. "Did … did you just say that I'm … hot?"

Back to being confused, he mumbled past his burger, "Yeah? You don't think so?"

So stricken with his frankness, Bree's brain went to static. "Uh…?"

Sam half laughed and said, "How can you be gay and not know you're hot?"

It all fell into place for Bree. Everything involving Sam for the past few weeks. Why he suddenly reappeared in her life. Why he so openly drooled about Amanda. Why he spoke with such candor. He viewed Bree as a buddy. "Sam. I'm not gay."

Sam shoved more food into his face as he looked at Bree with humor in his eyes. Bree returned a serious gaze. Sam's chewing slowed, the sparkle in his eyes fading. Bree's expression remained unchanged. Sam gulped and then his jaw went slack, realization settling in. "Oh … oh … my … God … but … but …."

"It was Amanda. She started the rumor."

"A rumor?"

"Yep, a rumor. It's not true, though." Bree offered a sympathetic smile, but Sam still looked at her like he was meeting an internet friend for the first time who lied about their profile picture.

"I … I can't … I'm—" Sam stuttered.

Bree reached out and patted his hand. "It's okay, Sam."

He yanked his hand from hers. "No. It's *not* okay. I thought you were gay. That's the whole reason I was able to hang out with you after … after all this time since our date."

Her face hurt from her forehead getting tighter and tighter throughout this conversation. "You were 'able to hang out' because you thought I was gay?"

"Well, yeah."

"And *now* you're weirded out because I'm *not?*"

"Yes!"

"What! Why?"

"I didn't want you to think I was flirting with you."

"Why would I think you were flirting with me?"

"Because I like you?"

"Then why *don't* you want me to think you're flirting with me?"

"Well, do you wanna go on another date sometime?"

"Umm—"

"See? *That's* why!"

Bree closed her eyes and shook her head. This was all too weird. Opening her eyes, she attempted to explain. "There's someone else in my life right now."

Sam's expression darkened, his eyes betraying his thoughts, ones accusing her of lying. They didn't live in a small town, but the school was small enough for everyone to know who dated whom. Even when someone dated outside of the school's walls, like Amanda, everyone knew. But no one had ever seen Lucien—except Chelsea—so no one could know that Bree was interested in someone else. Tone as flat as his expression, Sam said, "Someone else. Right. Got it."

"Sam, please. That doesn't change that we're friends and hanging out with you the past few weeks has been awesome."

"I'm sorry, but I gotta go," Sam said. He stood and headed for the door of the cafeteria, leaving behind his tray full of half-eaten food.

Blinking, Bree sat there and tried to make sense of the past fifteen minutes. All she could do was mumble, "What the hell just happened?"

CHAPTER 23

BREE LOOKED INTO the mortar and wondered if the powder was fine enough. Then she looked back to the book of potions, wondering how fine the book's definition of "fine" was. Still uncertain, she picked up the pestle and ground some more. When her wrist started to ache, she placed the pestle next to the small clay bowl and turned the page.

After the incident with Ryoku and Lucien in the greenhouse a couple weeks ago, Bree had decided to use her Wednesdays to learn more about mixing potions. Because one of her core magics made her a good healer, she wanted to learn some healing potions. The one she had decided to tackle today was a topical numbing agent.

Alone in one of the institute's laboratories, she found a sense of calm, which was vastly different from the heightened awareness and power—the *aliveness*—she felt when in the greenhouse. Even though it had work tables and running water and Bunsen burners and mixing containers like the lab at her public school, the vaulted ceiling and stone walls made her feel like a medieval alchemist. Although, she was certain a medieval alchemist would know exactly how much a "pinch" was.

Bree looked at the mixture in the glass bowl on the table. It contained about a pint of liquids, oils, and essences from various plants and herbs. She took a "pinch" of the finely ground powder from the mortar and added it to the mixture, and then, using a spoon made from birch wood, the *only* detailed request in the potion recipe, she stirred.

"Squeeze four aloe leaves," Bree read the next step. Frustrated, she mumbled to herself, "How much? How big should the leaves be? Would European alchemists even *have* aloe in the 15th century?"

Frustrated, she yanked four healthy chunks from the aloe plant next to her concoction. As she squeezed the drops into the mixture, she reminded herself that she should find this relaxing, the whole reason why she was here.

With a deep, cleansing breath, she tried to clear her mind and focus on squeezing the aloe. But her brain kept churning about how weird her life outside the institute's walls had become. She'd lost her two lifelong best friends, but recently got one back while the other one seemed to have gone full immersion to the dark side. Then a longtime friend disappeared, because he liked her, then came back into her life because he liked her, and then pushed her away again because he liked her. She just couldn't wrap her head around Sci-Fi Sam's logic. What was he thinking? Why were friendships so complicated? Why—"Oh, crap!" In her distracted state, she'd stirred a bit too hard and sloshed some of the mixture out of the bowl and on to the hand holding it steady.

She grabbed a paper towel and, reassuring herself, mumbled aloud as she wiped the solution from her hand and stuck her hand under the faucet. "Don't panic. Nothing in the mixture is dangerous. Everything was grown right here in the greenhouse." Her hand tingled a bit under the hot water, but it was nothing unusual. Then she wiped up the splattered mixture on the lab table, went to grab another paper towel and stopped. Wide-eyed, she lifted her left arm. Her hand dangled at the end of her wrist like a dead fish on a stick. With her right hand, she poked it and felt nothing at all. Her limp hand wobbled back and forth as she shook her arm. "What the—?"

"Bree?"

Like a whip crack, she spun and placed both hands behind her back. Lucien stood in the laboratory's doorway. "I'm on my way to the meeting. I thought you'd already be there."

Bree smiled and stammered. "Meeting. Yeah. I remember the meeting, but … but wanted to … to just work on … mixing potions."

"Is everything okay?" He walked closer, concern etched upon his face.

"Yep!" Bree's voice hadn't cracked this bad since her thirteenth birthday and embarrassment prickled all along her cheeks. "All good! Just fine, in fact."

Lucien frowned. He opened his mouth to speak again but stopped himself when he noticed she was hiding her hands behind her back. He smiled. "You were mixing a potion and spilled some on your hand, didn't you?"

"No! What makes you think that?" Bree tried to sound serious and convincing, but the warble in her voice destroyed all sense of conviction.

Keeping his eyes locked onto hers, he walked closer, toward Bree's right side. Unblinking, she shifted her position to keep her hands hidden. He said, "It's a nasty one, too, isn't it?"

"No!"

Lucien moved to her left side. Again, Bree shifted. "Your hand is all red and purple and bubbling, oozing pus everywhere, isn't it?"

"Ew! Why would you even think that?"

"You're hiding your hand from me, so you must have transformed it into something hideously disgusting. A tentacle. You turned your hand into a scaly tentacle, didn't you?"

"No! Maybe I'm hiding my diary!"

Lucien now stood so close she had to tilt her head back to look into his eyes. She could feel the warmth of his skin. The infinite depth of his dark, dark eyes. Warm. Inviting. She jumped a little when Lucien reached out with his right hand and put it on her left shoulder. "You're writing in your diary? In one of the laboratories? Dear Diary, I spilled a potion on myself and now I have a crab claw. It makes shopping more difficult but removing bottle caps has never been easier. I think I'll paint it to look like Hello Kitty."

"Jerk," Bree blushed and laughed in spite of her ridiculous predicament. A weird blend of excitement and comfort washed through her as Lucien's hand ran down her arm, gently coaxing her to show him the result of her accident.

Lucien was quiet as he guided her arm from behind her back. By the time his hand got to her elbow, her hand had come out of hiding. Once exposed, Bree moved her arm in front of her and flapped, her hand wobbling completely out of her control. Releasing her arm, Lucien moved his hand to cover his mouth while he watched her hand flop about like it was trying to escape her wrist.

Bree pulled her left hand close to her chest, cradling it with her right. "Stop laughing!"

"I'm not laughing," Lucien said, voice lilting with laughter.

"Are too."

"I'm not laughing at you. I'm laughing *with* you."

Brows furrowed, Bree replied, "I'm not laughing."

"On the inside. You're laughing on the inside."

"Really? I'm laughing on the inside? This is what you're going with?"

"Yes. I'm using my mystic Voodooness to sense that you're laughing on the inside."

Bree rolled her eyes and drew in a deep breath. "Okay, it's a bit of a chuckle. Not a full on ha ha."

Lucien removed his hand from his mouth and took her hand in his. "See? I knew you were laughing on the inside."

Had he truly been able to detect what was happening on the inside, he would have known she was ready to swoon. If not for her limp hand. She held up her arm, her hand looking like it could fall off at any moment. "Is there anything I can do? What if this is permanent?"

"Was it just a topical numbing potion?"

"Yes."

He lifted her hand and pressed his lips to her palm. "There. All better. You'll be fine by morning."

The warmth of his lips on her skin nearly made her lightheaded. She felt his kiss, but still unable to move her fingers. "I'm happy there won't be permanent damage, but

I wish I didn't have to wait that long for things to get back to normal.

"Well…," Lucien said, waiting until Bree looked back up at him before he continued, "I do have an idea."

"Yeah?" Bree's voice was hopeful.

Cupping his hands together, he brought them to his face and whispered into them while looking at Bree. Never taking his eyes from hers, he grasped her left elbow with both hands. Tenderly, he slid one hand down her forearm, over her hand, his fingers gliding over hers. He moved it back to her elbow while he used his other hand to repeat that action. He repeated the process over and over, and every time he caressed her arm, Bree gasped. Warm tingles skittered along her skin where his fingers touched her. Sensation returned to her hand. She wanted to say something, to thank him, but the way his hands skimmed over her skin left her inarticulate. Everywhere his fingers traced tingled, sending electricity through other parts of her body, even down to her toes. Was there a spell to stop time? To at least slow it so this moment could last longer? She wished her thoughts weren't so fuzzy, but relished the reason why.

Her fingers wiggled.

Smiling, Lucien cupped her left hand in both of his. Bree's fingers danced with his, tangling and untangling, tickling, twining. His right hand clasped her left. Their grips tightened as their bodies moved closer together. Then both hands were clasped together, fingers intertwining as well. Moving even closer, they looked into each other's eyes.

And then she closed her eyes and felt the warm, soft pressure of his lips on hers.

Bree didn't know how it happened, who leaned in first. All she knew was her heart was pounding so hard at the base of her throat that she wondered if she'd stopped breathing. The tip of his tongue skimmed along hers and she thought her knees might buckle. At first she couldn't think and then she couldn't stop thinking. Thoughts of how other people would react ricocheted through her head. Chelsea would cheer, Amanda would stew, Lord only knew how Sci-Fi Sam would react, her mother would be happy to know she liked boys, but disappointed that her daughter became so mushy for one. But what did her mother know? She had a full drawer of cotton underwear! *Oh my God! Why am I thinking about my mom's underwear NOW?*

To bring herself back into the moment, she squeezed Lucien's hands, more to prove to herself that this was *really* happening. It was and it was her kiss! No one else's! It didn't matter what anyone would think. Only now, *this moment*, mattered. Only her lips moving in time with his, the tips of their tongues flirting with each other like their fingers.

And then: "Bree? Are you in here ... Oh!"

Bree and Lucien jerked apart, turning away from each other. Face burning from the surprise of getting caught, Bree looked at her feet. After a moment of pure silence, she sheepishly looked up to see Siza's astral projection. Siza's grin spanned from ear to ear as she said, "It's almost time to meet in the game room. I was just looking for you."

"Ummm," Bree's voice cracked so bad, she had to pause to clear her throat. "Ahem. Yeah. Thanks. On my way."

Still wearing a smarmy grin, Siza purposely made the situation more ridiculous by turning to Lucien and saying,

"Lucien, I was looking for you, too. It's almost time to meet in the game room."

Keeping his head low, he cocked it just enough to look at Siza. Unable to stifle his smile, he said, "Yeah. I kind of got that. Be there soon."

Siza's smiling image floated in front of them just long enough to make them fidget. Then she winked at them and disappeared with an overly dramatic swirl of her cloak.

Bree glanced to Lucien then back to the floor just as he did the same. The action made them both laugh. Heads still low, they looked at each other with broad smiles. Lucien spoke first, "So."

"So," Bree replied. The kiss had made her year. Every problem, argument, misunderstanding, surprise, and issue she had with anyone and everything just melted away into a pool of nonexistence. Every cell in her body wanted to kiss him again, but she knew she shouldn't. For now. People were waiting.

"So," Lucien said again, standing straight, shoulders back. He turned to face Bree.

Feeling more confident, knowing that kiss was meant to happen, Bree straightened as well and faced Lucien. "So."

Lucien's eyes shifted from surprise to hunger as he slid closer to Bree. "So."

"So." Breath quivering as she exhaled, Bree moved closer to him as well. They stood toe to toe again, their fingers loosely intertwined. She hated the thought that popped into her mind, but knew she had to articulate it. "We should probably get to the meeting."

"I agree," Lucien replied. "Before 'Mom' comes back and catches us again."

Bree laughed. They walked to the door, the fingers of her left hand loosely intertwined with the fingers of his right. Before they exited, they stopped and turned toward each other for a quick, comfortable peck on the lips.

Once in the hall, they separated hands and smiled at each other. Bree felt an inferno blazing through her and said, "I'm blushing. Cartoonishly so, aren't I?"

Lucien cleared his throat and said, "I would use a euphemism like 'aglow'."

"Bright red?"

"Like a clown nose."

"Excellent," Bree said, nodding. The enlightenment of knowing herself so well didn't stop the blushing. "I'm gonna run to the bathroom first and splash some cold water on my face. See if I can get my cheeks to dull pink."

"I don't know if there's enough water for that."

Unable to stop smiling, Bree furrowed her brows and said, "Ha ha. Funny guy. Get going to the meeting and tell everyone I'll be there soon."

With a wink, Lucien turned and walked away. "Okay. See you soon."

Bree used every ounce of energy she had to keep from skipping down the hall to the nearest restroom. Giggling, a realization tickled her—she was seriously head over heels.

CHAPTER 24

THE OAR SLICED through the dark water like a blade, silent and smooth. Even the resulting ripples made no noise. Frightened, Bree took deep breaths through her nose and slowly exhaled through her mouth, fighting the heavy smell of decay hanging in the sultry air and focusing on Lucien as he paddled their small, flat-bottomed boat. His muscles ebbed and flowed like the water around them. Whichever side of the boat he used the oar, that side of his body tensed and torqued. Even when the glow from the circling ball of light didn't touch him, Bree could still see his shoulders, arms, and back move with the effort.

She tried to put up a brave front, and hoped no one else noticed her deliberate breathing. Every once in a while, she braved a glance away from Lucien, at the swamp surrounding them. Tall trees towered all around them, their roots starting well above the waterline, their leaves forming canopies. The mist rising from the water swirled with the darkness, touching every invisible fear Bree never knew she had. Things watched her, she felt. Living things. Dead things. Things she didn't want to think about. She shuddered and turned back to watch Lucien paddle.

The kiss. The memory of their first kiss was her safe space, her emotional embassy in a hostile, foreign land. Comfort. Warmth. Excitement. That memory calmed her, helped her breathe easier. She remembered afterward, too. Splashing her face with cold water, giddy and feeling ridiculous because she was giddy and still loving the feeling. She had hadn't wanted to enter the game room with scarlet cheeks begging for a barrage of questions she wasn't ready to answer. In retrospect, she doubted that there would have been any questions. She had entered the room to loud bickering.

"No!" Willem said emphatically. Seated on one of the stools at the bar, he swiveled all the way around saying, "How many times do I have to repeat myself: I. Am. Not. Going! I went on the last mission"

"Exactly," Siza said, her voice overflowing with exasperation. "Don't you see how it would be wise for one of us who has already gone on a mission to go on the next one."

"Then you go. You're the strongest, so why aren't you going?"

"Because my talisman is spirit. There are other talismans that would be more effective in the environment that needs to be traversed."

"My talisman is fire! The environment is a marshy, boggy, swamp. Did I mention that swamps are full of *water* and that my talisman is *fire?*"

"But like you pointed out in Egypt, one of your core magics is illusion."

"Bloody good that will do anyone if I'm getting chomped by an alligator's teeth."

Siobhan had had enough. "Use your illusion magic on the alligator, you daft git. Duh!"

Squinting as if she'd squirted lemon juice in his eyes, he turned on her. "What in our brief, yet ridiculously passionate, history together have I ever done to make you think I can use my illusion magics on alligators?"

"You mean you've *never* tried them on animals before?"

"Animals? 'Ello! I'm from bloody England! The most dangerous creature I might face on the island is a cross Billy goat! Or an ill-tempered sheep. Even then, I'd be more inclined to toss whatever food it might be after and run away."

"Run away," Siobhan huffed as she crossed her arms and slouched back into her chair. "Of course you'd run away."

"How about you go, She Bear?"

"Did you miss the part of the conversation where we think it'd be a good idea that we send someone more experienced?"

Slinking into the room as quietly as possible, Bree sat next to Siobhan at the table. "So … what'd I miss?"

"I told the group what will be waiting for us and we're trying to figure out who should go," Lucien said with a serious tone. Bree almost beamed at him. Not only could he be fun and whimsical, he was mature enough to know when to be focused and serious.

"So, what's the problem?"

"We can only bring four."

"Why?"

"Yeah," Willem snapped. "You never explained to us why the number is so limited."

Lucien leaned forward, resting his arms on the table.

His gaze grew distant as if watching a movie only he could see. His jaw muscles flexed as he inhaled deeply. "As I told you before, the Web of Anansi is kept by the Voice of the Loa. They believe Voodoo is more than just magics, but also about who they are and how they should live."

"Like the Mesos, right?" Siobhan asked.

Still focusing far away, Lucien said, "They are nowhere near as forceful or zealous in their beliefs and there are far fewer members, but their views on their magics are similar, yes."

"Just what we need," Willem mumbled. "Another crazy cult."

No one reacted to his comment. Instead everyone stayed focused on Lucien. "The members live throughout the bayou, but the center of the community is a small village on an island in the middle of a swamp. They believe this is a nexus of power, and the Web of Anansi is in a small temple in that village."

"So, we door-port in, grab the Web and get back out," Rumiel said. "Seems simple to me."

Keeping his tone calm and even, Lucien avoided eye contact with everyone in the room. "It would not be that simple. First, if they believe the island to hold such power, then we should assume that it does. A door-port would certainly alert them to our presence. Second, I know where the island is, but have never been to it, so it would almost be a blind door-port. However, I have been to an area where I know there is a boat. A small boat."

"A boat that can only hold four people," Bree finished his thought.

Lucien turned to face Bree and softened his expression. "Exactly."

"So far, we've come up with three people," Siobhan said to Bree. "You, Javier and obviously Lucien."

"Me?" Bree asked.

"Yeah," Willem said. "It's your bloody idea, so we thought you'd step up."

A cold sweat started to percolate across Bree's skin as she turned to Lucien.

As always, Lucien immediately gave her a sense of comfort. His dark eyes offered warmth and strength and understanding. "Since your talisman is flora, I thought you would be a good fit. The swamps are filled with plants and trees. Of course, if you don't feel comfortable, you can—"

"No," Bree cut him off. "I want to go. Willem's right. It was my crazy idea, so I should step up. But Javier…?"

A wide grin spread across his face. Almost joyously, he said, "Snakes! My talisman is snakes and reptiles. Lucien said there will be lots of those."

Lucien cracked a smile, easing the tension a bit. "I said there *might* be reptiles."

"Okay!" Javier replied, still beaming, still hopeful.

"Then Siza suggested Willem," Siobhan said, "But the cowardly dog tucked his tail and ran yipping to cower in the corner."

"Wow," Willem said, his voice holding genuine surprise. "That was cold. Even for you."

Siobhan shot him a gaze implying that he deserved her derision, no matter how harsh.

Trying to defuse that situation before it could get out of control, Bree asked, "What about Strongbow? He has experience. His talisman is air, so that could come in handy. Right?"

The room grew silent except for the subtle noises of uncomfortable shifting in seats. Strongbow flexed his chiseled jaw muscles before speaking. "It has been suggested that I might be too close to the situation to keep my emotions in check and might, therefore, pose a danger to the mission."

"Yeah, considering last time we found ourselves in a bad situation," Willem mumbled like he had no control of the words falling out of his mouth.

"How do you mean?" Strongbow asked, the brusqueness in his naturally deep voice smacked Willem harder than any spell he could conjure.

Eyes wide, Willem stammered, "I ... I just mean ... the mission on the beach ... was emotionally taxing."

The muscles along Strongbow's jaw clenched and unclenched and he shifted in his seat to look away from the group. He had nothing more to say about that topic. After Bree had heard the whole story from Ryoku, she thought she knew what Strongbow was thinking—that he'd choked on the beach, that he could have done more, that he'd panicked and made the wrong decisions. That friends had died and that now he refused to relinquish the burden of their loss.

Bree turned to Ryoku. "So ... what about you?"

Ryoku snapped her attention to Bree. Her glare hit Bree like a punch to the gut, hard enough to knock the wind out of her. Her mouth went dry, and Bree wondered if Ryoku had used a talisman spell on her. A tiny voice in the back of her head reminded her that Ryoku couldn't manipulate the water in living things. Ryoku's only response was an icy, "No."

"Hey!" Willem yelled. "She said 'no' too, so why aren't you calling her a coward?"

"Because cowardice is not her motivation for declining," Siza said.

"What is *that* supposed to mean?"

Ryoku turned to Willem and extended her hand, anger having carved a cold expression on her stone face. "It means you talk too much. Now give me a dollar."

Willem rolled his eyes and shook his head, but complied nonetheless.

Bree turned to Lucien, "Do you think we can do the mission with only three people?"

"What the hell?" Rumiel asked, frustration giving weight to his words. "I'm not as outspoken as Willem or commanding as Strongbow or as accommodating as Javier or as godly as Lucien, but I'm sitting *right here*."

Looking over to Rumiel, Bree saw that he addressed her directly. Surprised, she said, "Sorry, but Siza suggested that someone with more experience should go."

Still annoyed, he leaned forward, he hissed, "Just because I've never been in an institute like this before doesn't mean I don't have experience. I grew up with two parents who use magics and who have taught me since I was a baby. I assure you I can—"

Eyes glancing from Rumiel to Bree, Javier nudged Rumiel with his elbow and whispered, "Dude."

As if Javier's word was an off switch, Rumiel stopped ranting. Still glowering, though, he took a deep inhale and grumbled, "Sorry. I would like to come along on this mission. My talisman are insects and arachnids and one of my core magics is darkness. I think that could be useful."

Still unsure how to handle Rumiel's random outbursts, Bree didn't know what else to say other than, "Okay."

Sensing Bree's unease, Siobhan spoke up. "Now that that's settled, we need to get these four from here to the Louisiana bayou and back. That's quite a distance to wing it without the help of an instructor."

"I believe the five of us not going can create the door-ports," Siza said.

"That's good for getting them there, but what about getting them back?"

"'Ello?" Willem said, waving his cell phone around with his right hand. "Just send us a text."

"That would work if they knew where they were going to end up."

"Ever heard of GPS?" Willem snorted.

"What if they find themselves in a position where they don't have time to text and wait around for us?" Siza said. "It makes me nervous to rely on technology rather than magics."

"I know a way to get us back," Lucien said. "I'll need a few strands of hair from all four of us. And a couple drops of blood from Siza…."

Now, sitting in the boat watching Lucien row, Bree felt like that conversation happened months ago, even though it had only been four days. She took another deep breath and watched the golf-ball sized glowing orb circling the boat. Soft white with a subtle glow, it was weak enough not to seem too unnatural, but strong enough to cast shadows. It passed Javier, illuminating him and his rucksack, and then moved around the boat slowly, giving everyone an idea of what potential dangers were lurking. Rumiel had conjured it after they arrived at the boat, and Bree had commented that she didn't realize he could do that. In typical Rumiel response, he bit her head off, all but calling her ignorant.

The light completed another circuit and started around again, reflecting off the still, black water. As it passed Javier, Bree felt satisfied that he had his rucksack secured. It held escape plan after all.

An hour earlier, all nine students had been in the game room, readying themselves for the mission. The four going were all dressed in black jeans, shirts, and shoes. Bree almost giggled when Javier expressed disappointment that there would be no face paint, but he'd immediately perked up when Siza told him that his suggestion to bring a rucksack of food and first aid was a good one.

The butterflies in Bree's stomach had broken free and were fluttering through her whole body. Instead of stepping through a door port to potential danger, what she really wanted was to go back to the safety and excitement of Lucien's kiss in the laboratory. She wanted to feel his arms around her, taste his mouth on hers. She shook her head. What she wanted didn't matter. This whole escapade had been her idea and she needed to see it through, for Strongbow's sake. Still, just being near Lucien was enough for now. "So … it seems like we're ready. What's your secret plan for getting us back?"

"It's no secret, just a bit of magic." Lucien produced a thin, wooden dowel rod, about five inches long. It looked very much like a pencil to Bree. He collected half a dozen strands of hair from Rumiel and Javier. He started with Javier's, doing his best to twist the black strands around the wooden rod. Rumiel's strands were even longer, so

Lucien used them to keep Javier's in place as he spiraled the equally black hair along the dowel. Running his fingers over his dreadlocks, he produced a few strands of his own, not as long as the others, but just long enough to twirl them around the wood. Finally, he ran his hand through Bree's hair. Long strands of light brown glimmered in the light, stark and unnatural against the swirls of thin, dark bands. Hers were what held the rest together, long enough to wrap around the wooden dowel and secure everything into place. Lucien deftly tied at knot at each end and then handed a small needle to Siza.

Without hesitation, Siza pricked her index finger, just enough to garner a crimson bubble. Lucien dabbed each end of the wooden rod against her blood while whispering words in a language Bree had never heard and didn't understand. Then Lucien handed the stick to Javier to put into the rucksack. "Remember," he said to Siza and the others staying behind, "when the stick is snapped in two by one of us, you will feel the location of that person. That is where you guide the door-port."

"Understood," Siza said with a grim nod.

With good lucks, hugs, and handshakes, the five students staying behind opened the door-port for the other four, right into a murky patch of swamp with a small boat resting in thick weeds ten feet from the water...

"Bree?" Lucien said, snapping her from her memories. She looked up to see that they were gliding toward a patch of land. "We're here."

CHAPTER 25

The ground was spongey and Bree hoped quicksand didn't exist in the swamps. Lucien dragged the boat ashore with ease, unconcerned about where he stepped. If he wasn't going to worry about quicksand then she wasn't going to either. There were plenty of real dangers to stand guard against, so no need to manifest imaginary ones. She rolled her neck and cracked her knuckles. A mild sense of comfort trickled through as she thought about all of the amazing things she had done these past couple of months and a faint smile tugged at her lips. She took a deep breath and immediately regretted it.

The thick odors of the swamp coated the inside of her mouth. During the boat ride, she had grown accustomed to the smell. Rotting trees and foliage along with a pervasive fish smell and threaded with a hint of methane. Here the odors seemed to be even stronger, and she clamped her mouth shut, gritted her teeth, and frowned.

"Too much for you to handle, princess?" Rumiel whispered as he walked past, the small ball of glowing light hovering near him. The muted white light gave his already pale complexion a ghostly look. Forgoing any form of reply, she kept her mouth closed, not wanting to taste any more of the pungent night air. It made her feel better that even in the dim light she saw Javier scowl at Rumiel. Receiving the message, Rumiel turned back to Bree and mumbled, "Sorry."

"It's okay," she whispered on an exhale, forcing herself not tell Rumiel to stop being a jerk and that he had been acting more and more like a jerk over the past few weeks and she had no idea what she did to him to deserve it." Instead, she took the high road. "We're all a bit stressed."

"That's an understatement," he muttered as Lucien gave the boat one final tug. "It's only going to get worse from here."

Unsure what Rumiel meant, she ignored his comment and kept her eyes on Lucien. Strong, strong Lucien. She hoped and prayed that he knew what he was talking about.

As soon as Lucien joined them, Rumiel growled, "Now what?"

Lucien replied with a scowl and jerked his head in the direction he wanted them to go. "Follow me."

The path was worn and wide enough for them to walk two abreast. Rumiel's light, hovering just above the ground, provided enough light for them to see where they were going, and Bree fell in beside Lucien as the foreboding rhythm of insect chirps interrupted by deep frog croaks emanated from within the depths of the darkness surrounding them.

Bree marveled at how dark it was. The blackness seemed to ripple, but every time Bree turned her head to see the cause, the darkness was as still as death. There was no movement where she looked, but always in her peripheral. She'd look to the left. Nothing. Then to the right. Nothing.

Trying to keep her bearings, she looked down at the edge of the path where Rumiel's light was swallowed by the edge of the looming forest. There it was! Squirming. Weaving in and out of the bordering forest were snakes. Black. Long. She couldn't see heads or tails, just slithering bodies. She shivered and stepped closer to Lucien.

Eventually, small huts sprouted from the ground on either side of the path as if they had grown there. Smaller than even the tiny houses Bree had seen in magazines, the huts seemed to be just large enough for one person to lie down without touching the walls with head, toes, or outstretched arms. Was anyone at home? Bree shuddered at the thought of people watching them go by and hoped the glow from Rumiel's light wasn't bright enough to wake anyone.

Taking slow, deep breaths through her nose, she tried to calm herself, tried to focus on her magic. Commanding low hanging branches and brush leaves, she used them to swat at the snakes, trying to shoo them away. No effect. She even swore she saw more of them. And spiders. Fist sized spiders skittered around the huts. On the huts. Between the huts. They were big hairy ones, too, Bree just knew. She almost bumped into Lucien as a couple spiders danced across the path ahead of them while snakes made bigger loops from the forest, skirting along the path, then back in to disappear in the undergrowth.

Lucien looked over his shoulder to Javier and Rumiel behind him and gave a head jerk toward the surrounding darkness. The boys furrowed their brows in concentration, focusing their magics on their talismans. Rumiel had the spiders skitter off the path and Javier did the same with the snakes, but not before one of the snakes struck, eating a spider in one gulp. Even in the dim light, Bree saw Rumiel frown at Javier. Looking surprised, Javier simply shrugged. Bree would have chuckled if she weren't too afraid of making even the slightest noise.

As they approached the center of the village, the path split and encircled a large hut with a thatched roof and walls crafted from ramrod straight tree trunks. There were other huts nestled in the swamp's embrace on the outside of the path's perimeter. But the center hut was the only one to have a moat. Filled with alligators.

Six feet wide Bree estimated by the way the alligators lazily floated along, and it seemed deeper than it looked. She turned to Lucien, his face contorted in deep thought.

Dulling the glow of the light to reduce the world to muted shadows, Rumiel approached Lucien and whispered, "Now what?"

Lucien took a step forward, watching the alligators. "The Web of Anansi is in that hut. There is no other way but to sneak past the alligators."

"Why don't we just door-port?" Rumiel asked. "We can see exactly where we're going."

Taking another step forward, Lucien stared at the moat. "This is a place of strong, concentrated magic. If we use magic, it will be detected."

"Didn't Javier and Rumiel use magic to take care of the spiders and snakes?" Bree asked, feeling guilty that she, too, had used magic earlier.

Lucien cringed and looked at Bree. Emotions played across his face like actors dancing across a stage; surprise, realization, anger, frustration. "Damn."

As soon as the words left Lucien's mouth, dozens of torches lining the path lit; Bree jumped at the sudden bursts of flame. As if smearing midnight itself over their bodies, men painted in black oozed from the dancing shadows beyond the torches. Stark white paints formed rudimentary skeletons across their bare chests, arms, and legs, haunting skulls on their faces, hollow eyes watching. Thick smoke billowed from the ground in half a dozen different spots, roiling and black. Ominous figures appeared as the smoke dissipated, more painted men separating Lucien from Bree, Javier and Rumiel. Bree knew the smoke formed the door-ports, but the way the people appeared from the inky black terrified her, as if hell itself had spit them out. Bree huddled closer to Rumiel and Javier as each new column of smoke forced Lucien further away from them.

The final column of smoke plumed right in front of Lucien who was unable to do anything more than just stand there with fists clenched. The smoke gave way to an old woman. Resting her weight on a wooden staff capped with a human skull, most of her body was hidden by robes that looked more like layers of shredded rags. Unkempt dreadlocks fell past her shoulders, and lines of white paint circled her eyes while a lone streak started from under her nose and ended at the tip of her pointed chin. She cackled, a full body shrieking laugh that silenced all other noises of the forest.

"Oh, do not fret so, little brother. We knew of your presence long before your non-listeners used their magics," the woman said, Creole accent so thick that Bree needed to concentrate to understand her words. She spoke not only with her mouth, but with her hands as well, dancing fingers animating her speech. "We let you come. We let you walk through our village. We let you see our lives."

Stone faced, Lucien asked, "Why?"

"Why, to hear the Loa, of course. Hear the Loa speak. We are the Voice of the Loa. You hear the Loa, do you not?"

Lucien paused. "That is not why we are here."

"Ooooooh no," the woman hissed as she circled him, eyeing him as if his intentions were tangible, visible things. "You have come here to steal from us, little brother. We knew that, too, and still we let you come."

Lucien replied with a stony silence.

The woman continued to walk around him, but peered back into the open doorway of the hut filled with a dozen different items. She smiled, exposing missing teeth. Those that she did have were yellow and crooked, embedded in swollen gums. "You want a totem with strong magic. You want … the Web of Anansi."

"It does not belong to you."

Smiling, the old woman glided around Lucien. "Oh, little brother. You are both right and wrong. It may have come from Africa, but it belongs to us now. It belongs to us because we have it."

The Web of Anansi was not a voodoo totem, rather a powerful item from African magics. Why not? Just because Bree was learning about nine different magics didn't mean those were the only nine that existed. Every culture had a magic, and it made sense that every culture, every magic, had their own items of power. What items did her magic have? Was anyone trying to steal them?

Lucien straightened his shoulders and stood his ground. "We are here to reclaim it."

The woman looked up at him and cackled. "You say 'reclaim' as if you mean to take back what once belonged to you. You are no Afrikaner. You reek of Loa. We are the Voice of Loa. We speak to them and for them. We know them. You are a child of Loa. You are *our* little brother."

"The Loa may have blessed me with their magics, but I am *not* one of you!"

"Oh, little brother, you hear the Loa. *We* are the Voice of the Loa."

Lucien tilted his head subtly to Bree and shot her a hard look. Taken aback, she wondered what it meant. Panic started to swirl in her, even more so than finding herself in such a dire situation. What did he mean by that look? What did he want her to do? Run? Duck? Attack? Do something to distract their captors? Tensing her muscles, she concentrated on communing with the flora in the immediate vicinity and tried to ready herself for anything. Then Lucien glanced to Rumiel.

Bree watched Rumiel door-port into the hut, right in front of the Web of Anansi, thick cords of black forming a circular web a foot in diameter. He grabbed the totem and looked to Lucien as the old woman threw her head back and laughed as if that was the funniest thing she'd ever seen. Smoke formed around her body from the ground up and quickly dissipated, taking her with it, leaving her maniacal eyes for last. And her cackle. The damned laugh seemed to split the air like the sound of snapping bones.

The other members of The Voice of the Loa vanished in the same way, rolling smoke whisking them away. As soon as the last one disappeared, the forest came alive with noise, drowning out the disembodied cackling.

"The stick!" Lucien yelled to Javier and Bree. "Get the stick and break it!"

The rucksack! It was slung over Javier's shoulders and before Bree could reach for it, spiders and snakes exploded from the trees. Instinctively, Bree crouched, screamed and shielding her head with her arms. The mass of creepy crawlers split and changed course.

From the hut, Rumiel focused on redirecting the spiders, but there were so many that he was visibly strained. Javier did the same with the snakes, commanding them to return to the forest as his whole body shook with the effort, his brow covered in sweat and shimmering in the torchlight.

"Bree!" Lucien screamed.

Two of the alligators raced toward her with their jaws wide. She cried out again and threw her hands out. Her mind reached out to the plants and trees, begging for help. Just as the reptiles lunged, a web-work of roots burst from the ground while vines shot from the nearby forest. Caught in the newly formed net, the creatures hissed and twisted, thrashing their tails as they squirmed.

"The stick! We have to break the stick!" Lucien yelled again as he summoned smoke, laying a thick blanket of black over the other half dozen alligators. The cover did very little to hinder them as they emerged from the moat and rushed toward Lucien. Every time he commanded smoke from the ground to create a door-port, an alligator attacked before he could step through, forcing him to dodge or use a levitation spell to toss the animal aside. The choice being clear, he decided to abandon his attempts to door-port to his friends and opted to run.

Concentrating with every fiber of her being, Bree reached for every tree edging the forest to extend their branches toward the lunging beasts. She slowed them down, but they kept advancing.

Rumiel took a moment to door-port next to Javier, but the effort weakened him and he fell to his hands and knees as soon as he stepped through. Staying on his knees, he waved his hands in sweeping motions toward any skittering mass of spiders getting too close, commanding them to run back into the forest.

"Bree! The stick!" Lucien called again, running toward her. He almost tripped as he twisted his body to dodge the snapping jaws of a lunging alligator.

Bree could feel her pulse in every muscle and every joint. Commanding so much flora at once was too much, but she couldn't give up, not with Lucien in danger. If she stopped helping him even for a second, even to find the stick in Javier's rucksack, Lucien could get hurt. Or worse. She couldn't allow that.

Struggling to control the skittering, scurrying creatures, Rumiel remained on his hands and knees, closer to the ground, closer to the spiders. His eyes were closed as he concentrated his magic on his talisman. Javier stood still as a statue as he did the same with the snakes, and Bree poured every ounce of energy into commanding the vines and branches to entangle or swat away the oncoming alligators. Like a quarterback avoiding tackles while sprinting for the goal line, Lucien dodged snapping alligators and slithering snakes to reach them.

As a web of vines twined itself around an alligator snapping at Lucien's heels, Bree jammed her hand into the

Javier's backpack, past water bottles and energy bars and first aid materials, all the while keeping her eyes on Lucien. Just a few more yards ….

"Guys. Snakes and spiders. Snakes and spiders."

"Got 'em," Rumiel growled through gritted teeth.

"So many," Javier whimpering and dropping to his knees. "So many."

Bree wriggled her fingers to the bottom of the rucksack. Success! Feeling like King Arthur with Excalibur, she pulled the stick from the rucksack and snapped it in two just as Lucien reached her.

As planned, a door-port immediately opened in front of them and Bree looked in to see her fellow student standing in Siobhan's room.

"Go!" Lucien yelled, yanking both Javier and Rumiel to their feet. "Go! Move! Gooooo… !" They both tumbled through the door port just as Lucien let out an anguished cry.

"Lucien!" Bree gasped as he grabbed his leg. A vine whipped out of nowhere, curled around a snake, and threw it back into the dark forest as Lucien hobbled and fell into Bree's arms.

CHAPTER 26

HIS ARM AROUND her shoulders, Bree and Lucien stumbled through the door-port to a room full of surprised faces.

"Snake bite!" Bree shouted. "We need an instructor!" She held him up as best she could, but he quickly lost strength in his leg. Strongbow rushed to his side and ushered Lucien to Siobhan's bed as Ryoku helped Rumiel and Javier to chairs and handed them water bottles.

"No!" Lucien barked. "No instructors. Bree can fix this."

Every insecurity Bree ever had about herself turned to dust and blew away. Lucien needed her and she was *not* going to fail. Without thinking, she created a door-port to the greenhouse. Strongbow helped Lucien through and sat him on the ground where Bree pointed.

Here, in her familiar element, she was able to take control. First, she grabbed a pair of pruning shears and cut the leg of Lucien's jeans so she could see the wound. Two holes in the side of his thigh, just above his knee. She commanded vines to snake around Lucien's leg above and below the bite to stymie the spread of poison, and then made them contract toward the wound in an effort to push the poison out. It seemed to be working as trickles of blood dripped from where the fangs had pierced his skin. But it wasn't enough. Lucien's face had turned an ashen gray and he moaned and gritted his teeth in pain.

As deftly as if she used her own hands, Bree ordered two philodendron petioles to strip leaves from a nearby medicinal fern and wrap them around a small chunk of bark from a tree the next aisle over. Overwhelmed, Bree wondered if she really knew what she was doing or if somehow the philodendron was guiding her, helping her to pick the plants with the precise properties Lucien needed. No! It was she who guided the plants, she who was taking control of the situation, she who knew what she was doing. She hadn't just been learning spells and potions and salves these past months, she was learning about herself, about who she was. Right now, she was determined to be the girl who saved the day.

"Chew on this," Bree ordered. Doing as instructed, he took the small bit from the unfurled philodendron leaf and slid it into his mouth.

As soon as Lucien started chewing, Bree gave orders to her peers, sending each off on a different errand. When they disappeared, she commanded the plants to come to her aid, offering their essences and roots and saps.

Starting with a palm full of moss, she sliced open and wiped the juice from a piece of prickly pear and a few drops of San Pedro cactus into it. Then she stripped a frond of aloe and wiped it on top.

"How're you doing?" Bree asked as she scraped a root against the rough corner of a nearby table's wooden leg. Specks and chunks of the root fell onto the moss.

Lucien tried to prop himself up by his elbows. Sweat rolled down his face and he forced a smile past his grimace. "Good."

Siobhan, Strongbow, and Siza door-ported back with the other ingredients. Willem and Ryoku returned with pillows, and Javier and Rumiel came back with the specific spell book Bree needed from the library.

Rumiel opened the book for her as Lucien leaned back into the pillows. *I can do this,* Bree told herself. *He's counting on me, and I'm not going to let him die!* She hurriedly smeared lavender oil, turmeric, echinacea pupura root extract, coconut and tea tree oil into the moss and kneaded the mess between her hands. She looked back down at Lucien just as his body went rigid. Growling, he tried to grab at his leg.

"Javier!" Bree snapped. "Do you know what the snake's bite is doing to him?"

"The venom," Javier said, eyes wide as Lucien writhed in pain. "It breaks down the muscles. It stops them. Soon … soon he will lose breathing."

As if following a macabre script, Lucien wheezed. With exaggerated movements, his chest heaved up and down as he fought to inhale and exhale.

"Page 243!" Bree shouted. She held out her hands, now full of a greenish yellow gooey mess. "I can't touch the book like this."

Siobhan dropped to her knees and propped the book on her lap for Bree to see. She turned to the requested page as Lucien gave a pain-filled raspy gurgle.

Squeezing the moss between her hands, fingers interlocked as if ready for prayer, Bree looked over the words. Lucien moaned softly, his chest barely rising and falling.

"Bree?" Siobhan asked, her tone calm, but hurried. "If you're gonna do something, now is the time, girl."

Bree read the words aloud, annunciating each one distinctly, then pressed the dripping mess in her hands against Lucien's open wound. His body seized, his eyes snapped open, his jaw clenched. Muscles, ligaments, and tendons froze and flared again and again as his veins writhed beneath his skin like the very snakes that had just chased them. She didn't want to hurt him, but she knew that for the spell to counteract and eliminate the venom, he had to go through the cleansing fire of this intense pain. There were no other words to speak, so she filled her mind with every prayer she knew to every god she'd ever heard of.

The moss in her hands slowly changed color, going from the medicinal dull golden green to a sickly black. By the time it pulled the poison from Lucien's body, Bree held two fistfuls of gooey ink. Soon Lucien stopped shaking, his body relaxing into the pillows. He stopped sweating and his breathing returned to normal. Everyone stood or sat around him, waiting, watching. Barely breathing. Finally, a few minutes later, his eyes flickered open. A faint smile formed on his dry lips, and he struggled to prop himself up. After a raspy gulp, he looked around at his classmates and whispered, "Thank you. I'm good as new."

Bree let out a relieved sob and threw her arms around him, pushing him back against the pillows. She heard a few gasps, but didn't care. Right there in front of everyone, she planted a big teary kiss right on his lips.

Sniffling, she pulled away and used her thumb to trace the bottom half of Lucien's smile. He used the back of his index finger to wipe away her tears. "I knew you could do it."

"Thanks for believing in me," she whispered, unable to stop smiling.

"However," he continued, "I think I would like to take a nap now."

Bree sat back on her knees and looked up at their friends. "Can you help me get him to his room?

"Too his room?" Willem cracked, holding his hand out to help her to her feet. "To get him to bed so he can sleep off this magic snake healing thing you just did or to –?"

"Willem!" Ryoku, Siobhan, Siza, and Bree all said at once. It was classic Willem, but it served to break the tension. As one cohesive unit—except for Rumiel, who hovered at the back of the room—the group helped Lucien get settled. They door-ported him to his room, and while everyone else attended to getting him situated in bed, Bree used his bathroom to clean the mess from her hands.

"Thank you, everyone," Lucien said pulling up the covers. "But I really need to pass out now."

Before leaving, the girls gave Lucien hugs while the boys, except for Rumiel, clapped his shoulder and told him to sleep well. Bree stayed a bit longer to make sure Lucien was comfortable. She sat next to him on the bed and intertwined her fingers with his. "How are you feeling?"

Through tired eyes, he smiled and said, "Very good, actually. Your salve must have pulled out all of the toxins from my body including those found in potato chips, candy, cheese puffs, and soda."

Bree smiled and playfully leaned her body against his, shoulder to shoulder. "You don't consume any of that stuff."

"Oh, so you're my doctor now? Keeping track of my nutritional intake? Monitoring my trips to the vending machine?"

"Yes. Yes I am. That's why I know for a fact that you don't hit the vending machines." Still smiling, Bree unsuccessfully fought back the tears, her eyes stinging.

Again, Lucien wiped away a tear. "You were wonderful, full of magic and determination."

"I was so scared."

"So was I. But *you did it*, and now I owe you my life."

Bree wanted to say more, and wanted to hear more, but each time Lucien blinked it took longer than to open his eyes. She leaned in and kissed him one more time. Then she leaned her forehead against his. His eyes were closed, his breathing settling into a steady rhythm. "You let me know immediately if you need anything. I'm going to make some salves for to use for the next couple days."

Unable to get his eyes even halfway open, he smiled and whispered back, "Whatever you say, doc." He was asleep before she stood. Quietly, she turned off his light and shut the door behind her.

As Bree headed back toward the greenhouse to clean up the mess she'd made and make a batch of salve, the gravity of the evening's events began to fully sink in. *Lucien almost died!* she thought. *I saved someone's life! Lucien believed in me, and I saved him! My magic!* She had to stop and brace herself against the wall. Whether it was the overwhelming emotion of saving a life, the trauma of the experience in the swamp, the exhaustion from the concentrated use of magic on the island and in the greenhouse, or the sheer relief of knowing that Lucien believed in her—and the realization that she … well, she loved him—she had no idea. It was all almost too much. She leaned her head back, took several deep breaths, and tried to calm down. If today was this crazy, what would the future bring? Her plan to get their hands on the two magical totems that would help them find Lila had worked. Now what?

She looked at the time on her cell phone. She had about an hour before her mother would be home from her meeting, so pushed herself off the wall and kept walking toward the greenhouse. Keeping busy would do her good.

As soon as she entered the greenhouse, she stopped shaking. The now-familiar comfort of the flora relaxed her, like a warm embrace from her dearest friend. But she wasn't alone. Someone was in the area where she healed Lucien. After the events of tonight, she didn't know what to expect, so crept her way over there. She did not expect to find Javier on his hands and knees wiping up the mess on the floor with a wet cloth. Nor did she expect that he'd be crying.

"Javier?"

With an audible sniffle, Javier turned his head away from her and wiped his face with his sleeve. He stood and turned to her with his usual big, bright smile, his eyes still shining with tears. "*Hola.*"

Unsure how to proceed, she played it safe. "So … what's up?"

"I wanted to help clean up," Javier replied. To add validity to his statement, he held up the cloth as evidence.

"Actually, I meant why are you … upset?"

"I'm not upset. See? Big smiles!" He looked over to Bree to show his big smile just as a tear slid down his cheek.

Bree reached over and took the cloth from him. "Javier. It's okay. What's wrong?"

A second full tear followed the first and he wiped his face on his sleeve again. "It is my fault. It is all my fault."

Confused, Bree asked. "What is?"

"The bite. The snake that bit Lucien. I could not control him. I could not reach his mind until it was too late."

"Javier, that is so not true."

"It is! It is true. I controlled the many snakes, but not that one."

"I was there, Javier, remember? How many snakes were there?"

"Many."

"Not just many. Dozens! *Hundreds*, even. You did an *amazing* job keeping them away from us. I thought we were all dead. All of us. But you *you* kept us *alive* by keeping all of those snakes away from us."

"But ... but I failed. One bit Lucien."

"It could have been worse. *A lot* worse, if not for you. It's not your fault that Lucien got bitten. It's because of you that we all made it out of there alive!"

"Really? You think this?"

"No, I don't think this. I *know* this. And I know that we're going to use the Web of Anansi and the Eye of Ra to find Strongbow's sister. I know this, too. We're all in this together, remember?"

Javier's eyes lit up. He sniffled and nodded. "*Si*. Yes. I know this, too! Thank you!"

Bree stepped forward and wrapped her arms around him. "That's what friends are for."

He returned the embrace and whispered, "You … and the other girls are nice to me … accepting. You are like sisters to me."

The warmth of Javier's words spread through her heart. Bree didn't understand why boys reacted so badly anytime a girl said that they were like a brother. The sentiment was nice! It made her feel included, part of something bigger. Made her feel part of a family. Her mood shifted, though, as Javier continued, "And Rumiel is like a brother to me."

Bree pulled back and stepped away. "Too bad he doesn't like me."

Javier cocked his head and words he never intended to speak aloud came tumbling out. "You're wrong. He does like you. But—"

Bree looked to Javier to finish his sentence. At first, she thought there might have been a language barrier, but he put his head down and grabbed a broom leaning against a stand of plants. Prodding, Bree asked, "What were you going to say?"

Javier turned away and started to sweep the area as if Bree wasn't even standing there. "Nothing," he mumbled.

Bree didn't need any kind of truth spells or potions to know he was lying to her. "Javier. If you know something that will help me get along with Rumiel, then you should let me know. I don't want animosity to get in the way of our missions or our work at the institute."

"It's nothing," Javier repeated.

Bree decided to try the "Chelsea" approach. As fast as she could, she said, "You said he liked me. If he does, then why has he been acting like such a jerk to me? When he first got here, he seemed to want to be friends and hang out, but now he says mean things and makes nasty faces and—."

"He *likes* you," Javier said, looking to Bree with a worried look on his face.

Bree gasped and stepped back. "You mean *likes* me *likes* me?"

"*Si*. Yes."

Javier must have missed another snake, because it slithered up and down Bree's spine as she thought about the idea of Rumiel being attracted to her. Not only did she feel no spark between them, but also that there wasn't enough lighter fluid and matches in the world to create one. After her initial shock, she reminded herself that Javier and Rumiel were good friends, and she didn't want to insult Javier by appearing disgusted by the thought of his friend liking her. She must have done a poor job hiding her feelings when Javier's eyes turned pitying as he said, "Rumiel is a good person."

Squeezing her eyes shut, Bree shook her head, trying to not imagine Rumiel's skinny body, almost translucent skin, and stringy hair. She quickly reopened them and softened her expression. "I'm sure he is, Javier, but, as I'm sure everyone's figured out by now, Lucien and I are … together."

Javier smiled and blushed. "I know this. Lucien is a good person, too. He is also my brother."

Bree returned his smile. "Yes, he is a good person. And I want to be friends with everyone here. Well, Willem is a pain, but—"

With a laugh, Javier nodded. "Sometimes, yes, he is a pain, but I agree that we should all be friends." Then his eyes widened and he leaned forward. "Please do not tell Rumiel I said anything."

"It's okay. I won't."

His smile returned as he nodded. "Okay. Good. Good."

Bree put a hand on the broom. "It's been a very rough night, and I'm surprised any of us are still standing. I still need a few minutes to whip up some salve for Lucien's leg, and then I'm going to go home. Thank you for helping to clean up the mess I made, but I can finish up now. Why don't you go to bed."

Javier looked around the area and then relinquished the broom to Bree. "Okay. Bed sounds *muy bueno*." He gave her one more hug and smiled. "See you tomorrow?"

"Tomorrow," Bree said, and sent Javier on his way. She sighed, trying to wrap her mind around everything that happened, including the new information about Rumiel. No time to think about it, though. The last day of school was approaching and she had work to do.

CHAPTER 27

WIDE SMILE EXPOSING all of her braces, Chelsea chattered away as Bree cleaned out her locker. "Are you going to see him tonight?"

It was the last day of school, a half day to say goodbyes and clean out lockers. Chelsea had hers cleaned out by the end of the prior week, but Bree had been so wrapped up in the events at the institute, she hadn't given her locker a second thought until now. While failing to remember why she had a wadded up piece of paper with gum in it, she threw it out and smiled at the mere thought of Lucien. "Yes."

Impossibly, Chelsea's smile got wider and she bounced up and down on her toes. "Yay! I'm so happy for you! What are you guys gonna do? What's he like? Is he a good kisser? He looks like a good kisser. He's so handsome. Oh my gosh those shoulders! Are you two now boyfriend/girlfriend? When can I officially meet him? Does he have a brother?"

Trying to hide her reaction, Bree winced at Chelsea's last question. She knew the answer *used to be* "yes" until Tierney sacrificed himself months ago on a beach helping Strongbow and Willem escape a Meso ambush. Bree paused, trying to imagine what that kind of loss must feel like. A twin, someone so close, suddenly ripped away, especially at such a young age. There had to be some level of anger, but Lucien managed it so well. She made a mental note to talk to him about it the next time they could be alone, try to get him to open up about it.

Chelsea noticed Bree's stoppage in cleaning and speculated, "You don't know if you're boyfriend/girlfriend, do you? I guess you guys haven't talked about it yet, huh?"

Again, Bree's mind swirled. It had been three days since their escape from the bayou, three days since she saved Lucien's life. In those rare moments when her mom was not working like a fiend, Allyson had guilted Bree into spending quality time with her. So, no time with Lucien until after school today. Even though they had texted, emailed, and talked on the phone, he didn't like to spend time communicating electronically, saying it diminished the art and beauty of conversation, so their interactions had been sporadic and brief. However, he promised that he had been using the salves she had prepared for him and assured her that his wound was healing nicely. Even though they planned on using unpracticed and clandestine magic after school, Bree was still very excited to spend time with him. "No, we really haven't talked about it. I think we're just really savoring our time together."

Chelsea made a squeaking noise that could have turned into a squeal had she not shown great constraint. Well, great constraint for Chelsea. Bree knew this and was impressed, even though it made her giggle.

Grabbing the last handful of papers from the bottom of her locker, Bree exposed a small pile of dirt in the corner.

She immediately remembered the prank, and humiliation and anger welled up within her. She pushed those emotions down and reminded herself that after today, she would be free from Brittany for the summer. And Amanda.

Her recently estranged friend's locker was at the other end of the hallway. Like a full henhouse, Amanda and her new friends strutted and clucked and flapped their arms. Bree's stomach knotted as she realized that there would be no Amanda this summer, no more slumber parties or movie nights at her house. Her gaze was too longing and just as she started to turn away, she noticed something. It was subtle, but huge—Amanda was talking louder than Brittany.

Standing at the head of the group, Amanda gabbed away, tossing her hands about the air with a great flourish, the only interruption coming when she flipped her long hair. Even though Brittany stood by Amanda's right side, she was still relegated to the listening area with the rest of the nameless, lookalike drones. Had Amanda supplanted Brittany? Had Dr. Frankenbrittany's Monster turned on her?

Taking but a moment to eavesdrop, Bree couldn't hear the details, but concluded that Amanda went on and on about her new boyfriend. Bree knew that Brittany didn't have one. Was that all it took to become Queen Bee? Bree smirked, thinking if that were the case, she'd dominate them all, being involved with the most amazing guy ever. Then her brain froze when she noticed Brittany look over at her.

But nothing happened.

Face tight and serious, Brittany looked directly at Bree. Instead of the usual anger or hatred found within the cheerleader's eyes, Bree saw something different. A sadness?

Fear? If Bree didn't know any better, she would have sworn it was shame. The look lasted for only a second, not long enough for any of Brittany's cronies to notice. Bree blinked and Brittany was back to fake laughing through her plastic smile.

"It's gonna be weird, isn't it?" Chelsea asked, affectionately bumping her shoulder against Bree's.

"You mean a summer without Amanda?"

"Yeah," Chelsea sighed.

"Don't forget, we still have each other."

Chelsea giggled and did a small, jerky side-to-side dance. She soon stopped and a worried look spread across her face. "What about Sci-Fi Sam?"

Bree heaved a soul-shaking sigh as she peered into her locker one last time. Empty as the first day of school, she shut the door and turned toward the exit. "I don't know. After he got mad that I'm *not* gay, I haven't seen him since."

Putting her hands in her pockets, Chelsea walked beside Bree as they left the school together. Remorseful, she said, "Yeah, that was kinda weird, huh?"

"Very."

Once outside, Chelsea perked back up and said, "But I was right about him liking you! Too bad for him that you already have a sort of boyfriendish man in your life. Wow. Two guys liking you at once! That's so crazy."

"You have no idea," Bree replied. Chelsea thought the notion was romantic, and Bree didn't have the heart to let her know how truly conflicting it was. Especially after she learned about Rumiel. She still had a hard time processing that. What could he possibly see in her? He was so goth and morose. They had nothing in common, and

Bree wished she could convey that to him. Sure, he could be fun to hang out with when he was in a good mood, but ever since she became involved with Lucien, Rumiel had become *unbearable*. She wanted to talk to him about it, but she knew that ultimately, she'd say, "We can still be friends," and, being *a boy*, Rumiel would not react well to that statement.

So deep in her mental quagmire, Bree didn't notice how far they had walked until they approached her house. Chipper, Chelsea said, "Okay, you have fun with the rest of your day … on your *date!* With your *boyfriend!*"

Bree blushed at the words. "I told you, we haven't talked about—"

Finishing her sentence wasn't necessary. Chelsea turned and skipped away singing, "Bree's got a boyfriend! Bree's got a boyfriend! Bree's got a boyfriend!"

Bree blushed so hard she felt the warmth spread to her neck. Looking up and down the street, she checked to see if anyone in the neighborhood had heard her boisterous friend. Thankfully, the only potential audience were chirping birds flitting overhead on a powerline.

Once inside her house, Bree wasted no time. She dropped all her locker stuff on her desk in her bedroom, then went back downstairs to the kitchen to grab a protein bar and energy drink. Door-porting to the institute was getting easier with every trip, but the effort still left her feeling lethargic. As she munched away in between sips, she conjured the doorway and walked into the game room at the institute.

"Did you bring enough for the rest of us," Willem asked, sitting at his usual spot.

As usual, Ryoku sat next to him with her hand out. "A dollar."

"What?" Willem expressed his dismay but reached into his pocket anyway. "Why?"

"Bad joke."

"Bad? Why was it bad?"

"Because you're sitting at a juice bar. A bar that is stocked with protein bars of all kinds and a refrigerator with every kind of energy drink."

"I know! That's what makes it *funny!*"

"No. Not funny. Lame. The word you're looking for is lame."

"Bullocks." Willem paid the dollar. Everyone laughed nervously, one last grasp at levity before allowing the gravity of the situation to settle over them. As the smiles faded, all eyes focused on the small table where Lucien, Siza, and Strongbow sat. There, in the center of the table, Strongbow had placed the Eye of Ra and the Web of Anansi.

Lucien's usually stern face was soft with worry. He had supported the idea of using the totems to find Lila, but now, when the moment came, Bree wondered how he felt. His own brother had died on a similar mission, and he had just recovered from a near fatal snake bite. At the beginning of her journey with magic, he had been her rock. Now, she would now be his. "So," she said, trying to keep her voice even, feigning confidence to hide the same fear shared by everyone in the room. "The plan is to use these totems to find Lila. Once we figure out where she's located, then we have a few days to plan our next step. We get her on Saturday. Then we'll spend the rest of the summer reminiscing about how awesome we all are."

Her comment elicited few chuckles and smiles around the table. Despite the varying degrees of apprehension, Bree was satisfied that everyone was in this together. She knew in her heart that they were going to find Lila. This plan was going to work.

"Okay," she continued, addressing Lucien and Siza. "So what do we do next?"

"Well," Lucien said, straightening his posture. "It is believed that the Web of Anansi is the spider's web of the world. Like a regular spider web, what happens at one part of the web reverberates and can be felt throughout."

"And the Eye of Ra," Siza jumped in, "can see what you desire. However, it fails to show the *exact* location if what you desire is an object, or person in this instance."

"So, what we are going to try to do is combine our magics to combine these totems. To pinpoint Lila, we need something concrete, yet with emotional attachment," Lucien said.

All eyes turned to Strongbow. Ready, he produced a small five-pronged comb inlaid with turquoise. "This was passed down to Lila from our grandmother. She used it to comb her hair every day." He placed it next to the other items in the middle of the table.

Lucien looked to Siza and she nodded. He draped the Web of Anansi over The Eye of Ra, and then balanced the comb on top of the Web. Taking a deep breath, he held out his hands, one to Siza, one to Strongbow. They each accepted and joined hands themselves. Looking to Strongbow, Lucien said, "Don't use your magics. Just concentrate on your sister. Siza and I will use ours with the totems and use you as a conduit to find her location."

Flexing his jaw muscles, Strongbow gave a curt nod and closed his eyes. Taking one last look at each other, Lucien and Siza closed their eyes as well. The room fell silent. The only sound anyone could hear was the soft in and out breaths of the three around the round table as the concentrated and focused their magics.

Soft as whispers, Lucien began to chant and Siza whisper in Arabic. Their voices synced up, the two ancient languages harmonizing and creating a hypnotic rhythm. As the words flowed, a black mist crept over Lucien's shoulders and along his arms, and the gold pattern all along Siza's thin emerald cloak rippled and flowed along her arms like water. The creeping ribbons of gold and black met where Siza and Lucien's hands joined, and continued to flow, twisting around each other. The other set of black and gold strands met behind Strongbow's neck. They looped around each other and kept flowing. Then Strongbow gasped and jolted upright in his seat as if his chair had been electrocuted. So wrapped up in the ceremony, the six observers gasped and jumped in their seats as well.

The black and gleaming gold ropes wrapped around all three sets of arms, slithering over them. The incantation grew faster, louder. Strongbow opened his eyes, now pure black with pinpoints of lights, like two openings to the night sky. He moaned, "I see her."

"Where?" Ryoku asked. "Where is she?"

"I see her," he repeated, his voice hollow.

Bree's heart sped up as Lucien and Siza chanted faster and faster. A thin sheen of sweat formed along their foreheads. She didn't know how long they could continue like this or what would happen; she only knew that they needed to stop soon. She said, "Strongbow? Where is she?"

Again, his only response was a flat, "I see her."

Ryoku turned to Willem and whispered urgently, "You need to join your magics with theirs. Use your illusion powers to project what Strongbow is seeing."

Willem crinkled his nose and hissed, "Eeew! That means I'd have to … touch … him!"

"Willem!" the girls snapped in unison.

"Bullocks!" he snorted as he jumped from his stool.

"Hurry!" Ryoku growled.

Willem moved behind Strongbow and placed his right hand on Strongbow's shoulder and extended his left hand. Closing his eyes, Willem slowed his breathing and swirled his fingers through the air. Bree's skin crawled as her eyes bounced from Willem to Lucien to Strongbow to Siza, back to Willem. She wanted to scream at Willem to hurry but knew that would be counterproductive. Just as she contemplated leaving the room for her own sanity, the air rippled in front of Willem. A few feet in front of him, in the center of the room, a wavy image appeared. An image of a Native American girl, in her late teens. Tentatively, she exited a forest onto a lawn of manicured grass.

"Oh my God!" Ryoku gasped.

"I see her," Strongbow mumbled.

Sweat dripping down his strained face, Willem kept his eyes closed and asked through gritted teeth, "Where? Where is she?"

"Here," Ryoku whispered in disbelief. "She's right outside!"

CHAPTER 28

PANDEMONIUM ENSUED. Everyone not connected to the spell shouted ideas about how to break it. The idea of simply separating them won out, as Ryoku, no longer interested in listening to any other opinions, jumped from her stool and ran to the table.

"No!" Siobhan yelled.

"Stop!" Bree screamed.

Ignoring the other girls, Ryoku grabbed Siza and Strongbow's forearms and yanked them apart. An invisible shockwave radiated outward from the center of the table, knocking everyone around it to the ground. Willem's illusion disappeared as he stumbled and fell backward. Strongbow arched backward as if punched in the jaw. The black mist disappeared as Lucien's chair toppled backward. Siza flopped from her chair to the floor, the golden filaments of light snapping back into her emerald cloak.

"Lucien!" Bree screamed and ran to kneel beside him. She shook his shoulders and repeated his name until he moaned and opened his eyes. Sitting up, he shook his head and looked up at her. "That was … intense."

Around them, the other students moved with the same speed and flurry. Siobhan and Javier moved to aid Siza while Ryoku rushed to Strongbow. Rumiel stood frozen while Willem was left to pick himself up from the floor. As he stretched, he mumbled, "So good to be loved."

"I saw her," Strongbow shouted as he scrambled to his feet. He wobbled and Ryoku grabbed his arm to help steady him. "She's right outside!"

"We know," Ryoku said, worry in her voice. "We saw."

Stumbling forward, he said, "We have to get her! Get her *now!*"

"We'll get her, but first we need to—"

"No!" Strongbow snapped. He summoned a door-port to the patch of lawn shown in the image. Slipping from Ryoku's grip, he rushed through.

But his sister wasn't there. With the anguish of a wounded animal, he called out, "Lila! Lila!"

Being the closest, Rumiel maintained the door-port, keeping the gateway open to the expansive lawn behind the institute. Ryoku chased after Strongbow. Willem followed her. Once outside, they called out for Lila as well.

Siza stood, unfazed by the experience. She followed through the door-port, Siobhan and Javier coming after. Rumiel went through as well, but kept it open for Lucien and Bree.

Bree helped Lucien to his feet. Woozy, he asked, "Did they get her?"

"I don't think Lila is here."

"What? But we found her. Strongbow *saw* her."

"I know. We all saw her, but I don't know … I just have this gut feeling the vision wasn't true."

"Then we need to help them." Lucien grabbed Bree's hand and stepped through the door-port.

Rumiel closed it behind them and they all joined the search. Every few steps Lucien needed to pause and catch his breath, sometimes stopping to put his hands on his knees. Bree wanted to stay close, but he waved her on. "Go help the others. I'll be fine. The spell took a lot out of me."

"Okay." Bree joined the others, close to the forest line.

Ryoku stayed close to Strongbow as he ran across the lawn, shouting into the forest, "Lila! Lila!"

"She was *just here!*" Willem yelled, looking around. "We *all* saw her right here! Right? Or am I daft?"

Siobhan walked along the tree line, peering into the forest. "Let this be known as the first time I have *ever* agreed with you. We all saw her."

"I don't know … she must have gone back into the forest or something. We have to go after her."

"That won't be necessary—" a voice came from the trees.

Everyone stopped, as if the voice held the power to paralyze them. They all knew the voice, knew it belonged to the young man walking out of the forest straight toward them.

Talo.

Smugly, he strode further onto the lawn, a beam of sunlight shining before him, as if bowing to him, bending to his will to announce his presence. Behind him a dozen other Mesos followed, oozing from behind the trees. All of them wore only loincloths wrapped about their waists with images of snakes and skulls painted on their flesh. Bree remembered the story of Willem and Strongbow being ambushed on the beach. This was a trap.

Talo smiled, wickedness radiating from him as he continued from his last statement. "Lila's not here."

Strongbow morphed into a bear. Rearing up on his hind legs, front paws clawing at the air, he roared loud enough to rattle every bone in Bree's body. Fighting the urge to run, she had to remind herself that the bear was her friend.

Talo, however, was far from impressed. He raised his hand in front of him and waved his index finger as if scolding Strongbow. "Tsk, tsk, tsk. If you attack me now, my friends here wouldn't like that. And you'll never know where Lila is." Talo's minions chuckled and postured just as arrogantly. Except for one, who stared directly at Bree.

Amanda's new boyfriend.

Bree's heart sped up, throbbing in her stomach and beating behind her ears. She even felt it pound at the base of her closing throat. This was too much. This couldn't be happening. Her lifelong loyalty to Amanda resurfaced and thoughts of how to warn her one-time friend, if she survived this encounter, swirled through her mind. If? If she survived?

Fists clenched, Siobhan inched her way toward Bree while keeping a wary eye on the interlopers who were now taunting Strongbow. "What should we do?"

"I don't know," Bree whispered back, pushing aside the drama of Amanda dating a Meso. That was a future problem. The murderous look dancing within the Mesos' eyes was the current problem. Another thought caused her stomach to churn like a ball of squirming worms— if it came down to it, could she kill?

Every argument about morality versus survival crashed about inside her head. She knew that if a fight broke out, the Mesos would use lethal force. But could she? Did she have it in her? She loved her new friends, but she doubted they could resolve this situation peacefully. Especially when Strongbow shifted from bear back to human and yelled, "Where is she?"

Talo's smile twisted just as viciously as if his words turned a knife in Strongbow's chest. "Not here."

The rest of the Mesos laughed.

"Where is she?" Strongbow yelled again, spraying saliva while veins rippled under his skin and ligaments flared in his neck. Ryoku placed a hand on his shoulder, but he shrugged it off.

"Oh, she *was* here," Talo answered. "Your little spell to find her worked beautifully, but we were prepared. We were, how do you say, 'forewarned.'"

Bree and Siobhan looked at each other, dread in their eyes.

Talo laughed. "Oh yes. Your suspicions are true. There is a traitor among you."

Everyone from the institute looked around at each other and then turned back to Talo who shrugged nonchalantly and looked at Javier. "Isn't it obvious?"

"What?" Javier yelled, voice cracking. "No!"

"I knew it!" Willem spat, spinning to face Javier.

"It's not me! He's lying!"

"Of course you'd say that!"

"Willem! Stop it!" Bree snapped. "Talo *is* lying!"

"Of course *you'd* say that!" Willem yelled at Bree. "You're always defending him!"

"Because you're always accusing him of something he's not! He's *not* the enemy! Talo is!"

For the first time, Talo's smile disappeared. His eyes darkened as he glared at Bree. "No! *You* are the enemy!" He took a menacing step toward her. "Just as the Mesoamerican nations began to claim inheritance of the world, an inheritance we earned, the boats came from the East and white men took it from us. *Our* people were slaughtered, *our* gods destroyed. But we … what do you call us? Mesos? We Mesos will bring the gods back and take back our rightful place, our rightful power! My tribe will bring forth Tlaloc!"

After his outburst, Talo composed himself by puffing out his chest and returning the sadistic grin that looked at home on his face. Turing his attention back to Javier, he said, "So, Javier, which of our exalted gods is your tribe bringing back?"

All eyes turned to Javier. Bree saw his frustration grow, especially under the accusing glares of both Willem and Strongbow. Even Ryoku's expression held questions.

"I am not a Meso!"

Talo cocked his head and laughed as he said, "Come now, Javier. We are all brothers, all children of the ancient gods. Tell them the truth."

Bree's breathing hitched as she watched Javier. Clenching his fists, his whole body quaked. Eyes squeezed shut so tightly that his whole face seemed to bunch, his lips tight against his gums, exposing gritted teeth. Tears rolled over his reddening cheeks.

"Dude?" Rumiel whispered.

Javier opened his eyes. Throwing his arms out, aiming his open palms at Talo, he summoned a winged snake made of shimmering light. Striking like the viper it resembled, the beam of light slammed into Talo's chest and burst into countless pluming sparks of brilliant colors. The force of the blast threw Talo backwards. Landing hard, he skidded to a halt before landing against an old oak sitting on the border of the lawn and forest.

Laughing, Talo stood and went through the motions of dusting himself off. When he finished, he looked at Javier and said, "Nicely done. My turn."

Talo transformed into a snake, a twenty-foot long serpent with black scales that glimmered with a green reticulation when they caught the light. Glistening fangs exposed, Talo lunged at Javier.

Standing closest, Rumiel tackled Javier, both boys narrowly escaping the strike. Flicking its tongue, the snake coiled and rose up to dance in front of the two friends.

Talo actions were all it took to incite the rest of the Mesos to attack.

Air thickening around her, Bree gulped in desperate swallows. She didn't know if it was a Meso spell or her own fear paralyzing her. It became hot. Sweltering. Her mind barely registered what was happening around her, everyone moving and shouting.

Then the ground exploded upward. Covering her face, she stumbled back and fell. Adrenaline pumped and deadened whatever pain she should have felt, but she was stunned and disoriented. She fought through blurred vision to get her bearings and keep track of the advancing Mesos. Some ran for a better vantage point, some stood and chanted with their arms extended out from their sides. Small explosions erupted from random parts of the ground, flinging chunks of dirt and grass and pebbles through the air, leaving pockets of lingering steam in the craters.

Her friends retaliated, but sensory overload kept her from moving. Multi-colored lights flashed around her. Cracks of electricity and rumbles of explosions filled the air. Steam and smoke and shadows clogged her peripheral vision. Her stomach knotted. She felt like she might vomit.

The ground rippled next to her. Afraid it was part of an attack, she finally willed herself to jump to her feet. She held her hands in front of herself, ready to shield her face or her body. However, the waves of grass rippled away from her toward the Mesos. The mounds rolled, as if strange and mysterious creatures sprinted under blankets of grass and knocked two Mesos off balance. Siobhan ran toward them, following the flowing ground that she, Bree now realized, controlled. "Come on, girl, let's go!"

Snapping from her stupor, Bree followed. Siobhan ran to the closest Meso as he spoke quickly while working his hands together, trying to conjure a spell. Siobhan threw a right hook, connecting with his cheek. She didn't knock him to the ground, but it was enough to disrupt his spell. She pressed forward, continuing to throw punches.

Bree looked over to the other Meso, regaining his balance from Siobhan's ground attack. It was Amanda's boyfriend. He glared at Bree and worked his hands together, but before she understood what he was doing, he threw a fireball at her.

The velocity was slow and the arc had a lob to it. Bree easily avoided it, no magic needed. Why did he make it so easy to dodge? Was he taking it easy on her? Was he toying with her? Was he trying to lull her into a false sense of security? Confused, she decided to answer in kind.

With his back to the forest, it was easy for Bree to command a vine to sneak up behind him. Snaking along the ground, the tip of the vine wrapped around his ankle. Looking down, he barked a few words and made a slicing motion with his arm. The spell diced apart a two-foot segment of the vine. He turned to Bree and tossed another fireball at her, blasting the ground in front of her feet. Smoldering bits of dirt sprayed her legs, but nothing more.

Still uncertain as to what he was trying to do, Bree commanded a small willow tree at the edge of the forest to reach down and grab him. Lifting him from the ground, the branches of the tree bound his hands and feet. Trussed up, he dangled above the ground. And smiled.

Bree realized too late that he was just setting her up, distracting her. As soon as he smiled, she whipped her head around to see two Mesos fifty feet away working up a spell. As one threw a spear at her, the other performed the spell. Midflight, the spear split into two, then splintered into four, then doubled again. Fear locking her muscles in place, Bree watched as eight spears whistled through the air toward her. She couldn't even scream.

"*NOOOOO!*" Siobhan screeched from behind her.

Siobhan tackled Bree just as the spears arrived.

Then everything went dark.

CHAPTER 29

DARKNESS. Compact, confined darkness. Bree wondered if she'd been speared and if this was what death felt like. There was no bright light at the end of the tunnel, though. No life flashing before her eyes. Up until a few months ago, did she even really have much of a life? It hadn't been exciting. She hadn't been attacked by vipers or spiders or Mesos throwing spears at her. She hadn't been to Egypt, stolen priceless magical totems, danced with a boy, been kissed, or fallen in love. She hadn't known she was magical. That life had been … different. That's what Lucien had called it.

Maybe that's what death was. Just different.

Then she felt movement. *She was moving*. There was a scratchiness to her surroundings, whatever it was that she moved through was gritty, like that time at the beach when Chelsea and Amanda had buried her in the sand. The coarseness against her skin, the pressure against her body … no, she wasn't dead because she knew her eyes were closed and she felt whatever she moved through. Then she heard noises.

The sounds were muffled, but growing louder. Screams and explosions? She moved faster, less encumbered. The noises grew even louder. She recognized distinct voices, her friends calling her name and Siobhan's, too. The pressure around her diminished. The sounds filled her ears and then she burst from the ground.

And kept rising above it.

Opening her eyes, she saw that she was partially in a column of dirt rising from the ground, the battlefield below her. Everyone stopped and watched, even Talo.

The earth around Bree lowered her, gently placing her on the lawn. Covered in dirt, Bree turned to see what everyone was staring at.

It was Siobhan. Right next to Bree stood a fifteen-foot tall dirt and grass simulacrum of Siobhan.

Deep brown soil formed the figure of Siobhan while a thick carpet of grass made up her long hair. Wordlessly, the colossus swept a backhand at a group of four Mesos. The gargantuan dirt person swatted two of them and sent them backward, tumbling along the ground. The other two dodged the attack. The battle picked up where it had left off.

Bree wiped the dirt from her face to see what was going on. Swirls of steam and smoke partially obscured her vision. Bursts of colors and bright beams flashed all around her, no source, no destination. Explosions and snaps and cracks rumbled all around her and reverberated through her. Screams and shouts filled the air, but she couldn't hear words, only primal cries of quarreling animals.

Trying to stay near the earthen tower shaped like Siobhan, Bree focused on the forest. If any Meso wondered too close, she commanded a vine to trip them or a branch to lash out and hit them. Nausea roiled through her at the thought of hurting them, *truly* hurting them. She felt childish, knowing that they were trying to kill her and her friends, that they didn't have the same feelings of remorse or constraint. Watching Siobhan, Bree assumed that her friend had the same reservations.

Even though the Siobhan golem attacked the Mesos, she didn't use lethal force. She used sweeping backhands to disrupt and confound rather than injure. However, the disruption she caused was short lived. Three Mesos served as a defense perimeter while Talo and four others worked together on a spell. Bree tried to get vines and branches to strike at the five conjuring the spell, but Amanda's boyfriend, his sinister smile omnipresent, thwarted her attempts. Unfortunately, none of her friends could breach the defenses either. Talo finished the spell.

A blinding pillar of light flashed down from the sky onto Talo, in the center of the square formed by the other four Mesos. Talo angled the beam—as wide as he was tall—at the dirt version of Siobhan. With the muffled impact of dropping a boulder onto the ground, the beam of light decimated the dirt avatar, blowing smoldering chunks through the air. Instantly, the real Siobhan flew upward, out of the ground, landing with a thud, her limp body rolling to a stop.

The fighting between her friends and the Mesos continued as Bree ran to Siobhan while praying, pleading, for her safety. Skidding to a halt on her knees, Bree knelt next to Siobhan and cupped her head. "Please be alive. Please. *Please.*"

Siobhan coughed, her whole body jerking with the effort. She opened a heavy eyelid, her piercing ice blue eye looking alien against her dirt covered face. Bree stroked Siobhan's mud clumped hair, relief filling her chest so fast that it hurt.

With a pained whisper, Siobhan said, "I'm … sorry, girl. I did … the best I could. Wasn't … strong enough. So tired…."

"You did great," Bree said, but Siobhan didn't hear her. Bree pressed her ear against Shiobhn's chest. She was still alive. She had simply passed out.

Bree's relief was short lived. There was no time for it, not here, not in this situation. Siobhan saved her life, and Bree had to return the favor *now*. Bree got to her feet and looked over the expansive lawn turned battlefield.

Rumiel and Javier stayed close together, but didn't fight together. Javier did the best he could against two Mesos. Using simple levitation spells, he kept his opponents off balance. Bree assumed that he had little energy left after casting the spell he used to blast Talo. Small chunks of ground plumed from magic induced explosions while fireballs hurled past him, but Javier held his own and none of the attacks hit close enough to hurt him.

Rumiel had his hands full with another Meso. Standing tall like opposing kings on a chessboard, they faced each other, separated by forty feet of burnt and mangled grass. They couldn't have been more opposite: pale, skinny Rumiel in black clothes, his long, stringy hair reacting to his every movement versus a thick-muscled boy whose sun-darkened skin and shaved head were stroked with paints as yellow as the sun. Their magics reflected their looks.

With a wave of his hand, the Meso summoned a fist sized ball of blinding white light in front of Rumiel's face. Even though he brought one hand to shield his eyes, Rumiel remained aware enough to cast a quick spell to deflect the fireball the Meso hurled. Still shielding his eyes, Rumiel conjured his own fist-sized globe, one of pure black. Tendrils oozed from it and grasped at the miniature sun. The inky ball of darkness consumed the glaring ball of light. The Meso altered his attack.

With a surprising burst, the brightness intensified, bursting the darkness like popping a balloon, leaving only a black mist that quickly dissipated. Rumiel conjured darkness again, but this time over the Meso's face, enveloping his head like a hood. The bright light disappeared as the Meso clawed at the blackness.

Bree again assumed the spell used quite a bit of energy, because the darkness didn't last long, the Meso shredding it away like a flimsy cloth. Rumiel was ready, though. As soon as the Meso recovered, he stopped and looked down. Hundreds of black ants scurried up his legs. Panicking, he stomped his legs and ran in small circles. Summoning a small wall of short-lived fire, the Meso retreated, slapping at his legs. Bree felt satisfied that her assistance wasn't needed as Rumiel turned his attention to the two Mesos Javier tussled with.

A stream of fear flowing through her, Bree scanned the area realizing that she hadn't seen Lucien since the madness started. Weakened from the spell to find Lila, he could barely walk. He was strong, smart, and competent, but Bree would feel better if she knew he was okay. A thin haze of smoke silhouetted a tall, muscular figure and hope teased her. But the smoke cleared revealing Strongbow in a fighting stance.

He and Ryoku fought side by side as well, but they worked together. They faced three Mesos and focused more on holding them at bay than attempting to do anything lethal. They both worked their talismans, both using sweeping gestures. As usual, Ryoku's body flowed like the water she controlled. Two ropes of water rippled through the air, circling around her until she snapped them like whips to attack her opponents, or splash them in the face to confuse them, or douse a fire to defend against them. Strongbow moved about, too, but unlike Ryoku's lithe dancing, his movements were brusque and forceful.

Stomping his right foot forward, Strongbow extended both fists, as if punching. A gusty column of air swirled from him and slammed into a Meso twenty feet away. The pounding force knocked the boy off his feet, throwing him backwards. Another Meso threw a fireball, but Strongbow avoided it with blinding speed. He retaliated with another talisman spell, a cyclone only five feet in height, but powerful enough to spin the Meso violently and toss him aside like a broken doll. Bree wanted to help, but Strongbow and Ryoku handled the Mesos with ease.

Willem wasn't too far away either, exchanging fire attacks with another Meso. The Meso hurled a fireball, but Willem controlled it before it even got near him and threw it back. The Meso split the glob of fire into two and streaked one part along the ground back at Willem, the other part vanishing harmlessly. Willem gained control of the rivulet of flame and commanded it off the ground, whipping it through the air at the Meso like a living rope. With the wave of his hands, the Meso made it disappear. He then started the process again by throwing another fireball at Willem.

Bree thought about assisting when she saw a flash from the corner of her eye. She turned just in time to see a chuck of blazing dirt, a projectile aiming for Siobhan. Using a simple pushing spell, Bree deflected the attack. Amanda's boyfriend.

"You attack defenseless girls? Is that what they teach you in your cult? Is that why you're dating Amanda?"

He laughed. "No. I'm dating Amanda because she's hot. And easy."

Unleashing her anger, Bree let it flow through her like water rushing through a hose. She felt the emotion infuse with her magic, felt her anger through the vines and leaves and ivy she used to wrap him in a cocoon of green.

Arms pinned to his sides, ankles tethered together, he dangled a foot above the ground. Sneering, he said, "Do you know why *she* is dating *me?* To escape from *you!* To exert who she is without *you* holding her back. To claw her way out from under *your* shadow."

"I never held her back," Bree said, not sure why she was bothering to have a conversation with a guy who wanted to kill her.

"Says the girl who has me bound up." With a few words of an ancient Mesoamerican langue, a bright light glowed from the center of his chest. It only lasted two seconds, but it was long enough to char the stalks and leaves to a brittle brown. He dropped to the ground and deftly landed on his feet. He nodded to Siobhan and said, "You know, if you let me kill your girlfriend, I'm sure Amanda will take you back."

"You will *not* touch her," Bree growled. Nearby vines snaked toward him. He used a spell that he used earlier, slicing the vines into small chunks.

Bree didn't stop attacking. She couldn't. His vile words echoed in her head, echoing in a part of her soul she never knew she had. He had threatened her friend. A friend that she made on her own, one who liked and accepted her for who she was. A friend who had risked her own life to save hers. Bree was willing to do no less for Siobhan.

Emotions clashed, warring inside Bree's chest. Love and hate, fear and anger all swirled about faster and harder, forming strange feelings she couldn't define. Her emotions and her magics reached out from her to the forest, to the Earth itself. Vines and ivy wriggled around her as if she were a hydra with a thousand heads. Tree branches bowed to her. Blades of grass grew around her feet with every step she took. She gave herself to her emotions— and to her magics.

Striding toward her opponent, Bree commanded more vines to slither along the ground and whips of ivy to slice through the air. The Meso tried his spell again, but there were too many targets. Even though he stopped the vines from tripping him, the ivy lashed him about the chest, face, and back.

Swirling his arms, he summoned loose flames to swirl the same way in front of him. Withered and dried, some of the ivy fell to the ground. Branches from nearby trees reached in and swatted away the flames. Bree continued walking toward him.

Scowling, he conjured a fist-sized ball of piercing white light in front of Bree's face. Refusing to let it distract her, she summoned leafy ivy to wrap around the small, bright sphere. The foliage piled on until it extinguished the light. Bree walked forward.

The Meso hurled fireballs. Bree knocked them away with tree branches and continued to walk forward.

"You'll never win Amanda back!" he screamed as a wall of fire erupted from the ground, encircling him.

Squirming and twisting, lunging and lurching, vines and ivy and roots and stalks and even the grass attacked the flames between Bree and the Meso, making an opening large enough for her to storm through. Balling her hand into a tight fist, she reeled back. Connecting with a meaty smack, she punched him right on the cheek. Even though he didn't fall, she was proud of landing the first punch she had ever thrown in her life.

"Bitch!" he screamed, bringing his hand to his face. "I will make Amanda mine! Forever!"

No you won't, she thought as every memory of her friend, good and bad, raged through her like a flooding river. Allowing these emotions to sweep her away, Bree tapped into the full power of her magics. Foliage wrapped around the Meso, cocooning him from head to toe like an emerald mummy. Twisting and turning, he struggled. Bree fought against him and focused on tightening her extended grip. The flames flickered out. The twitching stopped.

Panting, she fell to her knees, exhausted. Slowly releasing her grip, the flora unraveled itself from the Meso and retracted back into the forest. Icy fingers of guilt squeezed her heart and cold sweat forming on her skin as she wondered if she killed him. His chest move slowly up and down and a warm wave of relief washed through her. She tried to stand, but she couldn't, her aching joints refusing to move right now. Unfortunately, she wasn't the only one giving way to fatigue.

Even though her friends were still able to defend themselves, they were beginning to tire as well. Ryoku's dancing slowed. Strongbow's movements weren't as forceful. Javier wore the pain on his face like a mask. Siobhan was still unconscious. Rumiel quaked and panted like a stray dog. Bree had lost track of Siza, and she still hadn't seen Lucien since they'd walked through the door-port.

Then the Mesos stopped fighting. At once, they disengaged from their skirmishes and simply walked toward Talo. Some of the other Mesos showed signs of fatigue, breathing heavily and sweating, but other than the one Bree rendered unconscious, they all looked capable of continuing, and winning. Especially Talo, smiling and brimming with energy. He stood in front, his minions all behind him. A bit of mirth in his voice, he said, "Well, that was fun, but now it's time for you to die."

"I do not think so," came from behind Bree.

Still unable to muster enough energy to stand, Bree could only turn her head. Siza walked past her toward Talo. When she got within ten feet of him, she stopped and lowered her hood. "My name is Siza."

The Mesos laughed. Talo sneered and said, "So?"

"I have been told that my name has meaning."

"I don't care what it means."

"You should."

"Okay, so entertain me, *Siza*. What does your name mean?"

"It means 'daughter of the lion.'"

Talo rolled his eyes. "So, you're the daughter of a lion."

"No," Siza said, a smirk sliding across her face. "I am daughter of *the* lion."

With that, Siza turned into the Sphinx.

CHAPTER 30

POWER. PURE, RAW POWER emanated from the sinewy muscles of the towering lion standing before Talo. Had Bree been able to stand, she doubted her head would even come up to its shoulder. Its mane flowed more like long hair, as black as Siza's with streaks of emerald from her cloak. The lion's eyes still remained human, bright green. Siza's eyes.

Muscles tensing, the Mesos backed away. Except for Talo. Bare chest glistening from sweat, bright tribal paints stark against his dark skin, he stood tall and firm. A wry smile twisted his lips. "Bad kitty."

Then instantly he transformed back into his snake form, hissing slithering around the lion, circling it. The lion growled, upper lip curling, salive dripping from sharp teeth. With cautious step, the lion faced the snake, following it at every turn. Until the snake stopped.

Coiling onto itself, the snake slowly rose up, stopping when its head was higher than the lion's. Then it attacked.

Jaws open, fangs gleaming, the snake launched itself at the lion. Siza easily dodged the attack, using a powerful paw to slap the snake as it passed. Slithering into a coil, the snake struck again. Again, the lion dodged with ease.

For the first time during the entire battle, Bree felt good. In Egypt, she'd learned that Siza was powerful. Of course, she had no idea that her friend could turn into a giant lion! If Siza could defeat Talo, that would be enough to send the Mesos running.

The two gigantic animals circled each other; the lion offered a rumbling growl with every breath, the snake flicked its tongue and hissed. Pouncing, the lion jumped and rose up on its hind legs, its front paws striking the snake. Bree wanted to cheer.

Trying a different approach, the snake retaliated, but not aiming for the face, instead for the legs. Trying to stay ahead of the quick strikes, the lion leapt around. Finding an opening, the snake wrapped itself around the lion's right front leg and chest. Before the snake could get a chance to constrict, the lion flipped over, throwing itself on the ground, landing with its full weight on the snake.

Retreating, the snake squirmed free and settled into a coil. Its head swayed back and forth as its eyes glowed yellow. The eyes of the ten standing Mesos glowed the same shade of yellow. Like the dancers at the club in London. Fear hollowed out a pit in Bree's stomach.

Faint rays drifted from the Mesos eyes, golden vapors floating with purpose. They intersected with each other and convened with the eyes of the snake. Talo controlled them, drew upon their magics.

The ten Mesos dropped to their knees while Talo siphoned their strength. He grew. A twisting ball of scale and fang, the snake writhed and folded in on itself. The lion paced back and forth, watching, ready to strike. But the snake struck first.

Twice as big as before, Talo lunged at the lion, mouth open wide as he attacked once again. The lion dodged, but the snake whipped its considerable tail and connected with a meaty smack. Landing on its side, the lion quickly got to its feet only to be hit again by the powerful tail. Again, the lion went rolling along the ground.

Siza, in lion form, got back to her feet, but wobbled. Like scaled lightning, the snake was on the lion. With claws extended, Siza swiped at the snake, but missed. In the blink of an eye, the snake coiled around the lion, constricting her within its embrace.

Something dark and fearful crushed Bree's chest as if the snake squeezed her instead. Still on her knees, she was unable to help the squirming lion. Different spells flitted through her mind, but each falling from her grasp as she reached for them. Panicked, she didn't know what to do. Until the lion's front legs turned from golden fur to the green scaly skin of a lizard.

Confused, Bree looked around and saw Javier. It was him. Dear, good-natured Javier was giving his magic to Siza. Bree followed his lead. Leaning forward, she pressed her palms to the ground, the grass sifting between her fingers. Concentrating, she took a few deep breaths and focused on the surge of energy coursing through her body, focused on her magic. She communed with the energy of the grass and the forest, the trees and plants. The feeling grew, building inside of her until her will was the only dam holding back the torrent of energy. She looked at the lion and released the power, directing it to Siza.

Almost deflating her, Bree felt her magic energies pour from her, rushing into Siza. Leafy ivy grew from the lion's mane and wrapped around its body. The lion fought against the snake's constriction by twisting its body, swiping its claws, and snapping its teeth. It still wasn't enough. Talo the snake was too strong. Then the lion's eyes changed from Siza's bright emerald to dark coal as black mist wisped from its mouth with every exhale.

Excited, Bree assumed it was Lucien lending his magic to Siza as well. Cocking her head slightly, trying not to disrupt her concentration, Bree peeked around, looking for him. But it was Rumiel who gave magic to Siza, the same black mist wafting from his ink black eyes. Disappointment hit Bree first, but she quickly replaced it with hope, hope that Rumiel's magic would make the difference. And then Bree's heart positively swelled when Willem join as well. He held a sturdy stance and extended his hands, palms facing the skirmish. The lion's mane burst into flame, licks of fire flowing with every twist and turn. The snake now struggled to contain the lion.

Bree drew strength from Javier, not from any form of magic, but from admiration. On his knees, sweat poured from him as he clenched every muscle in his body, giving everything he could give despite the pain and fatigue. Siza demonstrated that she had the most power of the group, but Javier had the most inner strength. The most heart. He was never going to give up, and Bree decided that neither would she.

Concentrating harder, Bree opened the floodgates. She pushed past the pain, fought off the fatigue. Every ounce of magic she could muster, she gave to Siza—and it worked.

With one final squirm, the lion broke free from the snake's hold and lashed at its head. The snake twisted and slithered away, readying itself for another strike. Looking like a chimera from the amalgam of talismans, the lion stalked, eyeing the snake. Pausing from its attack, the snake with the glowing yellow eyes drew more power from the other Mesos.

Clouds rolled along the sky, brewing above the lawn. Rain fell. It happened so fast, Bree assumed it wasn't natural. Strongbow and Ryoku held hands, their free hands extending outward. They joined their magics to make the storm. As the rain and wind intensified, they pointed to the Mesos.

A funnel of rain formed in the sky, aiming for the trance-like Mesos. Even though the whirlwind lasted only seconds, it was enough to toss them about, breaking their connection with the snake.

Glowing eyes flickering, the snake twisted and hissed. With a roar to rival the thunder of the storm, the lion pounced. Claws digging into the snake, the lion sunk its teeth deep into its flesh.

Thrashing in pain, the snake wriggled free. Too injured to continue, the snake turned back to Talo. Bleeding from his right shoulder, the boy collapsed. A few weak and exhausted Mesos crawled and scrabbled to his aid. Panting and coughing, Talo watched with defeat in his eyes as the lion transformed back to Siza.

Excited that the battle was over, Bree ignored her own pain and fatigue to jump to her feet and ran to Siza. "Siza! You did it! Siza?" But her jubilation was short lived. With a calm and grace beyond her years, Siza turned to greet Bree. In an instant, she went rigid. She jerked, soldier straight, her arms stiff against her sides, eyes wide with shock. Unable to even say a word, Siza fell to the ground like a chopped tree.

Thinking it another attack, Bree clenched her fists and looked at the Mesos. Half of them were scattered about, unconscious. The other half didn't seem to even notice what had happened, too busy trying to help Talo with his wound.

Confused, Bree turned to see if her friends had any ideas. Strongbow and Ryoku fell first and the same way—stiff as boards. Willem fell next. Then Javier and Rumiel.

Panicked, Bree reached out with her magic, commanding vines and ivy and branches to whip and lash blindly about, hoping beyond hope she could take down the source of these new, mysterious attacks. To no avail. A sharp, itching pain struck the base of her neck. Her arms and legs became as stiff as pipes. She couldn't move, couldn't scream. As she started to fall backwards, someone caught her. Lucien!

He was alive and unharmed and that was all that mattered to Bree. She was happy to see that he hadn't fallen to this new affliction and if there was one person who could figure out what was going on, it would be him. But something wasn't right.

Lucien lowered Bree to the ground, resting her on her back. Why? Why was he doing that? The way he looked at her wasn't right either—his eyes were filed with sorrow, pleading and pained. Was something in his hand? He stood, and Bree saw what he was holding. Voodoo dolls.

Figures crafted from sticks and wrapped in cloth, none taller than three inches, filled his hand. Each doll had strands of human hair on their heads; hair she remembered him keeping from her and her fellow students. Each doll had a needle sticking from the base of the neck.

Bree's stomach flopped. She couldn't move, couldn't talk. Trying to yell, she raged on the inside, but it resulted in nothing, no movement, no sound. She could only blink the burning tears from her eyes as she looked at Lucien, silently screaming at him, begging him to stop whatever it was that he was doing. At the very least, give her an explanation.

"I'm sorry," he whispered as he placed the pile of voodoo dolls on the ground. "This is because of Tierney. Please tell my father that I'm sorry."

Bree's head was tilted just enough for her to see everything that he did. His every step, a stab to her heart, his every movement a dream shattered.

Placing a hand on Talo's uninjured shoulder, Lucien said, "Focus on the destination," and opened a door-port. Black mist arose from the ground, swirling, forming the rippling frame of a door. A few of the Mesos helped Talo through the door. Lucien helped awaken the unconscious ones and aided them through the door. The last Meso was Amanda's boyfriend. Before he stepped through the door, he paused to glare at Bree. Lucian stepped in front of him and said, "Now is not the time." Still staring at Bree with hate-filled eyes, Amanda's boyfriend stepped through without incident.

Lucien stepped halfway through the door but stopped, his muscles flexing as if his entire body fought against what he wanted it to do. With a quickness in his step, he turned and walked back to Bree. He plucked her voodoo doll from the pile, crouched down next to her, placed it in her hand, and gently curled her fingers around it. He stroked her face, pushing stray stands of dirty hair from her mud-streaked forehead and cheeks.

Bree wanted to smack his hand away. She wanted to spit on him, wanted to spew every profanity she knew. Shout at him about losing his right to touch her by helping Talo and hurting her friends! People who thought they were *his* friends!

Lucien leaned in, close enough for Bree to feel his warm breath on her ear, and whispered, "I love you."

I loved you, too! she screamed in her mind. *But, why? Why are you doing this? Why?* No words came out of her mouth.

Lucien stood. He walked away from Bree. To the door port. Without looking back, he stepped through and disappeared.

"Bree?" She heard her name being called by Siobhan. In her head she screamed to Siobhan everything that happened after she fell unconscious. Again, nothing came out of her mouth.

"Bree!" Siobhan rushed to her and dropped to her knees. Bree rapidly shifted her eyes from Siobhan to the voodoo doll in her hand. Understanding, Siobhan grabbed the doll and yanked the needle from it.

Freedom came in a burst. Bree sprung to her feet and sprinted to the fading door port. As she got there, the last wisps of black were carried away on the breeze.

Crying, Bree fell to her knees and screamed, "Lucien! Lucien!"

He was gone.

And so was her heart.

CHAPTER 31

BREE SAT AT HER dining room table. With no walls to encumber her view, she stared absently into the kitchen. In a fog, she gazed at the refrigerator; the shining chrome mixed with the echoing tick-tock of her mother's hallway clock lent to the ease of a hypnotic daze.

Ten hours ago. A mere ten hours ago, Bree had stepped foot into her high school for the last time for the summer. Bree had every good feeling imaginable, and some she couldn't even categorize. Now, they were all gone. A life she had been introduced to a few months ago, a life that she had dared to dream about, crumbled around her in a mere ten hours.

How? Why? Bree pondered these questions, her chest aching every time she asked them. Betrayed, *utterly betrayed*, by the boy she loved. How? Why? Would she ever find answers? She didn't know. She only knew that she now had no help.

After Siobhan freed everyone from their paralysis, they contacted the instructors. The adults came and listened to what had happened. The students didn't lie and told every detail while the instructors used spells to heal and mend injuries and wounds. Distraught, the instructors held an impromptu meeting, contacting any member of the council they could find and left the eight remaining students by themselves in the game room. In retrospect, Bree realized that wasn't the best of ideas, especially with everyone's emotions running high. And with Willem's mouth running fast.

"Lucien was the traitor! I knew it was him!" Willem shouted as he paced around the room.

Leaning against a wall with his arms folded over his chest, Rumiel snapped, "You did not. You've been accusing Javier ever since he got here."

With his hands in his pockets, Javier stood next to Rumiel and whispered, "Dude."

Willem stopped walking and waggled his finger at Rumiel and Javier. "Doesn't matter. I knew it was one of you newbies."

Rumiel took a step away from the wall and pointed a finger at Willem, "No. You blamed Javier. You were wrong. Now, you need to apologize."

"Yeah? Sorry one of you bloody newbies was the bloody traitor. How's that?"

Rumiel took another step, but Javier grabbed his arm and whispered, "Dude. Not worth it."

"Seriously, you two," Siobhan said, sitting next to Bree. "Can't you stuff your testosterone in your pockets long enough to show some sensitivity."

Rumiel glanced to Bree, her shoulders slumped and sulking, and rolled his eyes. "Can't upset the princess," he mumbled.

Siobhan nodded toward Strongbow. "Not just her, you gimps."

Ryoku wasn't at her usual spot, nor next to Willem. She sat beside Strongbow. Ignoring the conversation, she whispered to Strongbow, "We'll find her. We'll find another spell and we'll find her."

Frustration still woven in his words, Rumiel grumbled, "A lot of good the last spell did us. It didn't even work."

"It did work," Siza said, sitting in her usual spot at the table. "Tell them, Willem."

Willem ran a hand through his mussed red hair and sighed. "It did. I ... I felt it."

"She was here," Strongbow said, his words heavy from despair. "She was here."

"It's bloody obvious what happened," Willem mused. "Lucien told those wankers what we were doing. They brought her here to mess with us and throw us off our game."

"Willem's right," Ryoku said. "Since she was here, that means she's alive."

Strongbow flexed his clenched jaw in response.

Ryoku continued, "We'll just keep meeting here over the summer and keep looking for her."

"Unfortunately, not, Ryoku," Came from the doorway. It was Miss Harkins, eyes red from crying.

Frown carving troughs into his face, Strongbow growled, "You *cannot* stop me from searching for my sister."

"Sorry. That's not what I meant," she said as she entered. She trudged to the nearest barstool and sat. Looking defeated, she slouched, her head low. "I meant that we're shutting the institute down."

Gasps filled the room as disbelief crashed through like a wave, even from the despondent Bree and agitated Rumiel.

Miss Harkins continued before any of the students could form questions, "Well, for the summer at least. The councils are very disheartened that the Mesos so easily breeched our defenses and walked right onto institute grounds."

Willem sputtered, "But … but … we determined that Lucien was a traitor. He did something."

"The instructors and council don't think so. Even as strong as he is, he simply wasn't here long enough to learn how to sneak past or undo the spells that were in place."

"What about his father?" Bree asked, voice dry and raspy.

A new trail of tears flowed down Miss Harkins' face. "Mr. St. Martin is very distraught. He had no idea Lucien was so angry about Tierney. He's promised to devote all of his time to helping us find answers. We still don't know how the Mesos did it. We don't know what to do from here."

"So, the council is shutting the institute down?" Siobhan asked.

"Definitely for the summer. I, personally, believe that they will reopen it for the school year. They want time to investigate what happened here today, and take time to think about what direction they—and us instructors —want the institute to go in. It was decided that it's in everyone's best interest to have you students go back home for the summer. Give everyone a break. However, for the summer, the school will be closed and we instructors will be indisposed."

Bree heard the word "indisposed" and her heart sank even farther. In what she viewed as an act of maturity, Bree had forgiven Miss Harkins, even though she never told Miss Harkins that she was mad at her. Though Miss Harkins had not told her of the potential dangers when they first met, Bree realized that her world had expanded; possibilities and potential had multiplied, all because of magic. She never would have had met Lucien, never known love, never known hope, if not for Miss Harkins. In the game room, Miss Harkins dashed that hope.

The heat of heartbreak burned right behind Bree's sternum. Lucien's betrayal nauseated her. His last words echoed through her mind. He said he loved her. His last words to her were those. Why? If he were *truly* evil, he would never have said that. If he were *truly* evil, he would have killed them all when he had the chance. She was just too hurt and exhausted to defend him to the others; they were all too angry and confused to listen. While Willem railed against Lucien and bickered with Rumiel, Bree simply sat, planning her summer to try to figure out who Lucien truly was. She had looked forward to coming to the institute for its resources, to practice and learn more, maybe meet a fellow student here every once and a while, and possibly research her family to find who had passed their gifts of magic on to her. She also admitted that she needed Miss Harkins's help. Now Miss Harkins was going to be "indisposed," dashing all of Bree's plans for the summer.

"What about finding Lila?" Ryoku asked for Strongbow's benefit.

"The institute council will be contacting Strongbow's home council. You said she was here, and we believe you. The councils will do whatever they can to find her." She turned to Strongbow. "They've never stopped trying since she first disappeared."

Bree was torn. Strongbow was going to have help finding his sister over the next few months. But what about her needs? What about her questions that needed to be answered? Would the council exert any effort to find out the truth about Lucien, or will his father have to work alone?

Two lines of tears rolled down Miss Harkins' cheeks and her voice cracked, "I'm sorry this is so sudden. It's time to say good-bye."

Since Bree and Ryoku didn't live at the institute, they helped everyone else pack. Everyone had already exchanged email addresses and cell phone numbers months ago, and they all connected with each other through every social media option available, but the promises to keep in touch over the summer were made anyway. Bree knew that after a week or two passed and the sting of what had just happened dulled, it was going to be nice to interact with her new friends. As she helped them pack, it didn't feel that way, though.

Rumiel was the first to leave, but with little fanfare. A quick shoulder-to-chest "guy hug" from Javier, and polite farewells from everyone else. Willem went next. Even he was sad about the way things were—he handed Ryoku one last dollar, but made no jokes as he departed. Strongbow left to a chorus of "good luck," but gave a very direct "goodbye" to Ryoku. Javier was next, apologizing on behalf of all Mesoamerican magic users and wishing that he could have done more. His humility and sincerity chipped another piece out of Bree's heart. As she departed, Siza offered a simple smile, one that held a million emotions and Bree felt them all. Siobhan and Ryoku called each other a few less-than-flattering names, and then hugged. Ryoku and Bree hugged as well, but as with every interaction with

Ryoku, it was cold and distant. Ryoku did shed a few tears as she left. Bree hugged Siobhan, squeezing so hard that she couldn't breathe. Through a tear streaked smile, Bree apologized, but desperately wanted something to hold on to, one good memory from the last few months that hadn't been tarnished. They promised to talk every day, but it wasn't going to be the same. She needed Siobhan's strength, to be with a friend who knew what she had gone through. But it wasn't meant to be, and Siobhan was gone.

Bree found Miss Harkins to say goodbye as well. More tears as they hugged and apologized: Miss Harkins for not being able to be there for Bree, Bree for not handling everything in the most mature way at times. Before Bree left, Miss Harkins told her she would be back before school started and promised, promised, promised that she would continue to help Bree, in any way possible, even if the council decided to put an end to the institute.

Now, Bree was at home, sitting at her dining room table. The dichotomy between mind and body had never been so prevalent. Her body was numb and unable to move from exhaustion, her mind abuzz with everything that had happened. She'd lost Amanda and Chelsea at the beginning of the year, found out she had magical abilities, regained Chelsea's friendship, made incredible new friends, survived the weirdness of Sci-Fi Sam and the rumors of her being gay, had gone to Egypt to find a precious artifact, gone to the bayou to steal another artifact, fought in a magical death match.

She'd fallen in love.

She'd been betrayed.

She'd lost everything.

But he'd said he loved her. He'd said, "I love you." Even though she was paralyzed, she knew what she heard. He loved her. Was it a lie? Was he lying the whole time? Did he recognize her as an easy target as soon as he got to the institute?

No. Bree admitted to herself that she wasn't the worldliest person and had few experiences to draw from. But she knew what she felt. She knew what he felt. He loved her. He absolutely did, and she didn't need to draw deeply from any past experiences to know that. His love for her was real. So were her new friendships. There were good things to be found from her time at the institute and she wasn't about to let them go.

The front door opened and Bree heard the familiar click of her mother's heels on the hardwood floor. "Bree? Are you home?"

Bree tried to answer, but as soon as she opened her mouth, her words shriveled and died at the back of her throat. She fought back the tears as long as she could, but as soon as her mom entered the dining room, Bree lost the battle.

"Bree?" her mom asked. "What's wrong?"

The first time her mother didn't ask the question that Bree hated was the first time she would have been right. Chin twitching and bottom lip quivering, Bree sobbed, "It's a boy."

Dropping her attaché, Allyson held out her arms and Bree ran to her sobbing. Allyson didn't say a word. Bree knew that she'd have to modify the stories, bend the truth and say things like, "He wasn't who he said he was," instead of, "He helped members of a death cult." But for now, she found comfort in her mother's arms.

ACKNOLWEDGEMENTS

WE LOVE TO LEARN. Part of the reason why we wanted to write this novel was to learn about different cultures. As with most research endeavors, especially when the internet is one of the tools being used, we may have received a piece of bad information or misconstrued something we had read. That means we may have gotten something wrong about your culture within the pages of this book. If we did, we definitely wish to apologize, but we would also love to know what the correct information is, so please feel free to let us know. Please don't yell at us or call us names if we made any errors representing your culture; just let us know how to correct it. Remember, the way to defeat ignorance is not with anger, rather understanding and education.

ABOUT THE AUTHORS

BRIAN KOSCIENSKI & CHRIS PISANO skulk the realms of south, central Pennsylvania. Brian developed a love of writing from countless hours of reading comic books and losing himself in the worlds and adventures found within their colorful pages. In tenth grade, Chris was discouraged by his English teacher from reading H.P. Lovecraft, and being a naturally disobedient youth he has been a fan ever since. They have logged many hours writing novels, stories, articles, comic books, reviews, and the occasional haiku. During their tenure as a writing duo, they even started Fortress Publishing, Inc., a micro-press responsible for the "TV Gods" anthologies.